Where Light Cannot Reach

Crusaders of the Lost Series
Book II

William Mark

Published by:
Southern Yellow Pine (SYP) Publishing
4351 Natural Bridge Rd.
Tallahassee, FL 32305

www.syppublishing.com

This is a work of fiction. Names, characters, places, and events that occur either are the products of the author's imagination or are used fictitiously. Any resemblance to actual persons, places, or events is purely coincidental.

The contents and opinions expressed in this book do not necessarily reflect the views and opinions of Southern Yellow Pine Publishing, nor does the mention of brands or trade names constitute endorsement.

ISBN-10: 1-59616-084-5
ISBN-13: 978-1-59616-084-2
ISBN-13: ePub 978-1-59616-085-9
ISBN-13: Adobe eBook 978-1-59616-086-6
Library of Congress Control Number: 2018956093

Printed in the United States of America
First Edition
August 2018

Dedication

To my beautiful family, you are what keeps the darkness away.

Other Works by William Mark

Crusaders of the Lost series

Lost in the Darkness - Book I

The Blue Line series

From Behind the Blue Line - Book 1
Crossing the Blue Line – Book 2

In the fight against darkness, the best weapon need only be a single ray of light. But there are shadows hidden within the deepest recesses of darkness where even the brightest light cannot reach.

Chapter 1

He detested this feeling. Vulnerability was for the weak and he had no tolerance for it. But, it was his own arrogance that led to this moment. Straying from the plan-not adhering to the rules-it all had proved foolish. He would not make the same mistake again. But there was no time to waste, he had to find her before all was ruined.

I should've never taken two at once. Dammit! I don't even desire the big one. I had no use for her anyway. Offering herself like that was just pathetic and shameful.

Concern turned into anxiety as his search of the house came up fruitless. She was gone. How'd he become so careless? He double checked the room again. The small one still lay on the floor. Now, *she* was desirable, he thought, as he gazed the length of her half-naked body. Lustful thoughts returned, but he ignored them as he moved about the house searching more thoroughly in all the small crevices she could have jammed her body into. With no luck, he surmised that she escaped. The vulnerability grew.

Outside, he scanned the back yard. The front was left secured, there was only one other option. There it sat. The basement access was left ajar. He thought about how long she was unaccounted for. How long had he been with the small one?

"Shit."

Chosen for its location, the house backed up to thick undeveloped woods. It added a layer of isolation and privacy he needed. He checked around the basement access and found footprints in the dirt that led toward the woods. He took off running.

This was not the hunting style he preferred, but he allowed himself to find the pleasure in its symmetry. It was cruder and more simplistic, but it was hunting nonetheless. He admitted, this made the big one more desirable.

Running for nearly half an hour, he passed through the bulk of the woods, over the small stream and came to a clearing. The setting sun shone brightly down on him, causing him to squint. He shaded his eyes and fixed his glasses to the bridge of his nose. He scanned the openness of the land. In a flash, he saw the big one disappear back into the woods on the other side. All was not lost, but there was much ground to cover.

After traversing the clearing, he entered the darkened woods after his prey. He looked feverishly for any sign of where she fled, ignoring the fatigue that was settling in his body. Figuring she kept the same heading from the house, he continued moving in the that direction. Thinking ahead, he realized for the distance he'd been going she would soon come across someone and that would prove disastrous. He picked up his pace, everything depended on capturing the girl.

From the crest of a hill, he peered over a small valley within the woods. Stopping briefly to catch his breath, he spied a scrub tree broken near the top. It swayed slightly even though there was no breeze.

She's close.

He galloped down the hill. Past the broken tree, there was an open drain tunnel. Perfect for hiding. He smiled and calmed his breathing as he crept up to the opening. Thoughts of how to bring the big one's demise flooded his mind. An idea came, a better way to instill terror. He backed away from the opening and noticed it ran underneath a nearby highway. He heard the traffic rolling nearby. He went around and climbed up the embankment toward the roadway, huddled in thick brush, waited for a single motorist to pass then crossed over the two-lane highway and back down to the other side.

Stealthily, he made his way to the mouth of the tunnel. She was as good as captured. He looked around, realizing how secluded and hidden the area was. It was as good as any place for a grave.

Waiting for her to emerge, he grew impatient. He had to get back to the house before the small one came around. He crept closer to the opening and jumped down to startle his prey. Only, she wasn't there.

"Ugh! Where the hell did you go?"

Off in the distance, leaves rustled and twigs snapped under weighted footsteps. He twisted around and saw the big one running unbridled. Continuing the chase, he realized she was proving a worthy opponent. He sprinted after her, barely able to keep her pink shirt in sight amongst all the green foliage. In her wake, he caught a whiff of her scent, a sweet and pungent mix of sweat and body odor which fueled his pursuit. She took an abrupt turn and he lost sight of her altogether. Catching up to the last spot where he saw her, he turned to see where she went. He saw nothing, but a slight noise rattled. Albeit faint, it was still alarming. He rushed toward the sound and broke the wood line.

The sun was again waiting on him, blinding him from just over the trees. Again, he shaded his eyes and fixed his glasses to the bridge of his nose. There it was. His vulnerability had graduated into exposure. He scanned the parking lot of the truck stop, restaurant, and motel parking lot situated across the highway for any signs of the girl. In her state, she would cause a stir, and he didn't see any such thing. Not yet. He stood behind a large grey boulder in the shape of a sideways heart. He used it to shield his presence from any patrons across the street while he watched. Large trucks came and left, families stopped and refueled and there were even a few potential beauties swimming at the motel pool. But the big one was nowhere to be found.

Anger boiled inside and only he was to blame. He slammed his fist down on the unforgiving rock, cursing to himself. This was a lesson learned, and he knew his punishment would have to be fierce. It would be imposed immediately. But first, he had to get back to the house and cover his tracks.

Chapter 2

Twenty-two years later...

She missed *him*. The only other person she missed was her sister, Rhonda, who was both the source of her weakness and her strength. She has been among the lost for over two decades, taken by a faceless monster and made to endure evils no person should ever know. Now, in Rachel Goodwin's world, she had made room for Curtis Walker.

In his absence, she moved into the de facto leadership role of the team. She battled with feelings of inadequacy but drew confidence from knowing that Curt had faith in her to do the job effectively. His support was all she needed. Her inner mantra when contemplating a move or decision was, "What would Curt do?" It had served her well for the past six months after she and the team helped Curt find his missing son and take down the man responsible.

It had been a wild experience; one she never would have fathomed a year before while working for an ineffective Children and Family Services. With the team, Rachel saw real and tangible results. Not being bogged down by the checks and balances of a bureaucracy, she was able to see the gift of their work displayed on the faces of the children they recovered. There was no glory or recognition for the work they did, but there was an internal satisfaction that kept the darkness at bay. It gave them purpose, a mission. It was a crusade against evil.

But no mission, despite its pure intention goes without setbacks. The team decided to move west after helping Joshua Walker to be welcomed back in his father's arms and putting the former senator, Thomas Pittman, in jail. Instead of sitting idle and enjoying the moment, Rachel wanted to find the next member of the lost. There was too much in this crusade to be done, she thought.

Stopped at a truck stop along I-10, just outside of Pensacola, Rachel ambled around the convenience store, fast food restaurant hybrid. It was just before sunset and an orange glow beamed through the store front windows. A rush of travelers lined up outside the bathroom while others scouted the candy aisle for a sugar fix. Rachel wandered around, trying to find the one lost soul amongst the lot.

Louis and Melinda remained in the van, standing by for logistical assistance, while Rachel and Beth ran point. Randomly picking this spot, Rachel could feel Beth's skepticism. She hoped to prove her wrong. Among the multitude of lost children in the world, this seemingly innocent truck stop was as good as any to look.

"We've been here for over two hours, Rachel." Beth complained. "They are going to make us leave if we don't buy anything."

"Hey?" Louis spoke up, his shrill voice was loud in Rachel's earbud comm. "I'll take a Mountain Dew, while you're in there."

"Sure, Louis." Rachel answered. "I just wanted to see if I could find anything we can act on. Any hint of trouble."

There was an awkward silence mixed in with the din of the truck stop. Insecurity gripped Rachel. Without Curt, she was just the new girl trying to be in charge.

"Let's give it ten more minutes." Melinda offered.

"Okay, ten minutes." A slight reprieve came to Rachel. But, what could she do in ten minutes?

Three minutes in, a woman clumsily bumped into Rachel.

"Excuse me, I'm sorry." The woman said. Her tone was flat, monotone, and robotic.

Rachel quickly sized her up. Her hair was tousled, like she'd spent the last few hours sleeping upside down. Her sweatpants hung loose off her waist and her feet slid heavily along the terrazzo flooring as she walked. The woman had barely looked at Rachel as she excused herself. Two heavy rings hung under her eyes, giving her a woeful disposition.

"It's okay," Rachel returned.

Stunned for a moment, it was the glimpse Rachel caught from the woman that gave her pause. There was a subdued pain, hidden behind her pathetic façade. The woman continued to the back of the store. Rachel noticed her shoulders were slumped inward and she stood hunched over while in the bathroom line. As the woman entered the ladies' room, Rachel took up a position just outside, watching.

"I may have something." Rachel announced.

"Okay, shoot," Louis said.

"This woman just bumped into me. She had this… look… about her. I think there's something hidden there."

"The female version of Eeyore that walked in a few minutes ago?" Beth asked. She had clearly picked up the same vibe as Rachel.

"Gray sweats and messy hair? Yeah, that's her."

"I saw her getting out of the truck parked next to us. We can run the tag real quick," Melinda added.

A moment later, just as the woman exited the bathroom, Louis announced what he had found.

"Selina Hastings of Milton, Florida. Recent divorcee, mother of one teenage boy. No criminal record and according to her Facebook page, she was just demoted from her job due to cutbacks. Her posts are the ramblings of a pissed off woman and an unjust system that has screwed her."

Disappointed in the initial information about her subject, Rachel let it soak into her thoughts. There were several reasons in the assessment that could explain that hidden pain, but Rachel saw desperation. Desperation breeds depravity, and Ms. Hastings was getting desperate.

"Where's the son?" Rachel asked. Thinking if she lost the kid in the divorce, maybe she would seek out a replacement. That was similar to the case in San Francisco and the high level of madness displayed by Francine Bennett.

6

Rachel heard a few clicks on Louis' keyboard. "At home. He just posted an idiotic selfie on Instagram with Emilia Clarke super-imposed as his girlfriend." Rachel's disappointment grew. Louis added, "Yeah, that guy wishes Daenerys Targaryen was his girlfriend."

"Huh? Who? I'm not sure what you just said, Louis, but..." Rachel answered.

"You know—"

"Hold on, Louis. She's moving."

Rachel followed the woman around the store. She grabbed a sleeve of powdered donuts and a bottle of Sprite and headed for checkout. She snatched a single dose of a sleep aid by the counter, paid for her items and sloughed out the door.

"I hacked her email. She's meeting her psychiatrist in the morning, and she put in her calendar as a reminder to pick up her prescription of Zoloft in the morning."

The air let out of Rachel. She felt as deflated and worthless as Ms. Hastings looked. She pinched out the earbud and stuffed it in her pocket.

"Damn."

As Selina Hastings backed out of the spot next to the Sprinter Van and pulled away, Rachel slid open the side door and climbed into the vehicle. She took her seat in the captain's chair and said nothing. Beth followed with Louis's Mountain Dew. She handed him the drink and moved up to the front seat.

"Thanks, Beth."

Rachel stared out of the large side window. Melinda cranked up the van and pulled out, heading for the interstate.

Beth turned in her seat. "She was just depressed, Rachel."

"Yeah, just another depressed, middle-aged divorcee. World's got plenty of those, too."

"It's okay. We'll just keep looking," Beth said.

Rachel didn't reply. It was said with sympathy, but the words carried the sting of failure.

As the hum of the interstate buzzed in her ears, Louis spoke from the back of the van. "Daenerys Targaryen…, she's the stellar blonde on Game of Thrones! The Mother of Dragons. She's a total badass chick!"

"Ah." Rachel nodded politely.

***

The next morning, they had arrived in New Orleans, Louisiana. After some needed rest the team spent an evening wandering the streets of the French Quarter. The outing quickly turned from sight-seeing into a hunting expedition off the main roads. Moving away from the inebriated tourists they took a detour into the poverty-stricken ghettos. Scars of Hurricane Katrina were still evident as the area they came across offered the allure of drugs and prostitution. The humid air carried the stench of desperation.

Indifferent about the lights and life on Bourbon Street, Rachel came alive as she and the team searched the neighborhoods tourists avoided. The drifters, drug users, and street walkers were all out looking for their next score. Rachel scanned the denizens, scrutinizing each face until she locked onto someone.

"*Her*," Rachel called out.

Melinda and Beth turned to look out of the passenger side window to see a woman standing under the orange glow of a street lamp. She stood in high heels and clung onto the light pole for balance. Whether it was the tall shoes or extreme intoxication, Rachel couldn't tell.

"Oh my, she looks rough. You sure?" Beth asked.

With an analytical stare, Rachel answered confidently, "Yes, I'm sure."

"She's strung out, for sure. That, I can tell from here," Melinda added. She had parked the Sprinter Van across a vacant lot to watch the subject Rachel had targeted. Her expertise in drug addiction ran deep.

"Melinda, swing around the block one more time," Rachel said. "I want to get a closer look."

After circling the block, the girl had moved down the street and stood unsteadily, talking to a larger black man. He was bald and wore an outdated, teal green track suit. Rachel noticed the girl's body was now tense and submissive. She seemed to plead with the man over something and then to finalize the argument, he shoved her violently back toward the spot under the street light. Rachel cringed at the violence.

"That must be her pimp." Rachel figured.

"Uh, huh." Melinda agreed with an edge of contempt. Rachel remembered Melinda's bitter distaste for pimps, having killed the man who had turned out her drug addicted sister during a violent confrontation.

As the girl walked back to her corner, the shine of the light caught her face. Rachel felt validated and Beth gasped.

"Oh my god, look at her face, she can't be but thirteen or fourteen!" "Jesus. She's just a baby," Melinda said shaking her head. "Never underestimate how strong of a hold that shit can have."

"No kidding."

"And clearly some people will do anything to get it."

"But she's just a kid." Beth complained.

"That's why we're going to grab her." Rachel stated.

A moment later, Rachel asked, "You ready?" There was uneasiness in Melinda's eyes.

"Yeah, I just hate what this reminds me of."

"I know. We can do something else if you'd rather not. Or I could…

"

"No," she snapped. "No, it's fine. If it helps get that girl off the streets before the drugs have completely taken over, then I'm good."

"Alright, then." Rachel submitted.

It was her least favorite, yet most convincing of her personas. A strung-out street walker, with desperation oozing out of her dingy clothes, a disheveled look and unhygienic odor. Melinda Dalton looked every bit the drug addicted prostitute. To walk amongst the wolves, you can't look like a sheep.

"Here Mel, here's your earbud." Louis Melton stepped away from his computer work station in the back of the Mercedes Sprinter and held his hand out for her to take the earpiece. She grabbed the earbud and inserted it into her left ear. Louis sat back down and spoke into a microphone.

"Can you hear me?"

She nodded.

Rachel stood nose to nose with Melinda to go over the plan one last time. She ignored the nerves and her feelings of inadequacy, hoping they didn't worsen the stress on Melinda.

"Alright, you got the plan? Easy distraction while we do our thing."

"Yeah, let's do this."

Melinda was dropped on the other side of the block. While she walked toward the direction of the pimp, Louis drove the large van down a narrow alleyway cut between two buildings that stood between the pimp and the girl. He parked short of the opening, keeping the van hidden from sight. Beth stayed poised in the front seat while Rachel directed from the Captain's chair behind her.

The sounds of footsteps on wet asphalt broke the silence as they listened to Melinda approach the pimp.

"Mel, cough if the girl is still by the street lamp."

She coughed.

The footsteps, light and purposeful, suddenly turned loose and sloppy. Melinda was getting into full character. A man's voice in the background suddenly became clearer.

"Hey baby, whatchu doin'?"

"I'm lookin'. You servin' or hustlin'?" Melinda replied.

The silence that followed bothered Rachel, she imagined the pimp sizing up Melinda, scrutinizing her with paranoid eyes.

"Why you wanna know?" He asked.

"I'm lookin' to get high, but I can work for it, you know? You got room in your stable?"

"You a hoe, huh?"

10

"Aren't we all?"

A deep, raucous laugh followed. It made Rachel cringe.

The laughing suddenly stopped and with a sharp tone the man asked, "You look like a dyke. You sure you a hoe? You gunna know what to do with a man?"

Rachel became embarrassed for Melinda; her sexual preference being called out by a callous street urchin. Without missing a beat, Melinda said, "So what if I am, I still got the parts that any man wants! Plus, it's about the green. I'm sure you know that."

More silence. He was mulling over the deal.

"Yeah, you right 'bout that."

"So, we straight?"

That was the cue. Rachel tapped Louis on the shoulder and he reached under the dash and flipped a switch. Red and blue strobe lights flickered from the front grill, the lights bounced off the walls of the alleyway spilling out into the street.

"Oh, shit. It's 5-0." Melinda warned.

"Fuck!"

There were footsteps heard walking away and Melinda piped up.

"Hold on, is that strawberry over there yours?"

"Yeah, why?"

"I got her. You stay here, dip out before they see you!"

"Yeah, a'ight... There's a gray house two blocks over, I'll be there. Bring her to me."

"You got it."

A moment later, Melinda passed by the mouth of the alley and caught up with the girl.

"Hey sister, come with me. The po-leece is down the alley."

"Heeeeeyyy, do I.... Heeeyy, do I know yeeeww?"

Rachel could hear in her voice that the young woman was far beyond the point of intoxication. Her high pitch was a tell-tale sign of her youth.

"No, but I got something for you. You want to party?"

"Oh shit! You're a girl... I... I don't do girls." The girl let out a playful giggle followed by a long sigh. "But, there's always a first time for everything."

"Mel, is the pimp far enough away?" Rachel asked.

"Umm, shit. I guess, I don't see him."

"Wha... who... you talkin' to?"

Rachel hesitated before proceeding. Not knowing where the pimp was, was disconcerting. This was supposed to be a simple distraction and scoop. It all hinged on the pimp being out of the picture. Without Curt there, Rachel had to avoid any physical and possibly armed encounters.

Again, Rachel tapped Louis on the shoulder. "Okay, let's go."

"Not worried about the pimp?" His concern was obvious.

"She doesn't see him, let's take the opportunity before it slips away."

Louis didn't reply. He turned off the police strobes, put the van in gear and squeezed through the alley. The large black van crept out between the two buildings and slowly turned on the narrow street. Rachel peered ahead and saw Melinda walking with the young girl who struggled to stay upright.

The van moved up next to Melinda, who struggled to keep the girl in balance. Rachel pulled the door back before Louis was able to come to a complete stop. The girl looked even younger up close. Her adolescent face was barely hidden behind a sloppy attempt at make-up and smeared, whorish lipstick. Her eyes were distant and glossy, a result of the drugs.

"Come on, get in."

Melinda repositioned herself behind the girl and her fight or flight instincts kicked into overdrive. She started to flail her arms and push against Melinda's efforts.

"No, no, no. We're not going to hurt you."

Slurring her words, but surprisingly sounding soberer, the young girl said, "I thought you said we were going to party?"

Rachel kept the guise going. "That's right, honey. It's a two for one deal. We'll pay extra, but we're going on a ride first."

The girl eased up as her dilated eyes fixed on Rachel's face. She must have seen something comforting.

"Okay, wha' the hell. Never been with a girl, might as well make it two."

Rachel gave a teasing laugh to appease the ruse as she helped Melinda get the girl in the van.

"Hey!" A loud voice from down the street yelled. Simultaneously, Rachel and Melinda turned to see the pimp running toward them. "What the fuck do you think ya'll doin'?"

"Shit. Drive, Louis."

"Are ya'll in?"

"What the hell?" The pimp shouted. "Get back here with her."

Rachel was still struggling to get the girl all the way in, and Melinda needed to follow. For some reason the girl's body suddenly went limp, like the drugs had just turned off the lights. The pimp gained ground fast. Thoughts of just dragging the girl in and having Melinda jump in on the run came fast.

"Go, Rachel. He's got a gun." Melinda warned. The fear in her voice was evident.

With a final heave, Rachel yanked the dead weight of the girl into the Mercedes Sprinter, pulling her body on top of her own. Melinda jumped in and fell on top of both of them leaving the door wide open.

"Go!"

Louis stomped on the accelerator and the large Sprinter van lunged forward. The pimp shouted out loud, but his voice faded as they sped off. Rachel tensed, waiting for shots to follow, fired in anger over them stealing one of his prostitutes. Thankfully, none came.

After clearing the area, Rachel shoved the passed-out girl off of her and took a second to check herself and Melinda.

"You okay?"

"Yeah." That distant look on Melinda's face returned.

"You sure?"

"Yes. Let's just get her to a safe house. She's a mess. It's going to take a while to dry her out."

Rachel nodded. She noticed the girl was lying unnaturally still. She reached over and put two fingers in the crease of her neck. There was a pulse, fast but weak.

"Beth, has Alexis made arrangements yet?"

"Yes, I just got a text from her. The safe house is ready." Beth read off the address for Louis, and twenty minutes later, they were pulling up to a small house in the outer suburbs of New Orleans.

Chapter 3

The school bell rang and the shuffle of feet went quiet in the hallway. The start of another day. The morning rush was over and Kathy Hield reached for her mug of coffee that read: World's Best Secretary. Still warm, she savored the hot drink, waiting impatiently for the caffeine to move faster.

The door opened. Kathy winced, dreading the first student complaint of the day coming this early. Another quick jolt of coffee and she looked up with a fake smile.

"Oh, hello." She answered, surprised.

"You looked shocked." The man said. "Were you expecting someone else?"

Kathy giggled. "No. Sorry, just wasn't ready to deal with some whiney kid's problem yet."

"Ah." The man smiled. "No issues here. Just gunna take a look at the network problems in the media center."

"That I can do." Kathy passed over a clip board for the man to sign. He signed it, passed it back, and took a generic visitor badge to clip on to his collar.

"See ya later."

The man exited the office and headed down the hall while Kathy went back to her morning coffee.

***

Patience and camouflage are the hallmarks of a good hunter. He'd perfected both, which is why he was still free to do as he pleased. Moving down the hall, he went unnoticed. Never a threat, he moved invisible among his prey. The cloak of invisibility was godlike. His patience had evolved over time, being rash and hurried at first, now he walked confidently, knowing that his prey would simply come to him.

Finding the media center, he scanned the openness of the space, the walls were lined with books, and there was a forced silence that gave the place a comfortable calm. He stood by the door, taking in what the field offered. A studious blonde, pretty, but not ideal. A curly haired brunette sat with her feet propped up on a table. *Too plump*, he thought. A group of boys in a hushed conversation didn't even register. Seeing nothing of interest, he moved on and made his way to the computer lab, staying under his veil of camouflage.

It had been a while since his last effective hunt, and he longed for the feel of another victim in his control. Their soft flesh and fear-soaked cries invigorated him to keep pushing, but he was on the prowl for a certain bounty. He was particular. The prize he longed for above all others was rare, and he often thought it would elude him for eternity.

Keeping his duality going, he ran the diagnostics on the computers in the media center and checked the network connections. First, he checked the spyware program of his own design he had installed during an earlier visit. He downloaded the necessary contents, then erased it leaving no virtual trail and reinstalled a new program to do the same thing. It provided him the necessary window in which to look into the lives of his prey, much like a well-positioned camera in the wild. It allowed him to stalk effectively. Finished setting his traps, satisfied they were hidden in the right places, he made his way back to the office. He had four other schools on the list.

Back in the office, he unclipped his badge and left it on the counter. He turned to the door when the secretary called out.

"Hey, you forgot to sign out." She held out the same clip board he signed in earlier.

"Oh, right." He smiled and did as she asked.

"Find anything?" The secretary asked.

"No. It just needed a little tweaking, that's all."

"Okay, glad to hear."

"See ya next time." He left, ready to bait the other hunting fields. But, in a flash, an angelic vision brushed passed him, making her way to the secretary's desk. Her beauty stole his breath, and he stood frozen in indecision. Being caught off guard was a foreign sensation. This vision came straight from his past. A vision for which he'd been patiently waiting. Could she be the prize he sought?

"Layla, honey, what now?" The secretary addressed the vision.

The girl answered with her back turned, but he had a name. Layla. The hunter found his prize.

Chapter 4

Alexis Vanderhill had spent the better half of the last decade making things happen. Through her self-motivated dedication and behind the scenes work, the crusading team was formed. Never seeking recognition or even payment when offered, she maintained that the only cost for her services was keeping the anonymity of the team. Only recently, under the threat of exposure from a dogged investigative journalist, did she reach out and ask for a favor. It was done out of pure desperation. The favor was returned without question and proved to be effective in protecting their secrecy.

Reassessing her stance on asking for help, Alexis vetted out several families who they had helped along the way in case there was something they could provide to the team, should the need arise. After a briefing by Rachel on the operation in New Orleans, Alexis made a call to a wealthy family in nearby Baton Rouge ready to put this idea to the test.

The family was devastated after their nine-year-old daughter went missing. The team looked into the matter and quickly located her in the clutches of a mentally unstable neighbor boy down the street. He had tied her up and sat her at a tea party setting with life-like dolls the boy made out of spare doll parts. After the girl was rescued, the eerie consensus was that the boy would, most likely, have killed her out of fear of discovery or neglect. The family vowed to one day repay Alexis and the team for the quick actions that saved their daughter.

"The Green family has agreed to take the girl in once you guys finish with the detox," Alexis told Rachel over the phone.

"That's awesome. Do they know her history? I don't want this to be a complete shock. This one is rough around the edges."

After getting the girl, Holly Maitland, to the safe house, Louis and Beth did their respective research finding out everything about her they could uncover. Maitland was one of four girls in her family, born in Slidell, Louisiana. Three days before the team grabbed her, she had turned fourteen years old. Louis found an NCIC hit on her name as she was listed as a runaway at age twelve. Beth found one blurb about her missing in the *Slidell Independent*, citing she was a troubled youth. Having seen girls like Holly before, Rachel knew she was considered more of a "throw away" than a runaway. Kids like these came from families of single parents, impoverished, rampant drug use and more commonly, abuse, both physical and sexual. They didn't know love and support like many normal kids. Life on the street brought them acceptance and freedom, and the short-term benefits taught them to ignore the dangers.

Louis found the police report detailing Holly's disappearance. She was listed as missing after five days of being gone. Her mother told the officers she thought Holly had been staying with a friend from school. When the investigators followed up at her school, they learned that Holly had been truant for weeks before running away. The notifications from the school to her mother had gone unchecked. Louis looked for any more police reports detailing her case, but that was all he could find. It was clear that no one was looking for Holly.

That's when Rachel called Alexis and told her they weren't going to take Holly back home.

"She'll just get neglected and leave again and restart this whole vicious cycle. She needs to go somewhere safe, where she'll be loved and taken care of."

"I agree."

"Do you know of somewhere we can take her?"

"I have an idea."

That's what prompted Alexis into calling the Green family.

***

Holly slept for the better part of three days. Occasionally, she woke up to vomit, shaking violently and demanding to leave. She was kept in an empty room outfitted with just a bed, no sheets. Various cleaning instruments were kept in a bucket and stored in the corner.

Melinda and Rachel had to keep her restrained to the bed at several points after she attempted to hurt herself by running into the wall head first. She would violently lash out, trying to fight the two women, but in her weakened state and with Melinda's background as a cop, her attempts were futile.

Any time Louis came in to help, Holly would make sexual advances toward him, trying to bribe him with sex in exchange for her release. A play she had learned worked at some point in her life on the street. When he declined, she would immaturely call out his manhood.

"What? Does your dick not work or something?" or, "Oh, I see. You must like boys, you limp-dick, butt-pirate!"

On day three, Holly seemed to calm down. Rachel checked in on her and saw she was awake, sitting on the bed, hugging her knees and staring out of the window. Holly finally changed out of her ratty street clothes into the clean, more appropriate jeans and a flowery blouse. Rachel sat down on the bed next to her and tried to explain that she was safe and didn't have to go back to the streets and sell her body.

"Why are you doing this?" Holly asked.

"Because we want to help."

"But why?"

"Why not?"

"I mean, why do you care?"

"Because you are worth caring about. Don't you think so?"

"No. Nobody has before. I mean, except my mom's sleazy boyfriend. He cared *a whole lot* when she wasn't home and it was just me and my sisters."

Rachel looked down. The inference that she was molested by her mother's pedophilic boy-friend turned her stomach in knots. It was easy to understand why she ran away.

"I'm sorry. You shouldn't have had to go through that. But that's why we want to help you."

"Whatever." Holly turned and stared back out the window.

"I know this all may seem surreal to you, but we want to see you safe and in a good home."

"Who do you think I am, little orphan Annie? You gunna send me to Daddy Warbuck's, and we all live happily ever after?"

Rachel smiled. She understood the girl's anger. Her life had never seemed fair so why should she believe her and the team were being genuine.

"Listen, Holly. Taking you off the streets like we did and keeping you here does seem like some kind of weird rehab center reality show, but I'll make a deal with you, okay?"

Holly turned and looked eager for what Rachel had to offer.

"We have a nice home and nice people who have agreed to let you come live with them for a while. You can go to school, make new friends, *real friends*, who knows? It's up to you."

"Okay, what's this deal?"

"The deal is, that you give it an honest month of living there. I mean really try for one month, and if after that, you don't like it and want to leave, I'll come back and take you to wherever you want. No questions asked."

"You're not going to be there?"

"No. I'll be a phone call away, but my job is to find more kids like you and help them too."

"So, what's to say I don't run away after you leave?"

"You could. But something tells me that you won't."

"I guess we'll see."

"So, you'll take my deal? We can leave first thing in the morning."

"Fine. I guess."

"Good. The family, the Green's, are excited to have you."

21

"Really? Excited about me?"

"Sure. You're beautiful, I can tell you're smart, and you're still so very young. You still have a chance to make something of yourself and leave that old you behind."

"Huh." Holly went into deep thought and hugged her knees tighter. "Leave it behind, eh?"

"I don't blame you for running away. Hell, that's why I want you to go to the Green's and not back home. You deserve a real chance. Everyone does."

A lasting impression was made on Rachel when she witnessed a young girl be reunited with her parents almost a year before. And again, seeing Joshua Walker reunited with his father, Curt, it was a special memory and feeling that would forever be engrained. That was the magic of this team. However, this reunion was going to be different. It was a blind date, with all the promise and allure of a meaningful relationship, but so too, the potential for disappointment of such high expectations.

Holly rode on the side bench of the Sprinter next to Rachel as they drove to the Green's house in nearby Baton Rouge. Rachel shared her apprehension. Putting herself in the girl's shoes, she appreciated that this was difficult to handle and could only imagine the tumultuous emotions swirling inside.

Rachel saw the girl nervously fidgeting with her hands. Beth had found a tasteful ensemble of designer jeans and a flowery top to wear instead of the stripper clothes she wore when they picked her up. Her face was clean with a minimal amount of makeup, not the painted-on mask she walked the streets in. She looked like the young lady she was supposed to be, although Rachel could tell the darkness still gripped Holly Maitland.

"It's okay. They're going to love you."

Holly let out a skeptical, *humph.*

"They will. You'll see."

"And if I don't like it there, I can leave. No questions asked?"

Rachel nodded.

The Sprinter van slowed and made a long turn up a short hill.

22

"We're here." Louis announced.

"Come on. You'll do great."

Rachel watched as Holly slowly strode up to the Green's. They waited with open arms and open hearts. Nearly losing their own daughter in a potentially deadly scenario, they had treasured the gift God gave them and were ready to take on this new challenge. Rachel knew they would show Holly Maitland the love and patience she required. The road to recovery would be long and arduous, but they would show her there is a better life in this world than what she had known. As Rachel watched the friendship begin, she saw Holly smile. It wasn't a pretend "just to be nice" smile, but a genuine smile, giving Rachel the satisfaction that intervening in this poor girl's life was worth every effort.

Chapter 5

"I may have something." Rachel said.

"What is it?" Louis asked.

"A man."

"… Okay? What about him?"

Rachel was distracted, trying to get a read on her target. "Hold on."

Rachel had followed a man leaving the soccer fields as teams of children walked to the parking lot after their games. The team had left Louisiana and the tribulations of Holly Maitland behind for a suburb outside of Houston, Texas. They had spotted a giant, sports complex busy with throngs of kids running around chasing soccer balls. It was a good hunting opportunity. Anytime that many children were in one place, the odds of finding one of the lost increased exponentially.

"Fine. A man…, no kidding. That narrows down everything. I mean, I just Google'd 'man' and boom, I found the Zodiac Killer!"

"Louis, stop whining," Beth offered.

"I was trying to get a tag, Louis. Geez." Rachel countered.

"Well? Did you get it?"

"No. You kept buzzing in my ear. You know I can hear you, right?"

Louis mumbled something along with an irritating static crackling. In the past, Rachel had seen him cover his microphone with an empty potato chip bag, crinkling it on purpose to mimic interference. She was positive that's what he was doing while he mumbled a snarky retort.

Rachel ignored him. "I watched this guy during most of his kid's soccer game. He positioned himself where he could watch the park entrance over the best advantage to see the game. Plus, when his kid's team scored, he didn't budge while the rest of the parents cheered."

"He could just be an uninvolved dad," Beth offered.

"Maybe, but then why even let them play soccer? Or any sport? It's like it's an obligation or for appearances sake." Rachel knew Beth could be spot on, but there was something else. "I mean, why not just wait in the car or not stick around at all."

The comms went silent and immediately Rachel felt insecure. Maybe she was trying to convince herself rather than the team. They didn't feel what she felt. She was about to move on from the suspicious dad when she remembered the encouragement that Curt had given her. *Trust your instincts.* Her instincts told her this guy was hiding a dark secret, but she'd been wrong before. She was wrong about Ms. Hastings but had been spot on with Holly. She hoped her instincts were right about this man.

"I know it's a stretch, but I walked by to get a better look and…"

"And what?" Beth asked.

"I saw something. In his eyes." Rachel felt awkward for even saying that. She agreed all of the paranoid tendencies could be explained away, but it was the darkness hiding behind his eyes that convinced Rachel. That part was transparent. That part was real. "He's hiding something. I can see it when I looked into his eyes."

Another silence fell over the line and Rachel felt foolish. She wondered if Curt had ever experienced this stage of self-doubt.

"Where is he?" Beth asked. "I'll try and get a picture of him."

Louis piggy-backed, "Yes, then send it to me, and I'll run it through facial recognition. See if anything pops." Rachel's uncertainty began to wane.

"The game ended so the guy and the two kids just got in a truck. It's backed in so I can't get a tag, but he'll be headed out soon." Rachel updated.

"Okay, I'm over by the entrance." Beth announced. "What kind of truck is it? I should be able to get a good picture from where I am."

Rachel described the truck and relayed the man's movements until he was in Beth's line of sight. A moment later Beth managed to get a good picture of him as he paused before pulling into traffic.

"Perfect." Rachel said. "Get it to Louis and let him do his thing."

The rest of the afternoon was spent following the nervous father. Melinda drove the Sprinter as the team kept a loose tail on him. Louis diligently plotted the points of the man's face to be entered into the facial recognition software. The program reads and compares the inputted plots to that of entered images and then matches up any hits, much like the FBI's Automated Fingerprint Identification System (AFIS). The success of finding a match depended on many different variables. The biggest was the target previously being entered into the system that is cross-referenced, such as jails, prison and drivers' license agencies. Louis was trying to tweak his own version of the software and trying to incorporate social media as a search medium to supplement all the government databases. Given all the different "selfie" poses that are constantly being uploaded, it's a viable option, but the variables to compare increased exponentially based on the multitude of different cameras used to post all those pictures. Clarity was never a constant among profile pictures and other posted images, and this proved to be difficult as the "fuzzier" the image, the more likely it would get passed over by the program's search engine. But it was a way to widen the search parameters.

Rachel waited anxiously on the results. They passed a street sign announcing they were entering the city limits of Houston, Texas. An unwanted feeling of nostalgia flooded Rachel. She had been so consumed with leading the team and uncovering the mystery of the dad that she failed to realize she was back home. It was like she absentmindedly walked into a school reunion where all of her past transgressions still existed. She had changed so much since she left, she was no longer the person she once had been. Hitting rock bottom in the hospital where she'd been treated for alcohol poisoning was the last memory she had of "home." With the exception of her mother and the memory of her missing sister, she had no reason to return otherwise.

"Boom! Got a hit." Louis shouted. He threw his arms up in success and then keyed back on his computer screen. A serious look creased across his face.

"What is it?" Rachel grew weary. A hit was good news, but Louis' reaction gave her concern.

"He's wanted for attempted murder and kidnapping out of Florida."

Shocked by the accuracy of her instincts, Rachel didn't know how to respond. The man clearly had plenty of reasons for being overly suspicious. He was a fugitive on the run. She felt like yelling out exuberantly, having her instincts validated, but thought better of it and remained silent, rejoicing internally.

"He's also tied to two missing children's cases in FCIC and NCIC." Louis paused to read more from his computer screen. "Yeah…, he kidnapped his own children."

"Wow, Rachel. You nailed it with this guy. Good job!" Beth praised.

"Thanks."

Louis found the warrant through the clerk of courts website and read off the document. The dad, Zeke Sheridan, while in the midst of a bitter custody battle, walked out of the courthouse during a break never to return. Anticipating losing custody of his two children, Zachary aged nine and Zoey aged six, he went to his ex-mother-in-law's house in a fit of rage. He was an abusive and angry man who thirsted for control. He forced his way in the house, demanding his children. The woman tried to fend him off, but his larger size allowed him to quickly over-power her. He beat her unconscious and left her for dead. The judge granted custody to the mother, and when she went to pick up her children, she found her mother nearly beaten to death. Initially listed in critical condition, she was able to recover enough to provide the police a detailed account of what happened.

"That was last summer, so he's been on the run for almost seven months."

"Yeah, seven months." Louis answered.

"And the police have no idea where he is?" Rachel asked.

"Looks that way."

27

"So, how do you want to handle this?" There was an expectant tone in Beth's question.

"Let's follow him and see where they live. We could probably grab the kids at the house if we can figure a good way draw the dad out."

"He's got a long history of violence, Rachel. We're going to need to be careful." Louis was referring to the absence of Curt. He had always been their protection when violence was a possibility, and in his absence, it was a weakness of the team.

"Let's see what we have to work with first."

***

Melinda followed Sheridan to the outskirts of a small west Houston suburb of Ranchero, Texas. He pulled into a small mobile home community with dirt roads and a depressing look of despair.

"We're going to stick out way too much in there." Rachel said. "Keep going down the road a bit and see if we can't hide the van somewhere better."

A few blocks away there was a strip mall with a discount store, a Chinese take-out restaurant, and a pawn shop. Melinda pulled around to the back and parked. Only about a quarter mile from the trailer park, they would be able to run reconnaissance without interruption.

"Hey guys, I found this on the net." Louis turned his screen to face the front of the van so the team could watch.

It was a video of a woman, distraught and holding herself with arms crossed as she stood behind a podium staged in front of a police station. She wore a purple knit sweater, and her hair was stringy and moved wildly with the wind. The name on the bottom of the screen read Linda Sheridan. The team watched as she begged the public for assistance in finding her children. She even pled directly to her ex-husband, asking him to do the right thing and turn himself into the authorities. It was appropriately heart-wrenching. The video concluded with the agency's Public Information Officer reminding the public that Zeke Sheridan was wanted for attempted murder, and he was considered very dangerous.

"Beth, can you dress down and go find which one is Sheridan's house?""

"Sure. Won't be needing these." Beth kicked off her shoes with a smile.

"It's a little chilly outside, you sure?"

"It's a trailer park, so yeah, I'm sure."

"Fine." Rachel didn't argue with the assumption.

Ten minutes later, Beth was feeding Louis and Rachel information over the communication line.

"He's in lot number thirty-seven. I'm pretty sure it's just him and the kids in there. No girlfriend or anything like that."

"Where does that lot sit in the park? Near the entrance?" Rachel asked.

"No. It's about half-way down on the east side."

Rachel thought about her answer. She mulled something over in her mind, trying to get a clear picture of how she wanted this operation to go.

"Have you seen the kids?" Melinda asked Beth over the comms.

"No, not yet."

"The warrant says they are nine and six years old," Louis stated.

"Something we need to consider, and we've seen it before." Melinda turned to Rachel. "Sometimes, the kids won't want to go with us. Most times in parental abductions, the kids are brainwashed into thinking the other parent is the bad one. We need to be prepared to deal with that."

"Wow, well…" Rachel let the possibility soak in. "Let's cross that bridge when we get to it. We can't let them stay with him any longer."

Beth managed to send back a few pictures taken covertly that would help Rachel formulate her plan. As Louis uploaded them onto his screen, Rachel saw something at the neighboring trailer that gave her an idea.

"Beth, come on back. I have a new assignment for you. We're going to grab them tonight."

What spawned Rachel's plan was a photo of the handicap ramp leading up to the door of Sheridan's neighbor. Along with the flower gardens out front, albeit somewhat neglected, the image told Rachel

29

there was an elderly woman living there, most likely alone. Louis was able to verify that Agnes Stanton, age seventy-three, lived there.

"Beth, I want you to get cozy with Ms. Stanton and see if you can get her to call over to Sheridan and ask him to fix something. While he's out, I'll sneak in and grab the kids. Louis, you be ready with the van in case he gets wise to what we're doing, and we need to make a hasty escape."

"You want me to befriend a seventy-three-year-old woman? Whatever shall we talk about?"

"I don't know."

"Crocheting? Knitting? Wearing dentures?"

"C'mon, I thought—"

"I'm kidding," Beth giggled. "I'm giving you a hard time. I'll just pretend I'm a long-lost relative stopping by to chat. I'm sure that will buy us all the time we need to get ol' Granny Stanton on board with us."

Rachel playfully scoffed back at Beth. She took the ribbing as a sign of acceptance. Beth dove into a duffel bag, removed conservative clothing, and began to change in the front seat. Rachel turned to Louis to address another need and caught him leering toward the front of the van. She forced a cough and he snapped his focus back to Rachel.

"Louis, I need you to get on the scanner and monitor the police."

"On it."

"What do you want me to do?" Melinda asked.

"I want you to show me how to use your stick thingy?"

"My 'stick thingy'? You mean my Asp?"

"Yeah, whatever it's called."

Melinda smiled at the request. She checked a small bag, pulled out a collapsible baton, and followed Rachel outside.

"First thing is to expand it, like this." With a violent jerk, she whipped the small stick at a downward angle, and it popped out to three times it's length. Melinda demonstrated the move two more times for Rachel.

"You need to make sure you use enough force to expand it or else it won't lock."

Rachel nodded, unsure of herself. She gave the baton a few swings trying to get a feel for the weapon.

"You got it?"

"Yeah, I think so. How do you get it go back down?"

"Here." Melinda took the baton and banged the head of it against the cement ground, collapsing it down to the compacted size.

Rachel took the Asp and practiced a few more times, expanding it and closing it back down.

"Okay, so to hit someone, try and hit them with this point of the stick." Melinda pointed to the knobby end of the baton about the size of a half roll of quarters. She gave her a few more pointers and told her to store it in her back pocket.

"You good?"

Rachel nodded, "Yeah."

Beth stepped out dressed in jeans, a hole on the right knee, and a navy-blue hoodie with the word "College" stitched across the chest. It was an homage to John Belushi's character in *Animal House*. With her youthful looks, she would pass anywhere as a college co-ed.

"I'm ready."

"Okay, go ahead." Beth took off on foot toward the trailer park and tested the comms as she left. Louis acknowledged her and wished her luck.

Rachel tested her comms as she prepped herself for the mission.

"Loud and clear." Louis said.

"Not going to wish me luck, too?" Rachel said with an accusatory grin.

"Oh..., yeah.... Good luck."

"Thanks."

***

Thirty minutes later, Rachel managed to sneak close enough to Sheridan's trailer. There were still a couple of lights on inside. Dusk gave way to the veil of night. The faint orange glow of the street lamps cast long shadows, giving Rachel extra concealment in her hiding spot. During the wait, she slipped off a back pack and double checked the contents, hoping she didn't forget anything. Satisfied everything was there, she zipped it up and sat it on the ground beside her. She waited, listened to Beth convince the old lady that she was a distant relative passing through town. The old lady was cautious at first, and at the point which Rachel thought Beth's act wasn't going to work, she was invited in by Mrs. Stanton and offered hot tea.

During the quiet, Rachel's thoughts turned to Curt. She felt as if she was hanging out on a ledge, about to give way and fall into the abyss. Grateful for the opportunity to be a part of this team, she feared she would mess up and ruin what Alexis and everyone had worked so hard to accomplish. Curt had been a stronger leader, way more confident than she. In moments like this, she wished he were there to guide her and the team. She wondered if he would ever come back.

Finally, Rachel saw the lights in the back of the Sheridan trailer go dark. She figured they were in the kids' bedroom, and it was bedtime. Further confirmation came as she could hear heavy footsteps leave the back of the trailer for the front. She took the opportunity to move closer to the back door.

"I'm set up, and I just saw the kids' lights go out," Rachel noted.

"Okay, we're on our second round of hot tea with Granny Stanton over here," Beth said.

"Alright, the plan is simple. Have the old lady call and get him over there to fix something, whatever, and then stall him while I get the kids out."

"Copy that."

As Rachel waited for notification that the phone call was made, the familiar voice of Curtis Walker came over the ear bud comms, "What do you need me to do?"

Rachel instinctively grinned from ear to ear at the sound of his voice but checked herself before speaking.

"Couldn't stay away, could you?"

"No, I guess not."

Without further hesitation, Rachel ordered, "Good, well, come meet up with me, and you can help me take the kids out. I'll brief you in person."

"Alright, I'll be right there."

Rachel couldn't believe he was there. Moments later, she spied his form walking through the shadows of the trailer park and over to her location. She erased the smile from her face and fought away the urge to hug him. She noticed he wasn't wearing his trench coat, which seemed strange. With the exception of that time in the hotel after his run, she'd never seen him away from the house without it. He gave her a crooked smile and knelt down next to her.

"What?" he asked.

"Nothing." Rachel decided not to ask about the trench coat.

"What do we have?"

"Got a guy who kidnapped his own kids from Florida and brought them here. Apparently, he beat up his ex-mother-in-law pretty bad after he lost custody. Louis was able to confirm he has warrants for his arrest."

"So, a real prince, this guy!"

Curt asked about the particulars in the case from Florida. As Rachel explained, he began to nod his head.

"Yep, I remember that case in the news. Out of the Jacksonville area. Wow, how'd you spot him?"

Rachel hesitated before answering from embarrassment. She blushed but didn't fully understand why. Curt waited for an answer.

"Well, we were hunting around this giant soccer complex, and I spotted him in the crowd. He was just standing off to the side, not really paying attention to his kids, and he seemed paranoid." Curt nodded as he followed her reasoning. "So, he stood out to me and then—"

"What?"

"Then, I saw something in his eyes."

Curt seemed impressed. "What did you see?"

"It was strange. It's like I could tell he was hiding some dark secret, like he was pretending to be someone he's not." Rachel saw Curt smiling at her and looked away, embarrassed. "Like I said, it was strange."

"Rachel, Granny Stanton just made the call, begged him to come fix the heater. And I mean, begged. This guy's an ass."

"Okay, Beth. As soon as he's clear—"

Rachel shushed herself as the aluminum door of the trailer flung open, and Zeke Sheridan stepped out. He was mumbling to himself as he walked over to Mrs. Stanton's lot. She was sure she heard, "stupid old bitch," muttered under his breath.

Looking back at Curt, Rachel asked, "You ready?"

He nodded. Rachel began to ease around the trailer to the back door. Curt stood behind her. After trying the door knob, she hesitated at what to do next. She looked back to Curt.

"It's locked. Should I knock? If we bust through, it'll scare the kids and alert Sheridan. What would you do? Pick it?"

"This is your show. I'll follow your lead."

Put off, she didn't like that answer and gave him an irritated glare. She wanted direction, not encouragement.

"Fine. If you're not going to help…"

Rachel lightly knocked on the door. While waiting for a response inside, she zipped open the back pack and removed a small tablet and powered it on.

"What's that for?" Curt asked.

"Back up."

Rachel knocked again, this time a bit louder. Lighter footsteps inside the trailer moved from the back to the other side of the door. But whoever was on the other side, just stood there. Blanked, Rachel wasn't sure what to do.

"Use their name." Curt whispered. Rachel turned and gave him a confused look. He returned with a silent urge and head nod toward the door. Now, she understood.

"Zach? My name is Rachel. I want to give you a message buddy. Can you open the door?" Rachel took a guess it was the older boy, not the younger girl, Zoey, who chose to investigate the knock. There was no movement inside, but she could tell the boy was still standing there.

"Zach, I'm here to help you, but I can't give you the message unless you open the door."

Rachel began tapping at the screen of the tablet. The glow illuminated her face in the dark shadows of the trailer.

Curt tapped her and nodded at the door. The doorknob was slowly turning. As the door cracked open, the light flooded out and half of a small boy's face poked out.

"Hi, Zach. I'm Rachel. I'm so sorry to wake you up, but I have a message for you and Zoey. Is she awake or sleeping?"

"Sleeping." His tone carried skepticism and curiosity together.

"Okay, well, since you don't know me, I won't ask to come in, but the message is really for both of you. Do you think you could go get her?"

The boy didn't move or respond. He only stared back at Rachel studying her like she was a new species of animal. Curt moved and Zach noticed, turning afraid.

"It's okay, Zach." She said in a friendly tone. "This is my friend, Curt. He's helping me. Can you go get your sister?"

Without acknowledgement, Zach pushed away from the door and ran down the hall. The door slowly swung open, revealing the inside of the home. A slight rotten smell emanated out which caused Rachel's nose to crinkle. There was trash strewn around the kitchen floor and she noticed overall uncleanliness. She turned her head for better air to breathe.

"Gross."

Two sets of footsteps came back to the door. Zoey, rubbed her sleepy eyes and stood at the threshold looking down at Rachel and Curt. Zach didn't say anything, but held an expectant look on his face.

"Okay, here." Rachel tapped the screen of the tablet a few more times and then spoke to the device.

"Are you ready? They are right here." Rachel twisted the tablet around to face the children. The glow was now on their faces.

A woman's voice spoke out from the tablet. Rachel saw Zoey's face light up, but Zach's seemed to grow angry.

"Mommy!" Zoey cried.

"Hi, my angels. Hi. Yes, it's mommy and I miss you so very much."

"Mommy, where are you?" The girl asked.

"I'm at home, baby. Waiting for you."

"You are?" The confusion in Zoey's voice was obvious.

"Dad says you were going to give us away, that you don't really love us and don't want us to be a family no more." Zach spat with as much rage as a seven-year-old could muster.

"No, son. That is not true. I would never do or want such a thing. I love you and will always love you with all my heart. The *only* thing I want is us to be together."

"Then why'd you go to the judge's courthouse and ask for us to be given away?"

"Zach, I didn't do that. Is that—"

"I don't believe you!"

Zach reached for his sister, but she pulled against him to keep looking at her mother on the tablet screen.

"Zach, buddy. I think your dad has been lying to you and your sister." Rachel offered with sincerity.

"Yes, he has Zach. Please, listen to me. I need you guys to go with her, please." Curt added.

"No! You'll just try and give us away again." Zach began pulling at his younger sister. She began to whine that he was hurting her and that she wanted to see her mommy.

"No, Zoey. Dad said that it's a trick. We have to stay here and hide."

"Okay, that's enough." Curt said. He pushed past Rachel and stepped inside the trailer. The young boy was dwarfed by Curt's size. Zach tried to punch Curt as he reached for him, but there wasn't enough umph behind the blow to do anything. Curt spun him around and picked him up over his shoulder. He began to kick and flail uselessly. Rachel handed Zoey the tablet letting her speak to her mother over Skype.

"Come on, Zach. You got to know deep down, your dad is lying to you." Curt said.

36

"No, he's the only one that cares." Zach let out a screeching yell that pierced Rachel and Curt's ears. It was no doubt loud enough to alert Sheridan.

In a hushed tone, Beth's voice came over the comms. "Um, Rachel, I don't know what the heck is going on over there, but the dad heard something and left out in a hurry. Is everything okay?"

Rachel corralled young Zoey in her nightgown while Curt carried the flailing Zach. As they reached the corner of the trailer, it shook with the weight of Sheridan busting in the front door. He yelled for the kids, but went silent. Rachel figured he saw the back door left open.

"Shit. Go, Curt."

"I'm coming to get you." Melinda responded over the air.

"No!" Rachel snapped. "You won't be able to get the van in here and turned around. We'll make a run for it."

"Okay, I'll be waiting at the entrance."

Rachel looked at Curt, "Let's go."

"What the hell?" Zeke Sheridan's large frame filled the threshold of the back door. "What the fuck do think you're doing?"

"Go, Rachel. I got this."

"No." Rachel directed Zoey toward the entrance just as Melinda arrived with the Sprinter. She handed the tablet to Zoey, pulled out Melinda's ASP and flicked it down to full length. "I got it. You get the boy to the van."

"You sure?"

"Yes. Go!"

Still carrying Zach, Curt headed for the van while Rachel stayed behind.

"And you think you're going to stop me? Those are my goddamn kids!"

"Who you took from their mother!"

"Is that who sent you? The bitch?"

Zeke advanced on Rachel, but she stood her ground, ready with the ASP. "You're going to need more than that little stick, honey!"

Rachel jumped forward with the speed of an experienced fencer and swung at Zeke's knee's. She swung as hard as she could at the large man, but the blow didn't knock him down. He reared back and countered with a punch from his large hand, but Rachel ducked and stepped back out of his range. She regrouped, repositioned the ASP and swung again for the same knee. This time it buckled, but Sheridan still didn't fall. He reached out to grab her, but she remained nimble and out of his clutches. Once again, with more confidence, she swung at the same left knee. This time Zeke let out a painful howl as the small metal tip landed against his knee cap. This time he went down. Rachel was sure she felt a corresponding crunch of bone and cartage from the hit.

Rachel lifted the ASP up high for a final blow, hoping to take Zeke out of the fight. As he writhed in pain, she reveled in his underestimation of her ability. As she brought the baton down with all her might, it was met with only empty air. The momentum of her swing knocked her off balance, and Zeke Sheridan grabbed her and slammed her down to the ground. He kicked at her ribs as she covered them in defense.

"You messed with the wrong guy, lady!"

Confused as to how the tables turned so quickly, Rachel felt trapped with Sheridan's massive frame standing over her. His mass blocked out the street lamp and made everything immediately dark.

Suddenly, his arms flung up toward the sky and his body lurched backwards. Rachel craned her neck looking up for the reason. Curt appeared at his side after delivering a swift kick to the same left knee. Curt twisted back and punched the large man with a vicious right hook before he could get his bearings. Sheridan fell to the ground with a solid thud. Curt positioned himself for a response, but Zeke remained on the ground, knocked unconscious.

Curt turned and held out his hand for Rachel. She winced at the shooting pain in her ribs but pulled herself up with his help.

Looking down at the unconscious man, Rachel asked. "What should we do with him?"

With a grin, Curt said, "I have an idea."

38

Five minutes later, Curt and Rachel casually strode from between Sheridan and Mrs. Stanton's trailer toward the Mercedes Sprinter waiting at the entrance. Zeke Sheridan was going to get what he deserved and his children were going to be returned to their mother where they belonged.

The ache in her ribs caused Rachel to favor her left side.

"You alright?" Curt asked.

"I think so. I hope he didn't crack a rib." Rachel took in a deep breath and grimaced in pain. "So, what the hell happened? I mean, I had that guy on the ropes, and all of a sudden, I missed with the ASP. I don't get it."

"It collapsed on you."

"Huh?" Rachel turned to Curt. "But I flicked it out like Mel said."

"Yeah, but if you don't flick it hard enough after hitting something, it has the tendency to collapse."

Curt took the weapon from her, expanded it, hit hard against the sole of his shoe and then wiggled it in the air. After a few gyrations, it fell down to its hand-held size.

"Oh, well damn."

"Won't make that mistake again, will you?"

"Nope."

***

The patrolman saw the trailer park entrance and advised dispatch that he was in the area. He was acknowledged, and he soon found the lot number displayed on the side of the mobile home. The call notes sounded far-fetched, which piqued his curiosity, and he was eager to find out what had really happened.

He grabbed the printout and exited his patrol car. He clicked on his Maglite even though the street light gave enough illumination. Making his way up to the destination lot, he came upon a clearing between two trailers. On one side was a slightly overgrown garden area with potted plants and a sense of order. The other had dirt, a trash can with flies hovering over it, and a depressing look. But in between, was a whole other sight. One that lived up to the odd call notes, and one to surely be retold for the coming months.

On the ground, sporting a bloody lip and dirty clothes, was a large man handcuffed around the base of a light post. His face was scowling in defeat, and he could barely bring himself to look up at the patrolman. Full of shame, the man had clearly lost some sort of physical confrontation. The patrolman shined the beam of his Maglite on the man's face and compared it to the printout in his hand. Another confirming look, and he was positive it was a match. The man was Ezekiel "Zeke" Sheridan, wanted on Attempted Murder from Jacksonville, Florida.

"Well, damn. It's not your lucky day is it?" The patrolman said.

Sheridan didn't respond, only sighed in humiliation.

However unusual it was to find a wanted felon such as Sheridan handcuffed to a light post at random, it was who was standing, or sitting rather, next to him that made the call for service much more intriguing.

"Are you Agnes Stanton?" he asked.

"Yes, officer."

"And you apprehended this man?" The disbelief in his voice was overly apparent. "On your own?"

With a beaming smile, she replied, "You bet your sweet ass, I did. Got a little rough with me, too. So, I had to put him down."

Dumbfounded, the patrolman didn't know how to react other than to smile and nod at the old lady in the wheelchair.

"I'm sure you did, ma'am. I'm sure you did."

Chapter 6

The final test was upon Layla, and although she was completely unaware, he felt certain she would pass. She was too much like *her* for it not to be fate. With excitement brewing in his stomach, he clicked the mouse to open up the window into Layla's life. He pushed his glasses up the bridge of his nose, waiting for what his machine would reveal to him. She was like the rest of them. Putting her world out in the open for anyone to see. Sifting through the stockpile of endless selfie's and inane comments, he found what he was seeking. She passed.

Maneuvering through her virtual life, he gained an understanding of how his prey worked. She was complicated, smart, but remarkably easy to predict. A time and place quickly calculated and constructed in his mind. It would work perfectly.

A satisfaction draped over him giving him the sense that she was the prize he had searched for so desperately. He leaned back in his chair, a king at rest on his throne. He held his arms behind his head, interlacing his fingers. Looking away from the computer screen, his gaze moved up toward the memories. All of them, frozen in time for him to relive at any moment. Each one held their own special place in history. Each one had brought him closer to *her*, but never close enough.

He took in the lot and then narrowed his focus on one specific memory. It was *her* memory. Unlike the rest, her memory was incomplete. But now, with this prize falling into his trap, his satisfaction turned to anticipation that there would be an ending.

Chapter 7

She pushed away the bothersome odor permeating in the backseat of the taxi cab. The stench was irritating, like burnt pasta and stale incense, but it wasn't strong enough to distract her from where she was going. Staring outside the window, in what under normal circumstances would be a welcome sight, all Rachel felt was disgust. Seeing the city limit sign of her home town was anything but nostalgic. After leaving years ago, she never desired to return, but after debating whether or not to go see *her* over a sleepless night, she gave in and called a cab.

"Make the next left." She directed.

The cabby made the turn. Knowing it was coming didn't ease the anxiety, it made it worse. She inhaled deeply, taking in a mix of fresh air from outside and the odd aroma inside the car.

"Can you stop here for a minute?"

"You get out here?" Rachel couldn't tell if he was Mediterranean or Middle Eastern with his accent. It didn't matter.

"Yes, but I'll only be a minute. Can you wait, and then we can go to the other location."

"Oh, okay. Meter still on."

After the taxi stopped, Rachel stepped out. The dawn sky was in transition from a deep, dark blue to a lighter cyan with hints of orange hues that lined the horizon. The morning air carried a chill and Rachel tightened her jacket around her body for warmth. She stepped onto the sidewalk and looked up and down the street. She had come back to this spot a few times before, each time seeking answers that never came.

There was no reason to think this visit would be any different. She remembered the day as vivid as when it happened. She and her sister were pushing their bikes, nibbling on their favorite candy when the faceless man appeared out of nowhere and forced them into a van.

In an instant, images from the next few terror-filled days flooded her mind. A hazy van ride where her body felt like it was drowning in quick sand and being held captive in a dank room with her sister who was repeatedly violated by the faceless man. Her shamelessly offering herself to her captor so he wouldn't take her sister.

A shudder broke her from the unwanted reverie. The disappointment of unanswered questions didn't sting as bad as it once did. She looked around again, trying to focus on the area. She noticed the trees that lined the road were much bigger. Evidence that she'd been gone a while.

"Okay, we can go to the address I told you now."

"Okay, not a problem."

Rachel checked her cell phone. There were no messages. She hoped everything back at the hotel was going according to plan. After leaving the trailer park, they checked into a nearby hotel. Melinda and Beth were doing their best to talk to Zachary Sheridan. His father had done a number on him, convincing the boy that his mother had truly wanted to give him and his sister away. He also convinced Zach that his grandmother was in on the plan which is why she was beaten. The only reprieve was for him to take the children off to another state so they could hide from their evil mother.

Alexis had arranged for the kids' mother, Linda Sheridan, to catch the first flight out of Jacksonville bound for Houston. She had arrived at George Bush Intercontinental after midnight and Louis had brought her to the hotel. As expected, Zoey ran to her mother with open arms in a tearful embrace while her brother stood angry and skeptical in the corner avoiding eye contact. Rachel had knelt down and talked to the boy until he finally agreed to at least listen to his mother. Linda had begged her son to give her a chance and to come back home where he belonged.

Rachel wiped away a tear watching the exchange. Not knowing that power of a mother's love for the last twenty years made the scene tough to witness. It forced her to recall the loveless relationship with her mother.

"Pull over here."

The cabby slowed and pulled next to a curb. He typed something into the meter and twisted around in his seat, looking through Plexi-glass.

"You get out here? Total is fifty-three dollars and fifty cents."

Rachel fished out sixty dollars and slid it through a slit in the divider.

"Keep the change."

Rachel got out and peered down the street. Her mother's house, her childhood home, was at the end of the block. The sun was now fully above the horizon and warming up the brisk day. Taking in the houses, she realized they were so much smaller than she remembered. Everything looked worn and tired.

Across the street was a small playground. It was still too early and too cold for it be in use, but she walked over and sat down on a swing, angled to see the front of her mother's house. She hadn't seen her or spoken to her in over ten years. She had tried her best to be open minded and sympathetic to her mother, but that never erased the blame. In a volatile time in her life, Rachel learned that when she needed love and compassion, she was made to feel guilty for surviving against the faceless man, instead of her sister. Not being a mother, she couldn't fully grasp this rationale, but even so, she felt cheated out of what could have been a salvaged childhood. Rather, it led to promiscuity, binge drinking and anorexia. For that, Rachel couldn't bring herself to knock on the front door. But yet, inexplicably she still wanted to see her.

A short, blonde woman exited the house, bundled in a jacket and mittens, and began walking away from where Rachel sat in the playground. She was moving slow, but with purpose. Instinctively, Rachel followed. Even though she was facing away, Rachel knew it was her mother.

Keeping a distance of a half-block between them, Rachel tailed her for about two miles. They came upon a shopping center. It wasn't there when Rachel was younger, so it must have been built since she left. Sitting in the middle as the anchor was a grocery store. Her mother walked into the store and out of her sight. Next door was a coffee shop. The chill was biting so she stepped inside but kept an eye on the entrance and exit of the store. She would wait her mother out in the coffee shop and see where she would go next. Maybe, after she found more courage, she would approach her and say hello.

An hour went by and Rachel still hadn't seen her mother exit. Her cup was empty and her bladder was full. The Grande latte' lived up to its reputation. She contemplated whether or not she missed her leaving, but remembered surveillance was now her day job. She was good at it.

Rachel pulled out her ponytail and let her hair fall to the tops of her shoulders. She pulled out a pair of over-sized sunglasses from her jacket and put them on. It would buy her a moment of anonymity against an inadvertent glance.

Walking in the store and ignoring her bladder, she scanned the checkout area in case her mother was about to leave. Not seeing her in line, she moved to the front runway so she could visually search the aisles. Starting on the far side of the store and making her way to the other, there was no sign of her mother.

Frustrated, she cursed herself for losing her mark. It was the personal connection that must have clouded her ability. As she turned around to find the restrooms, her eyes immediately found the saddened face of Amelia Goodwin. She was working as a cashier. Entering from the far side, her back had been to Rachel, but now she was facing in her direction. She had removed the jacket and wore a bright green smock with a nametag pinned to her chest.

Frozen, she watched her mother innocuously scan food items and punch a key board in front of her. She only spoke when spoken to. There was no fire, no passion, no life to her mother. Maybe it was because of the intimate knowledge Rachel had, but it was clear that darkness hid behind the desolate eyes of Amelia Goodwin. And for good reason. She had known the pain of losing two daughters, one to horrific circumstances and the other as an aftereffect.

45

Suddenly, Amelia looked up and noticed she was being watched. Rachel snapped from her trance and turned down the nearest aisle. With the sunglasses and down worn hair, she hoped that she registered as a random customer and not her estranged daughter. She pretended to study some merchandise at the edge of the aisle, spying on her mother. She was back to scanning more items for another customer. If she had noticed, she didn't care to react.

Utilizing the time, Rachel grabbed a basket and set out to grab a few personal items while she loosely surveilled Amelia. From a favorable angle, Rachel watched her mother in between customers when she had dead time. She looked hollow. She would superficially smile when someone acknowledged her or said hello, but the darkness would quickly return. Rachel imagined that for her mother, not too many moments passed without her thoughts going back to that tragedy.

A few hours more of casually strolling around the store, a quick bathroom break and slowly filling up her basket, Rachel saw that another cashier was waiting behind Amelia with a cash drawer. Figuring it was nearing her lunch break, Rachel made for a checkout line to her mother's back. She watched as she took her drawer up to an office and then clocked out. After she threw on her jacket, she headed straight for the exit.

Rachel quickly finished her transactions and made it to the exit just in time to see Amelia pull the door open to a neighboring liquor store and go inside. This gave her pause, feeling an even lower level of pity for her mother. Moments later, Amelia exited the liquor store and walked to the far end of the shopping center. Rachel hung around the parking lot and followed her mother from afar, knowing her obvious intentions. Amelia found seclusion, or so she thought, leaned up against the side wall of the corner business, furiously twisted the cap off the small bottle, turned it up, and held it there for a few seconds. Rachel looked away.

It was another few hours before Amelia came home. Rachel had let herself in through the back door. The hide-a-key was still under the second potted plant to the right of the back door. The plant had long since joined the afterlife, but the key was still there. Uncertain as to why she wanted to look around, Rachel thought maybe some part of home was still there for her to come back to, one day. Not much had changed. Matter of fact, after a walk-through, Rachel was sure nothing had changed within the house. The furniture, the carpet, the dishes, the towels, the beds, the bedspreads, everything was the same as when Rachel had left for college. It had just aged nearly two decades. However, the stench of stale urine and sour liquor hung in the air. The drapes were drawn and there was an overall melancholy feel to the house.

Rachel peeked in her old room. Most of it was as she remembered, but there was a box shoved in the corner with the word *Mail* scribbled on the side. She flipped open the flap and saw a pile of envelopes and postcards all addressed to her. She pulled out a fistful and just let them fall back in the box. They were from a lifetime she no longer wanted to be a part of and letting them go unread kept it that way.

Rachel slipped out the back, replaced the hide-a-key, and strolled back to the playground. She chose to sit on a bench with her back turned to the house now that a few parents stood by while their kids played.

By mid-afternoon she had ignored her phone long enough. There were dozens of missed calls and text messages from the team. They started out casual but quickly grew more worrisome based on the amount of exclamation points Louis used. She noticed none were from Curt. She wasn't sure if that meant anything or not, but it hurt a little on some level.

She dialed Melinda.

"Hey, I just wanted to let you know I'm fine. I just needed some time away."

"Okay, well…, you could've told someone, but take your time if you need it. We're headed out in the morning."

"Alright. How's it going with Zoey and Zach?"

"Fine. Zach is a stubborn one. He's going to need some major therapy. Dad did some real psychological damage to that boy."

"Oh, that's a shame."

"Yeah, but Zoey is doing good. Mom is ecstatic. Oh, and I had Louis check. Sheridan is being extradited back to Florida in the morning to stand trial for the attempted murder and kidnapping charges."

"That's good." Her answer was flat. Rachel realized she inadvertently let her emotions come out through her tone.

"You sure you're alright?"

"Yes and no. I'll be back to the hotel tonight. Don't leave without me. Goodbye."

"G'bye."

Rachel stowed her phone. One of the kids on the playground was staring up at her with an ear to ear smile. Despite the depressive day, Rachel couldn't help but smile back at the child, who giggled and then ran off toward her mom. Rachel's past was so clouded with darkness, she couldn't remember if she'd ever laughed like that.

Movement out of the corner of her eye drew Rachel's attention. It was Amelia walking back home. Her pace was slower and she swayed side to side while she cradled a small paper bag in the shape of a bottle. Up the sidewalk and onto the porch, she entered the house and shut the door. Rachel didn't want to see her mother like that. She debated further if she should go knock on the door or not.

Another hour went by and she found herself standing on the front porch. The television was on with the volume up loud. Only out of some unknown obligation did Rachel finally knock. There was no answer. She knocked again, this time deliberate and loud. Nothing. She peeked in the window, but the drapes, however ratty and thin, blocked a clear view inside.

Is she hiding? Doesn't she know who it is? Rachel beat on the door again, but there was still no movement.

"Mom, open up." She announced. "It's me, Rachel."

Frustration set in and Rachel walked around back. She snatched up the hidden key and entered through the back. The television was obnoxiously loud and covered her movement. She felt like an intruder even though at one point this had been home. From the kitchen, she peered into the living room and saw a pair of feet dangling off the couch, faced down. They were still. Something was wrong.

Quickly, she stepped into the living room to check on her mother. As she stood at the end of the couch she looked down. That feeling of pity returned and sank another notch lower. Amelia was passed out. Drool seeped from her open mouth and her right-hand clenched a near-empty bottle of cheap whiskey. It was a pathetic sight, and she felt sorry for her mother.

Rachel pried the whiskey bottle from her hand and drained the rest in the kitchen sink. She found a blanket and carefully draped it over Amelia. She wondered who this woman was? This was not the person she knew as her mother. It looked like her, only older. *She is a shell of who she used to be, a consequence of her past.*

Rachel knelt down, only inches away from her mother's face and spoke soft and tenderly. "Goodbye, Mom."

Chapter 8

Ripped awake, Rachel sat up breathing heavily, her brow drenched with sweat. The vivid dream left her with one strange thought echoing in her mind, *the faceless man had a heart of stone*. Falling back against the hotel pillow, the phrase resonated as she tried to decipher it's meaning. She remembered running from the faceless man, terrified for what seemed like forever, and then hiding. She tried to recall any other parts of the dream, but suddenly it evaporated.

It had been late in the evening before Rachel made it back to the hotel. Exhausted from the long, emotionally draining day following her mother around, she just wanted a hot shower and to crawl into bed. She headed straight for her room seeing only Louis in the lobby, his face buried in a laptop. After the hot shower, she wrapped her naked body tight in the plush hotel towel and climbed into bed. Her thoughts remained on her mother and what she had become, but as she closed her eyes, sleep soon followed.

"Heart of stone?" As she heard it said out loud, Rachel shook her head, unsure of its meaning. She shook it off like all the other unanswered questions having to do with her kidnapping. That wasn't anything new. She had come to expect it and simply moved on with her day.

She dressed, packed her bags and went downstairs in search of breakfast.

Curt was finishing up a plate of eggs and toast when Rachel strolled into the hotel dining area.

"G'morning."

"Good morning." She forced a tired smile.

"Didn't sleep that good?"

"No, it was fine. It's just…" Rachel sat and thought again about the bizarre phrase from her dream. "Just a weird dream is all."

"Have anything to do with what happened to you when you were a kid?"

Impressed that Curt could tell that right off the bat, she held an amazed look on her face. "How'd you?"

"C'mon, we're like one town over from where you were kidnapped and then you disappeared all day yesterday. Doesn't take a rocket scientist to figure that may have been weighing on your mind."

Rachel smiled. "Yeah, I guess you're right."

"That and when they couldn't find you, Louis pinged your phone. Showed you across the street from where you grew up."

"Ha!" Rachel said. "Should've known."

Rachel placed an order with the waitress as Curt finished up his breakfast. He sat with her while she ate.

"Thanks for your help the other night."

"I'm glad I was able to be there." Curt added a smile. She had noticed there had been several smiles from Curt, much more than before.

"I didn't get a chance to ask why you came back. Is everything okay at home? I mean, with Josh and all?"

Curt's mood changed. "Well, things are fine and not fine. It's complicated."

The frustration with his son's recovery and integration back into his old life was obvious. Rachel gave him a probing look.

"What?"

"Curt, it's me. You and I share a bond remember?"

He conceded, but he searched for his words first. It was weighing heavy on him, she figured, as he fidgeted and rearranged the salt and pepper, a spoon, and his coffee mug before answering. She waited patiently.

51

"It's not going very good at home." He started, embarrassed of his situation. "I tried going back to work at the police department, but all I could think about was being out here with the team. I mean, the only reason I was out here in the first place was because of Josh, but then I actually find him, and for some reason, I'm not satisfied. That doesn't make a lot of sense."

"You did a lot of good out here with this team. That should not be overlooked at all."

"I know, but…" There was more, she could tell. "It's been tough with Tracy as well."

Inexplicably, Rachel felt guilty. She only nodded.

"But, what's been the hardest is getting Josh the help he needs. He actually tried to hurt himself."

"Oh my god!"

"I walked in his room and he was holding a knife. Now, he didn't do anything or say anything, but I could see it in his eyes that he was damn sure thinking about it."

"That's terrible. Why aren't you home then? Shouldn't you be there with him?"

"Well, actually, the reason I'm here *is* him."

"How so?"

"Well, one thing that he's responded to positively, and the doctor said it could be beneficial, is when he asks about the kids we saved, you know, before him. He constantly wants to hear stories about how we swooped in and saved a kid."

"Really? That's good, right?"

"Yeah, I mean, he gets into the stories. I mean, really absorbed, and afterward, he shows improvement. He gets happier, functions better, actually shows affection towards me and Tracy. It's great. But then that eventually wears off and the depression sets back in. At one point, he asked if I would ever go in search of more missing kids."

"What did you tell him?"

"I told him no, but then he got even more depressed. He didn't want to hear the same stories I had already told him. He knew there were more kids out there like him, and he needed to know that someone was looking for them. So, after talking it over with Tracy and then Alexis, we worked out a deal that I could run with the team every so often."

The promise of seeing Curt with some regularity excited Rachel, but she kept that to herself.

"So, here I am, with Josh's blessing."

"I'm glad that worked out."

"Me too." Curt replied. "On the good days, I just look at him, knowing what he's been through and the horrors done to him, and think 'he's got such strength to go on'."

Rachel noticed Curt's eyes water up and smiled at the sentiment. He casually wiped his eyes and went back to rearranging his silverware.

"What else?" She asked, sensing something else.

Curt looked up through watery eyes. "You know, he went through the unimaginable."

"Right. It's understandable that his recovery would take time."

"Yeah, I know that. It's just…" Curt swallowed, looked down and back up. "It's just that I wonder if he's strong enough."

Rachel could see the worry. It was consuming and unforgiving. She imagined that he still carried the burden of his son's disappearance.

"If he's anything like you, he will be."

"Yeah, I hope so."

***

Leaving the hotel and heading for the highway, Rachel took the Captain's chair behind the front passenger seat. It had become *her* seat. It gave her a sense of stability. Something that had never been abundant in her life. Plus, it offered a great view through the large window.

It didn't matter where they were going, only that the team was leaving the Houston area. Rachel had been apprehensive about being home since their arrival, but that subsided as they started to put distance between them. Following the distant horizon, Rachel reflected back on her mother and the dismal life she led. For Rachel, it was a glimpse of an unchosen path. One she was glad went unknown. However, she felt an internal satisfaction, knowing that she did try to reach out to her mother and didn't let the opportunity pass. In the case of her mother, the last thing she wanted was regret.

Reaching under the seat, she pulled a small hydraulic lever, allowing her to twist her seat at an angle to better see out the window. She kicked off her shoes, pulled her knees to her chest, and slid down in the seat for a comfortable ride. As her eyes focused on the world passing by, something odd caught her attention. It looked like a novelty at first, but as the van got closer, the image became clear. It was a giant stone rock in the shape of a heart.

Instantly, Rachel was sent back twenty-two years. A memory forced its way out of her subconscious and played vividly in her mind. Running through woods, tired, thirsty…, so thirsty, and terrified. He was chasing her and he had gotten so close. But she found a place to hide. It was in a small nook of a huge rock. In the shape of a heart. *A heart of stone.*

She broke into a cold sweat, panicked and stricken with fear. As the van passed by, her eyes clung to the rock like they were tethered by an invisible link. She began panting, unable to catch her breath. She could no longer control anything, as if her brain had disconnected from her body.

"Hey, Rachel? You alright?"

Her head whipped around to see Curt, his face was filled with worry. She spoke, but only strained air managed to get out. Curt grabbed hold of her.

"Hey? What's wrong? Talk to me." Melinda, Beth, and Louis all turned their attention toward Rachel.

"St… st…, st…"

Curt couldn't decipher what Rachel was trying to say.

"St… *Stop!*" she screamed.

The abrupt turn into the gas station parking lot nearly threw Rachel out of her seat, but Curt, still holding her shoulder, kept her in place. She was on sensory overload, processing repressed memories that were flooding back with the force of a tsunami, trying to make sense of it all.

Was it from a made-up dream? Or was it from the actual nightmare of her abduction?

Unable to communicate her thoughts, she pushed past Curt and stepped outside for fresh air.

"What's wrong with her?" She heard Beth ask.

"Not sure, but something scared the hell out of her."

Rachel turned around in a circle, searching for the heart-shaped rock. Spying it across the street, she took off in a run straight toward it.

"Hold on, Rachel!" Curt shouted.

She ignored him and the rest of the team. The rock held answers to long overdue questions, and she wasn't leaving until she had them. Blinded by the situation, Rachel failed to see the traffic didn't share her epiphany. Several cars blared horns and swerved out of the way as she crossed the street in a manic run. A near collision clogged up the intersection, while Curt followed, apologizing to the stopped drivers for her erratic behavior.

"Stop, Rachel! You're going to get yourself hurt."

She didn't stop until she reached the other side. She stood back as if a force-field hovered around the rock, keeping her from getting closer. Replaying the unlocked memories, she tried to get a better understanding of why she was drawn to this strange object.

Curt and the team caught up with her and stood by, waiting for an explanation. A few minutes of silence went by, while she stared at the rock.

"Rachel? What's going on? Does this have some significance to what happened to you?"

She didn't respond, continuing to stare down at the rock. Her eyes glared, and her chest heaved, heavy with breath. Traffic rushed by, entering and leaving the gas station across the street. The smell of charbroiled beef emanated from the restaurant as they geared up for the lunch rush. Life was moving, but Rachel was reliving a nightmare.

"I hid from him right there." Her eyes never averted from the rock.

"What?" Curt sounded incredulous.

"I thought you didn't remember anything about your escape?" Melinda asked.

"I didn't." Rachel finally looked up. The team stood there wide-eyed. "Until now. I saw this rock and suddenly all these memories came back. Images so real it couldn't have been from a dream. Could it?"

"What do you remember? From the memories?"

Rachel closed her eyes. "I remembered running for what seemed like a day. It was through woods and mud and trees and bushes. I hid here for hours until I was sure he was gone. Then I kept running. I remember, I could hear him panting from the chase just on the other side of the rock. I was so scared he'd find me and take me back. I knew I had to find help and come back to get Rhonda. I heard him curse himself. I… I…" Rachel crossed her arms and hugged herself tight.

"It's okay. What else do you remember?" Melinda was gently rubbing her back, trying to ease the troubling memories out into her conscious.

She gasped and her eyes flicked open. "There was a tunnel and his house, there was a basement. That's how I escaped. It was through a basement."

"That's good, Rachel. Real good. Anything else?"

Rachel locked eyes with Curt. "I remember catching a glimpse of him in the woods. He wore glasses."

"Do you remember seeing his face?"

For so long, her captor was the faceless man. She had tried so many times to put a face to the monster and unveil his evil mask. She constantly wondered if it was the man behind her in the bank line, seated across the aisle from her on the bus or even the older guy who served her at the coffee shop. The not knowing was paralyzing. So as Curt asked if she now remembered his face, she concentrated hard, mentally enhancing the newly recalled memory.

"Yes."

It sounded impossible as she said it out loud, but she believed within these new memories, there was a face to the faceless man. A confident smile creased her face. It was contagious as the rest of the team shared the potential.

"You said you ran through a bunch of woods during your escape?" Louis asked, looking down at his smart phone.

"Yeah, a lot of woods."

Louis looked up and nodded just beyond the rock. "According to my phone's map, these woods go on for a few miles to the west. Toward a town called Sweetland, Texas."

"So, what do we do now?" Beth asked.

Rachel was too stunned by this monumental revelation to think about anything in the present.

Curt studied Rachel's face, looking to her for an answer. She shrugged her shoulders, making way for him to decide. He looked over his shoulder at the wood line, back to Rachel and scanned the team. With a crooked smile, he squinted up to the sun as it was ascending toward the zenith.

"Great day for a hike in the woods."

***

Going on pure instinct with no plan was something new for Rachel. When she worked for the Department of Children and Families, she always had a plan when it came to her job. Since joining the team, if not she, then someone came up with a plan of action. Not this time. Curt seemed a little more at ease, which was comforting, but trekking through the woods in hopes of finding a trail that had been cold for twenty-two years was as far-fetched as it got. Add in that this came about from previously unknown memories repressed in a fragile psyche, the chances of it actually leading anywhere were next to none.

"So, let me get this straight. We're just going to trounce through the woods hoping to find a clue after all this time?"

Busy packing basic survival gear in a backpack, Curt stopped and looked up at Louis, "Something like that."

57

"But we don't know how far she ran back then? Which direction? Nothing. All we do know, if we give these dreams credit, was that she was here at some point. Which according to her report, she was found a few miles to the east in another town."

Curt shot a glance to Rachel who was tightening the shoelaces of her boots. She shrugged her left shoulder.

"She could've gone anywhere between a mile or ten. She could've come from the east, north…. Hell, she could've come from anywhere and wound up here at this rock."

"He's got a point," she said.

"And another thing, it's been over twenty years, and no offense." Louis turned to Rachel. "All this is coming to light just because of a dream or something?"

Curt stood up and let out a sigh. "He makes a point, but that's not what he's asking."

"Huh?"

"I'm not?"

"No." Curt looked over at Louis. "You're not."

"So, oh great mind reader and decipherer of plain English, what am I really asking?"

"The answer's yes."

Rachel was confused. She looked at Louis who was studying Curt's face, trying to clear up his own confusion.

"Yes, you can stay in the van and not go through the woods with us."

"Oh, thank God!" Louis immediately loosened up. "I mean, I'd be happy to go, but you know, I'm more of a stay-in-the-van kinda guy. You know?"

"Whatever. Just try and follow as best you can with the van."

"Will do." Louis fist-pumped to himself and jumped in the van while the rest of the team finalized their gear for the hike.

"Give me one of those trackers, Louis. I'll put it in the back pack so you can follow us easier."

Louis moved to the rear of the van where his work station was fashioned. Bolted to the floor, the small desk held a computer screen and keyboard. On the shelves above, there was a collection of hardware, modems, radios, hard drives, and other computer components on standby for whatever was thrown at them during an operation. Behind him was a thin cabinet that he unlocked, removing a small black device. He pressed a button, waited for the tiny screen to light up, pressed a few more buttons, and handed it over to Curt.

"It's all good to go. Batteries should last a while."

Curt put the tracker in his back pack and looked to Rachel.

"Ready?"

"I guess so."

He unholstered his Glock and removed the magazine. After inspection, he slid the magazine back in and racked the slide loading the weapon. "Alright, let's go."

For the first ten minutes, Rachel felt like she was pulling some type of hoax on the team. Only, it was a hoax that even she wasn't privy to. The heart-shaped rock had triggered such a vivid memory from her escape, but she had no clue as to where to lead the team. She was humbled by their willingness to at least try.

"Thank you." She told Curt. She walked in front of him while Beth and Melinda trailed several yards behind.

He smiled. "I know what it's like to be in search of answers."

"Yeah, but we're operating on nothing more than blind faith. I feel like we're on a wild goose chase."

"All faith is blind. That's why it's called Faith. You can't see it, can't touch it, can't smell it. All you need is to believe it."

"But it's like you guys expect to find answers that I'm not even sure are there."

"Hmm." Curt thought a minute as they moved up a wooded bluff. "Well, did you have anything else better to do today?"

"Ha! No, I guess not."

"Then I guess unlocking the mystery of your abduction will just have to do."

Trekking through an open field and thick patches of woods, the morning gave way to the afternoon.

"You know, repressed memories have never been scientifically proven." Louis' voice broke the silence over the comms.

"Do you think I'm making them up, Louis?" Rachel sneered back.

"No, no, no. It's not that. There's been recent research saying that there's no science behind the theory of repressed memories due to trauma."

"So, what are you saying, exactly?" Curt asked.

"Well, the phenomenon came to light back in the '90s after a series of arrests were made when several women 'uncovered' memories of sexual abuse while being treated for other psychological issues. After several convictions were made on these alleged abusers, the women came forward saying that the abuse was 'suggested' by their psychiatrist rather than proven."

"Then how'd they get a jury to believe them?" Beth asked.

"Apparently, these women believed it themselves and were very convincing on the stand. It was well after the trial when the women became convinced the memories were suggestions of the therapist."

"Wow!" Beth said.

"Yeah, but this is different." Curt offered.

"How so?" Rachel asked, earnestly.

"I had a case that dealt with that and I was able to make the arrest, because I was able to corroborate part of the victim's account." Curt looked at Rachel as they walked. "The cases Louis is talking about lacked confirmation, and they later found out that the women pieced the 'abuse' together based on facts they already knew about the case. Like from news articles or commonly known facts about the case. Nothing intimate, only generalities."

"And I have corroboration?" Rachel asked skeptically.

"I would say so." Curt stopped and started to count his points. "First, you were in fact kidnapped. Second, it occurred in this area outside of Houston. Third, you can recall other parts of your experience, whereas those women were revealing everything at once, some ten or twenty years later. You seem to be filling in the gaps is all. Plus, I don't see where you could have been 'suggested' by anything from your experience."

Rachel let Curt's argument settle. The comms went silent as Louis had nothing to counter.

"Plus, I believe you," Curt added.

Rachel smiled "thanks" back at him and kept walking.

"Just wanted to mention that, guys. Not start a coup or anything," Louis said.

Rachel stopped abruptly. Curt halted and started to look around, searching for a threat.

"What is it?"

"That sound."

"Sounds like a car." Beth offered as she and Melinda caught up.

"Yeah, like a road is nearby."

"There!" Rachel pointed off into the distance. "That way."

Curt strained to see through the woods, bare and gray from the winter season.

"You see it?" Rachel asked.

"No, what?"

"That dark spot over there. It's a tunnel. I remember a tunnel."

Chapter 9

Life hardly seemed fair. Over halfway through her freshman year of high school, Layla Bragden, had been through too many ups and downs. More than most adolescent teenagers, she swore. She hated the way she looked: her underdeveloped body, her board straight hair, and one of her front teeth slightly overlapped the other. For the most part, she shied away from mirrors and never smiled. School was boring, and her so-called friends had become gossipy bitches, more concerned with what someone said about someone else than carrying on a meaningful conversation. The only refuge for Layla was in her boyfriend, Lucas Millwood. He had been the first boy to tell her she was pretty and give her a first kiss. One night, she snuck out of the house to go see him, but it got late, and she accidentally fell asleep at his house. It was so embarrassing when the cops came and took her home.

Both had gotten into deep trouble and put on restrictions. Luke had been so angry with her, he didn't talk to her for a week. But he agreed to meet with her at the Spring Dance. Layla sent him a flirty text that she would make it up to him, including a winky face emoji. Finally, feeling like things were back on track, Layla felt positive.

However, her mother felt different, as usual.

"No, Layla, you can't go. You are still grounded from the last stunt you pulled. You know this."

"But, Mom! Luke is going to be there. He just started talking to me again."

"I'm sorry. You can't just sneak out whenever the hell you feel like it and expect there to be no consequences."

"Yeah!" Layla's pesky little sister chimed in, backing up their mother's tongue lashing.

"Shut up, Lily. This is none of your business." Layla snapped.

"Lily, this is between me and your sister." Mom said and turned to Layla. "You can't go and that's final."

"Ugh, you are being so unfair!"

"I'm not the one who broke the rules."

"You're ruining everything! Sometimes, I wish I lived with Dad!"

Layla stormed off running upstairs to her room. She put all her strength into slamming the door, making her point even louder. She felt bad about mentioning her father, which she didn't mean, but she knew it would hurt her mother's feelings. That she wanted. Layla's father was a workaholic who barely had time for his daughters and was the main reason her parents split.

After their divorce was when she felt her lowest. She lashed out and broke a few items around the house, but nothing too major or expensive. They took her to a psychologist and explained that she was allowed to be angry, but there were "irrational" reactions to divorce. Layla knew it was all a waste of time. The cuts to her wrists were for attention only, she knew this deep down, although she never admitted it. They all had overreacted saying it was a suicide attempt. Layla told them what they wanted to hear, but after she met Luke, everything got better.

Plopped down at her desk, she grabbed her cell phone. She reread the text message thread between her and Luke from earlier that afternoon.

R ur parents letting you go 2 da dance?

Yup

She replied with two heart emoji's, and a kiss emoji.

I'm sorry about getting U in trouble. I promise I'll make it up to u

Oh???

Smiley face emoji.

Like what?

U'll see. Winky-face emoji.

C'mon, tell me!!!!

Layla's heart fluttered before she had sent the picture. It caused a new sensation that she welcomed. She felt like it was the beginning of a sexual awakening. She became aroused. Making sure her bedroom door was locked, she stood in front of her closet mirror and took off her shirt. Careful not to smile, she aimed her phone toward her image, pushed up what little cleavage she had and snapped the photo. She repeated this until she was happy with what Luke was going to see. She watched the pic upload and send, for his eyes only. She added another winky face emoji for effect.

He replied back with a barrage of love-struck emoji's along with, *OMG!*

Layla relived the sensation, thinking about her upcoming night with Luke and when she took the photograph. More than anything, she wanted to be with him, and she didn't care what her mother said. School wasn't that far away and there was plenty of time.

She pulled her dress from the hanger and slipped it on. After messing with her hair for about ten minutes, it was finally acceptable for the dance. She liked her hair pinned up with volume, a change from the boring straight look. Checking herself out in the mirror, she twisted and turned to see how the dress fit and flowed. It hugged her thin waist and she liked the way her butt looked. She hoped Luke did, too, giggling at the thought of him grabbing it. Facing her mirror image, she decided she needed something else. She opened up the jewelry box that sat on her dresser and looked for a complimentary piece to wear. She groaned, annoyed that it only contained *little girl* jewelry.

An idea popped in her head. Layla crept to her door and eased it open, checking on her mother's whereabouts. The sound of her mother's television show echoed off the back wall and up the stairs. Layla slipped out of her room and tip-toed across the hall to her mother's room. Using the light from the hallway, she lifted the lid of her mother's jewelry box and sifted through her collection. After a moment of consideration, she found a pair of large silver hooped earrings with a sapphire stone setting at the bottom. They were perfect. They matched her dark blue dress with a sparkling silver trim.

She picked them out of the box and slipped back into her room. With the earrings in her ears, she smiled back at herself in the mirror. She looked and felt beautiful. Luke was going to like the way she looked. An inadvertent smile crossed her face and Layla noticed the ever-present overlap in her front teeth. Self-consciously, she covered the smile with her top lip.

The clock read seven forty-eight.

"Shoot! I gotta go."

Layla grabbed her shoes and climbed out of the window, onto the awning, and down on the trampoline in the back yard. Her dress flew up on the way down, giving her a sense of freedom and playful joy. Escaping her teenage prison to spend the night with the love of her life was exhilarating. She took off in a slow jog down the street and sent a text to Luke that she was on the way. Tonight, she was going to be the belle of East Tampa High School.

But everything was for nothing. Layla sat alone in the first-floor science wing, crying. With the thump of the music still audible from the gym, she wallowed in misery. Arriving late because she had to walk, she had strolled in the open double doors fashionably late, ready to find her prince charming anxiously awaiting her arrival. After scanning the darkened dance floor, she saw Luke's arms wrapped around the waist of Sarah McGill, his ex-girlfriend and evil temptress.

He's just being nice to her, Layla tried to convince herself. *He's just killing time until I get here.*

Once he sees me, he'll drop that slut like a bad habit.

Layla moved through the crowd, her stare fixed on Sarah McGill and her unseasonably large chest. As she got close, Luke's attention moved from Sarah to her, but nothing changed. It was like he didn't even see her standing there in her blue dress, looking beautiful, just for him. He turned his back to Layla and just kept dancing.

For the second time that night, she ran away. She kept the tears hidden for the moment, until she was alone. Then, uncontrollably the tears streaked down her face. She sobbed, hoping that Luke saw her leave, felt awful, and changed his mind about wanting to be with Sarah McGill. Soon he would come looking for her, and they would live happily ever after.

But it wasn't meant to be. Luke never came. She sat there alone, reading social media highlights from her classmates' posting and commenting on pictures from the dance. She wanted to "dislike" all of the comments, but not having that option, she settled on ignoring them. She snapped a quick selfie with a disgusted look on her face to show Luke how upset she was after he ignored her. When they stopped updating, she felt like such a loser and wanted to go home.

Staring at her phone, the only person she wanted to see was her mother. Queued up on the screen, she stared at her mother's contact. There was a picture of them cheek to cheek during a shopping spree over the past summer. Both had smiles so wide they would make the Cheshire cat jealous. A simple touch would dial her cell phone and she would hear her mother's voice. She hesitated, knowing that hell would follow once she did. Hopefully, her mom would understand.

A metal clink echoed down the hallway. Layla jumped. The sound was deliberate, like someone knew she was there. She stood up and looked back to the end of the hallway, waiting for some immature jerk to jump out and scare her.

"Real funny, asshole!"

There was no reply.

The music from the gymnasium had stopped. The dance was over and most of the kids had probably already made it home. As an eerie sense of worry enveloped her, she had an overwhelming desire to get home. Pushing the bar to the door, it didn't give. It wasn't locked when she walked into the hallway. She pushed it harder, and it cracked open, but stopped again. Through the crack, Layla could see chains on the outside.

"What the hell?"

Another metal snap resonated loudly, but this time it came from the other end of the hallway. She twisted and stared down in the direction of the noise. Worry transformed into fear. She ran down to the corner of the hallway and stopped short to spy around the corner. Whoever was playing this joke had gone too far.

"This isn't funny!"

Still no reply. She peeked around the corner and nothing was there, only the shadows within the darkness. She quickly ran to the other exit and slammed into the push bar on the run. The door was unforgiving and knocked her down to the floor. The terrazzo floor was equally unforgiving and her wrist smarted from the hard landing. Another heavy clang resonated throughout the corridor.

Fear now gripped her insides. She grabbed her phone to call her mother, but the screen was shattered from the fall. She tried to press through the cracks, but it didn't register the commands.

"No, c'mon, work dammit!"

Layla popped up looking for another way out. She ran down the corridor, checking the classroom doors, but they were all locked. She turned to study a window and how to unlock it. At her height, she couldn't reach the latch. Searching for something to stand on, she stepped up on the cast iron pipes that ran the length of the hallway, but it wasn't tall enough to give her the needed boost. She only managed to move the clasp halfway before it got stuck on something.

Panicked, she abandoned the latch and pulled off her shoe, with a two-inch heel, and used it as a hammer to try and break her way out. Whacking it as hard as she could, the window didn't budge. Not even a crack. She reached back as far as she could for maximum force, but the distinct sound of footsteps broke the silence. They were heavy and methodical, not quick and light, like that of a prankster.

They were coming from the far end near the stairwell. At the corner of the hallway was a set of bathrooms. Layla dropped her shoe and sprinted for the girl's room. She quickly moved to the last stall, sat on the toilet and pulled her feet up. The footsteps quickly moved to just outside the bathroom. As the exterior door creaked open, Layla stepped off the toilet and slid the interior lock shut. She huddled on top of the toilet, frightened beyond belief and tried to get her phone to work again.

The cracks still kept it from reading the static friction of her finger. Tears automatically began to stream down her cheeks as she sat in silent hell.

There was a pause before the creeper pushed open the interior door. She heard some odd noises, like someone was fixing something mechanical. Confused as to what was going on, she remained squatting over the toilet rim, trying to be as quiet as possible.

Layla's eyes began to water, but it wasn't from tears. There was an odd smell filtering in the small bathroom that was causing her eyes to burn. Initially, she thought it was the strong remnants of a recent pine scented cleaning, but her breath became shorter. Suddenly, she couldn't get any air to her lungs and she began to wheeze. The wheeze turned into a cough which grew uncontrollable. She tried to stifle the sound inside the bend of her elbow, but the lack of air intake led her to desperately gasp for air. She started to feel light headed. She stepped off of the toilet and out of the stall. She was going to have to face whatever or whoever was on the other side of the door. She squeezed her remaining shoe in her right hand for a weapon, but suddenly, a hazy feeling engulfed her and she collapsed in slow motion down to the hard tile floor of the bathroom. She tried to lift herself up, but her limbs felt like they were mired in concrete. She was paralyzed.

She struggled for air, but for every labored breath she sucked in, the need to cough amplified. Trying her phone one last time, she lost the ability to use her fingers to dial out.

A light from the hallway suddenly flooded inside the dim bathroom. A man appeared in the threshold. He was the source of the noise, the odd smell, and the onset of her paralysis. The apparition was fuzzy, backlit by the ambient light in the hallway, his silhouette standing tall. His face was hideously shaped and grotesque with an abnormal black, rubbery growth protruding from his mouth. With a cylindrical center and small gray pockets on both sides, it caused him to breathe like Darth Vader in *Star Wars*. Trying to look into his eyes, she saw the glare of the hallway light reflect in a pair of old fashioned glasses, like what her grandfather used to wear.

68

With every last ounce of her being, Layla tried to move, but the man hovered over top of her, keeping her pinned down. She wanted to fight, she wanted to live. She wanted to see her mother. But no matter what she did, she couldn't move.

Chapter 10

A solemn silence fell over the woods. Rachel ducked her head inside the muddy culvert that ran under a two-lane highway while the others stood back, giving her space. The muck ran deep and there were patches of weeds, reeds, and other green stuff growing within. It was noticeably cooler inside the damp tunnel, and it was the opposite of inviting. It had seemed right when she spotted it moments before, but now it seemed unfamiliar and foreign.

Clearing away a spider web, she stepped over some foliage growth and into the tunnel. The walls were dusty but otherwise absent from the vegetation. Leaning against the cement wall, she closed her eyes and concentrated on her memories. Nothing came.

"Maybe this is wrong." Her voice echoed inside.

She listened to the surrounding environment, hoping to hear something that triggered another memory. She needed something to tell her she was on the right path.

The dull and hushed sound of a car approaching in the distance grew louder and louder until it passed overhead. The sound of rubber tires sticking to the asphalt as it sped over the small tunnel was loud and obvious. An image flashed and Rachel let out an excited gasp. She whipped her head to the other side of the tunnel expecting confirmation.

"The tree!" she shouted.

"Huh?" Curt had stepped to the tunnel's opening. "What tree?"

Pointing through to the other side Rachel said, "That one."

Electing to climb up the embankment and cross the road instead of traversing the sludge-filled pipe, the team stood on the other side waiting for Rachel to explain.

She wrenched her head up, looking in the distance until she found something that felt familiar. There was a brighter patch of woods ahead, up a slight hill, that caught more direct sun than the other way. Rachel pointed in that direction.

"There. I think I came from there and ran down here to the tunnel. I tripped or stumbled, or something and grabbed this tree breaking the top of it."

"This tree?" Beth said, heavy with skepticism. "This tree is huge!"

"Yeah, but honey, it wasn't twenty-two years ago," Melinda explained.

"Right, look at the top. It's split in two like it was broken at one point," Curt's voice carried an air of excitement.

Stunned, Rachel held a surprised look on her face. It was unexplainable, but yet it felt right.

"So, where to next?"

"Up that hill."

As soon as they broke the tree line, the sun's warm reach beamed down, caressing their faces like that of warm blanket. Before them was a vast open area that stretched for several acres. A few majestic oaks dotted the middle, making the natural beauty of the scene near breathtaking.

"Must be old farm land or something," Curt offered.

"Maybe."

"Which way from here?"

"I'm not real sure." Rachel started walking. "I think I just ran straight across, so I'm guessing this way."

The team fell in line with Rachel in the lead. She heard Curt fiddling with his gear behind her.

"Hey, Louis? Yeah, do you have us on the tracker?" Rachel heard a tiny voice respond, but she couldn't hear what was said. "Okay, good.

How far is that town from us now? Oh, about two miles. But how far is that development?"

Curt waited for an answer. He told Louis to start driving the van toward a location and then walked next to Rachel keeping in stride.

"He said that town of Sweetland is just to the northwest of us, that way." Curt pointed to his two o'clock. "But, there is a neighborhood about a mile and a half straight west from our position now."

"Okay." The news should have been comforting, but for some reason, Rachel felt the opposite. This wasn't some treasure hunt where at the end they were going to be celebrating some type of victory. It was a journey that led straight back into the hellish nightmare that had been haunting her since she was a teenager. It was hard to get excited about.

"We don't have to do this, you know? We can turn around if you like?"

"No. I know where this might lead, but I want answers."

"Good."

"But above all else, I want to find my sister."

After the clearing, the team entered another set of woods. Rachel stayed in the lead, but her pace grew fast and motivated. There was a magnetism that drew her in and guided her way. It seemed as if she'd been there before, but the scenery looked alien.

After crossing a valley and jumping a thin watery stream, there were signs and sounds of civilization. A hefty dog bark was heard in the distance, followed by a car engine starting up. The echo of a mother's voice calling out for her children let them know there was life nearby. Strangers in the woods, they slowed, careful to tread lightly as they got closer.

"This is going to be the hard part." Rachel stated. They stopped at the base of a small slope, looking up to the backs of several houses.

"What else can you remember about the house? We'll need something to narrow it down."

She shook her head. "I'm not remembering anything."

"What about that?" Beth asked from a few feet back. Rachel turned and followed her line of sight up into the trees. "Does that spark anything?"

Up on top of a thick limb of a tall oak tree was the remnants of an old tree house. Clearly, abandoned and ignored, the wood was faded and looked structurally weak and dangerous. Rachel didn't feel anything as she stared up.

"No, I'm not getting anything." Turning back to the houses, she asked, "So, how do we figure out which one? Assuming this is where it all started."

"We can go one by one, see if anything stirs a memory and go from there?"

"Okay."

"Mel and Beth, you guys hang back and we'll sneak up closer to take a look."

Beth looked put out by Curt's suggestion.

"Or, we can head down that way." She spotted a clearing down the hill where there were no houses. "And have Louis come get us."

"Yeah, alright."

Beth made the request of Louis, and he responded with an ETA.

"You ready?" Curt asked of Rachel.

She took in a deep breath, summoning some needed courage. "Yes."

They started at the bottom of the hill and slowly made their way up to where it flattened out and then turned back to the east. There were at least fifty houses that bordered the woods, and Rachel had to determine which one was the house where she and Rhonda had been held captive over twenty years ago.

As they moved along, they attracted the attention of several dogs, which would complicate matters if their owners were alerted. Having to vet out each house, they needed to get close enough to see the back of each one. Because houses, like people, can change appearances over time, Rachel needed to study the back of each house to be sure. Not finding anything remarkable up the hill, they trekked on, hoping to avoid further detection while they completed the search. It was getting later in the afternoon, and the sounds of kids playing in the backyards were heard. Another hurdle Rachel and Curt had to overcome.

Making their way around the bend, the setting sun cast a bright orange glow in the trees overhead. The cold air of the evening was starting to bite. Rachel rubbed her arms trying to generate heat.

"It's getting chilly."

"Yes, it is." Curt stood behind Rachel and began to rub her arms.

Stemming from his touch, the moment turned intimate. He is just being friendly, she thought. But there was a sense of familiarity she welcomed. She relaxed her shoulders and felt safe in his hands. He stopped abruptly and then rubbed his own arms.

She figured he must have realized what he was doing and stopped. Rachel didn't say anything and concentrated on the next backyard.

"That's not it."

"Okay. Do you remember anything about the house or are you just hoping it comes to you when you see it?"

Rachel thought for a moment. She tried to dive deep down into her subconscious mind trying to uncover the repressed memories. If she had learned anything that day, it was that there were memories in there somewhere. But nothing was coming, at the moment.

She shook her head, "No. I can't remember anything." She took a step and froze. "Wait!"

"What?" Curt studied her face in anticipation.

"A basement. There was a basement. I do remember that."

"Okay, well. We haven't seen a basement yet, so that's good."

"Right."

They moved on and checked three more houses. On the fourth, Rachel stopped and stared wide-eyed at the back of a pale green with faded white trim, one-story home. There was a back porch that overlooked a wide set of stairs and a flat back yard. It was unassuming and fit in with the rest of the houses, albeit slightly dated, but normal. Her instincts told her to pay closer attention. She moved around a large pine tree to focus on the back porch and the windows that were facing the rear.

74

"What's that over there? Below that second window?" Curt asked.

Rachel stepped forward to see around the tree, and nestled on the ground, just below the second window was a basement access. Two large hatch doors were shut and padlocked. She closed her eyes and the fateful day she escaped came back in full color.

***

It had all started with the faceless man leaving the door to the room unlocked. He had been too focused on taking Rhonda for what turned out to be the last time. Rachel beat on the door for what seemed like hours. Too absorbed in her frenzy, she failed to try the doorknob. When she grabbed it, inhaled a deep breath, and twisted, the door fell open. Rachel nosed her way out of the room and into the hallway. She could hear awful noises from the faceless man coming from the other side of the house. She tiptoed as soft as she could toward the sound but caught a glimpse of herself in the mirror. Startled at the sight, she looked emaciated, dirty and tired. Instantly, she felt weak and knew she was not strong enough to fight the faceless man. The only alternative was to escape. That was the only way she could help Rhonda. Retreating, she found a door at the end of the hallway. She opened it slowly, in case there was another monster lurking inside, but the room was filled with televisions, VCR's, and a computer on top of a desk. Photographs of girls, some she knew, some she didn't, were plastered all over the wall. She tried the window, but it was locked and she abandoned the room. A third door in the hallway was her last option. She pushed it open and was met with a vast darkness. Scared to go on, she fought against her fears for Rhonda's sake, knowing she had to find help. Stepping into the void, she was surprised to see a staircase materialize leading downward. As she slowly crept down, a small line of light broke through the shadows illuminating the room just enough to tell it was a basement. She ran toward the light and could see through a crack between two hatch doors that led outside. She could smell fresh air filtering inside. She nudged it with her shoulders, but it only gave an inch before going taut from the lock. There was something keeping it closed on the other side. Freedom was only a hatch away. Determined, Rachel searched the dusty basement and found a metal bar with a hook on it, the end of it looked similar to a pig's hoof. She jammed it between the slats of the hatch doors and pulled with every muscle in her body. She gained enough leverage and kept pulling until finally, something popped and light flooded the basement. She shoved the doors open and sprung from out of the darkness and into a dead sprint for the woods.

***

Twenty-two years later with tears rolling down her cheeks, Rachel Goodwin stood behind the tree line of the house where she had been held captive.

"That's it." Her voice was unwavering and precise. She continued crying and wiping away the tears as Curt stood next to her, silent. "Goddamnit, that's it."

Rachel didn't move from behind the large pine tree for several minutes. She didn't know what needed to happen next. More questions began to flood her consciousness. Was the faceless man still there? Was there another little girl held captive in there? Should we storm the door and face whatever evil lurks inside head on?

"What do we do now?" she asked.

"Well...," Curt replied, "that's up to you."

Chapter 11

Everything around her felt surreal, like it was a dream and she would soon wake up before all the questions were answered. Curt led Rachel out of the woods, and the team reconvened back in the van to assess their options. Staring down at the carpet for no apparent reason, it was hard for Rachel to focus. Only by chance, she passed by that heart-shaped rock which triggered a cascading memory free-for-all. It was too much to process in such a short time, but part of her wanted to press forward and find out what happened to Rhonda.

"I'm running background on that house as we speak. Property appraisers, liens, police dispatch records, blah, blah, blah. You know, the usual stuff," Louis chimed.

"That's a good start," Curt said. "How should we play this?"

Rachel noticed an odd quiet had materialized in the van. The silence broke her from her trance, it was that obvious. She replayed what Curt said and realized that it was *Curt* asking, not telling the team what should happen. Usually at this point, he would have already come up with a plan to storm the house and to do whatever was needed. Curt not having any ideas was outside of the norm. Melinda and Beth shared equally furrowed looks as Curt waited for suggestions.

"We should probably watch the house for a while. I mean, if this is the house, then he may still be operating, and we should gain as much intel as we can." Beth sounded sensible.

"I like it," Melinda agreed.

"Looks like the house was sold a few times in the last two decades. I'm trying to back track through." Louis didn't look away from his monitor. "There's nothing on the dispatch notes. I'll try to get inside the police department's report management software and double check."

"I want to go in," Rachel said. Her tone was serious and flat, not to be debated.

"What do you mean 'go in'?" Curt asked.

"I want to go inside. Take a look for myself. I'll know for sure if that's the house, and then we can figure out what to do next."

"I don't think that's a good idea. What if he still lives there? Obviously, the detectives on your case didn't even find him as a suspect back then. Hell, what if he actually recognizes you?"

"After twenty-two years, I don't believe he'll recognize me."

"You remembered him."

The point was made, true enough, but Rachel wasn't going to back away. "But only after repressed memories surfaced."

"That doesn't matter. It's all memory. I still don't think it's a good idea."

"Neither was torturing one of your son's kidnappers, but you did it anyway." Rachel got defensive and snapped at Curt. He retreated back into his seat, hurt by her words. He swallowed his anger, and he avoided eye contact by looking out the window.

"I'm sorry. That was harsh. I didn't mean that. But, listen, this is unchartered territory for me and you always told me to listen to my gut. My gut is telling me that I need to go in."

Curt turned back and nodded in understanding. "Fine. But not alone."

***

An hour later, her nerves were still a turbulent mess. Standing on the base of the front porch while Curt stood at the door poised to knock, she felt as though she might faint. She took a deep breath to collect herself. Facing the darkness that had swallowed up so much of her innocence was a once-in-a-lifetime opportunity, and she willed herself to be strong. She glanced up at Curt, then back down the block to the van. With the team by her side, she could face whatever evil that waited.

However, Louis confirmed that a woman in her late twenties now owned the house. The presence of well-worn children's toys stacked by the garage let them know the likelihood of Rachel's kidnapper still living here was slim. But, Rachel hoped, no matter the inhabitants, inside still bore answers to her past.

While they waited, a navy-blue Volvo pulled into the driveway and a woman dressed in pink striped yoga pants, a matching work-out shirt, and tennis shoes emerged from the driver's seat. The team watched from the seclusion of the tinted windows of the Sprinter van. She slung a large flower-printed bag over her shoulder then reached into the back seat. Emerging again, this time she hoisted a little girl, no more than three, onto her hip. She gave the back door a side bump of her hip and walked into the house.

Giving the woman ten minutes to settle in, Curt and Rachel approached with a plan. The knock was impersonal, like that of a salesman. Curt still carried himself as a cop and had been warned to avoid his usually authoritative knock. They needed answers before they took action.

The woman from the car poked her head around the door. Her short black hair cupped her small round face. She was pretty and gave Curt a polite smile.

"Can I help you?" she said.

"Well—"

"Hi, my name is Rachel." Rachel stepped around Curt and cut him off completely. She was going off-script. "I know this is going to sound really weird, but I grew up in the area and had a really good friend that used to live here."

Curt glared at her, which she ignored and kept going.

"We lost touch after my family moved away while I was in high school. I was wondering if you by chance are related to the family that lived here back in 1993?"

The woman gave the question thought. "No, no. We bought this house about two years ago from a family that moved to Michigan. They were the Sewells. I'm not sure how long they had the house before us. Was that your friend's family?"

The name meant nothing to Rachel, but to continue the ruse, she had to respond. "Yes!" She feigned excitement. "Yes, that was her last name. Oh, that's wonderful."

"Oh, good." The woman shared in the joy, unwittingly.

Rachel shot a glance back at Curt. He stood there with a cautious but impressed look.

"And you said they moved to Michigan? Oh, please tell me you have a forwarding address or something?"

The woman creased her brow and then turned, letting the door swing open all the way. "Yes, I think I have it written down somewhere. Please, come in for a minute. Excuse the mess, I have a two-year-old who thinks the whole house is her play area."

Rachel and Curt stepped in and stood in the foyer. Rachel immediately scanned the living room, a short hallway that lead to a kitchen in the back and then another hallway that led presumably to the bedrooms. *It's all warm and homey*, she thought. Light blue walls with white trim, tastefully arranged pictures, and a pleasant floral odor mixed with baby powder was anything but a depraved house of horrors. Nothing like the den of terror from over two decades ago. No memory was coming to her.

"So, are you and your husband visiting Texas, or do you still live in the area?" The woman called out from another room.

Husband? The word sounded absurd to Rachel. She gave Curt a puzzled look and then figured the woman must've assumed they were together.

Curt gave a broad smile. Rachel mouthed quietly, "Don't flatter yourself."

"Um, yeah. We're here on family vacation, and I dragged him all through my old stomping grounds."

The woman reappeared with a folded slip of paper and handed it to Rachel.

"Here, I found it. The Sewell's. Hopefully, they're still at that address or you'll have to do this again, huh?"

Rachel smiled politely.

With business finished, an awkward silence between the strangers fell on the room. The woman had been more than hospitable, but Rachel wasn't satisfied. There were still questions left unanswered.

"Anything else?" The woman said.

"Um, well…" Rachel put on her best sheepish face. "Would it be too much to ask for a stroll down memory lane?"

Confused, the woman didn't react, but then something triggered, "Oh, you want to look around?"

"I know it's odd and we're strangers, but just a quick stroll? It'd mean a lot to me."

"Um…." The woman looked at a clock hung on the wall. "Yeah, I guess it'd be okay. Just a few minutes though." She was clearly uncomfortable, but Rachel wasn't going to let that get in her way.

"Oh sure. We've intruded enough. Thank you so much."

Rachel walked down the hallway, trying to get a feel for the renovated house. She transported herself back twenty-two years, trying to wade through the murky darkness and bring more memories into the light. The multiple coats of paint, laminate wood floors, and decorative window treatments served to block out those memories. It was hard to believe this house could have hidden such atrocities once upon a time. Rachel grew skeptical too and wondered if she had found the right house. She had been so sure from the woods, but now inside, doubt was piling up.

There were three doors down the hallway. Rachel turned to the door on the right, feeling drawn to that bedroom. She eased open the door. A flash of her sister, still age thirteen, lying on the floor waiting to be rescued, hit Rachel as she entered the room. The room was the same as she remembered, but yet nothing was the same. The smell was clean, not a putrid stench of sweat and urine that she remembered now so vividly.

The carpet was soft, the linens were laid out perfectly, and the drapes matched in a colorful ensemble that was inviting and comfortable.

It felt wrong. Her skepticism weighed heavy, and she was getting irritated that the answers weren't coming.

She stood in the middle of the room trying to focus on the freshly returned memories. She blocked out everything that was pleasant. The light fragrance, the airy breeze, and the pitter patter of the two-year-old ambling along somewhere else in the house. She allowed the memories of seeing her sister being taken by the kidnapper for the last time back into her consciousness. She focused on the room, the walls, the door, the floor and the ceiling. Then it was dark. She had been frightened beyond belief and wanted desperately to escape. She remembered the panic of seeing her sister's eyes as she was carried out by the man. The door slammed shut, and the sound of his heavy footfalls resonated down the hall.

Lifting her eyelids slowly, she was met again by the welcoming bedroom fit for a princess.

"Damn." She said to the empty room.

Rachel turned to look out of the window. She didn't remember a window back then. Maybe it was blacked out, or maybe it wasn't there. Or maybe she had the wrong house. Rachel's shoulders sank. She had been so sure looking at the house from the outside.

She lifted her head and closed her eyes one more time. Someone behind her stepped down the hallway and stopped just outside the bedroom. Their weight shifted, causing the floorboard to creak.

The sound paralyzed Rachel. The noise echoed all around her as if it were the darkness ready to engulf her soul. She gasped and stood frozen, unable to move. Instantly, she was transported twenty-two years earlier, and the faceless man stood outside the bedroom door. His heavy foot squeaked the creaky floorboard just before he unlocked the door and would take Rhonda. Her breathing grew rapidly and her skin was hot and flushed.

Mustering just enough strength to turn around, she saw Curt standing in the threshold.

"Hey, you okay?" he asked.

Rachel shook her head, fighting off tears. She ran to Curt and he grabbed her in a tight embrace.

"Shhh. It's okay. He's not here. You're safe. Shhh," Curt said, comforting her. "Hey?" He rubbed her arms, trying to jostle her away from her emotional breakdown. "Hey, don't forget how we got in here. Let's keep it together for just a bit longer."

"Yeah." She wiped her tears, stowing the emotion for later. They needed to uphold the pretenses. "You're right." She sucked in a deep breath in an attempt to steady herself.

"Everything alright?" The woman asked. She now stood in the threshold of the bedroom.

"Yes, sorry. So many memories from this room. Ya know?"

"Awe. I can imagine it holds a special place in your heart."

Curt spoke for Rachel. "Thank you for your hospitality. We've taken up enough of your time."

Curt thanked the woman again for allowing them inside and led Rachel down the sidewalk and back to the van. He slid open the door to let Rachel get in first. Louis, Beth, and Mel were waiting for answers.

"Well?" Louis asked.

It was the hell she once knew, only now it had been decorated and repainted. "It's the house. No doubt in my mind."

Chapter 12

It was like no other dream she had ever had before. The nightmare felt so real. As Layla began to recover, her body ached and shook from the cold. Her eyelids were heavy, and she could barely open them to take in her surroundings. Everything was dark and blurry. She tried to move her arms, but they didn't respond. The air was damp and carried the pungent smell of a murky swamp. A shiver rushed through her body as she realized she was somewhere unfamiliar.

As her grogginess wore off, Layla's eyes adjusted to the dark. She was in a small room with a clammy breeze coming from underneath. It had the feel of a dungeon. She gasped as she remembered the *Darth Vader* man had come for her after she collapsed on the bathroom floor. She had been kidnapped and the nightmare was real.

Layla tried to fling her arms, but they didn't move. Pain developed in her wrists, and she looked down to see the cause. Her arms were bound behind her as she sat in a wooden chair. There was no give to whatever held her hands together. They were clamped together and there was nothing she could do about it. Layla realized that she sat in the chair wearing only her bra and panties. She felt so vulnerable and exposed. She began to weep.

She fought vehemently against the restraints, testing their strength, but grew exhausted from her efforts as they proved durable. Out of breath and sweating, Layla tried to figure out what was happening.

Looking around the room, it was empty, but the shadows in the deep recesses of the corners held a foreboding darkness. Behind her, she could see the beginning of a staircase leading up above the ceiling. A worn wooden stick stood erect from the floor next to the staircase, seemingly out of place, Layla couldn't figure out its purpose. There was a work bench on the wall behind the stair case, and a single light bulb fixture hung from the crossbeam in the center of the room, just above her head.

A strange noise, wet and moving slow, came from somewhere below. She turned her focus to the floorboard and noticed there was faint light coming up between the slats. She managed to lift her foot up only a few inches and stomp down. The return sounded hollow like walking on the deck at her aunt's beach house. She leaned forward, as far as her bound hands would allow, and peered between the wooden planks. It was too dark to make anything out. She heard another slow wet movement. Something was down there, something alive.

At that moment, Layla saw the square outline that surrounded her chair. To her left, on the floor was a small metal flap, as if it were a tiny hatch that led underneath the room. It was too small to use as an escape route. Confused, she didn't know what this was or what purpose it served. Her fear level rose to the point of suffocation. Her weeping grew into sobbing, and she yelled out, as loud as her young lungs would allow.

"HELP! HELP, ME! HELP ME, PLEASE! ANYBODY!"

Layla continued until she was exhausted. She waited for a response, but nothing came. Another wet breeze blew up through the slats, chilling her half-naked body, turning her skin to goose flesh. She pulled again at the arm restraints, and there was still no give. She pulled both feet up, managing to slide the rope up the leg of the chair about halfway. With all the strength she could muster, she stamped down her feet and arched her back. Her shoulders protested in pain as her hands didn't budge. She flung her head wildly, hoping she could free herself. The large hooped earrings she borrowed from her mother bounced against her neck and cheek during her efforts, and the left one broke free and flew somewhere in the room.

This calmed her. It gave her an idea. Her abductor didn't completely strip her down, and a plan began to formulate in her mind. She shook her head, feeling the right earring dangle against her neck, ensuring that it was still attached. *Careful*, she thought, if she could try to remove it and use the sharp end to cut through the ropes, she could try and escape this nightmare. It was her only hope.

A whisper came from somewhere in the room. Layla froze, trying to hone in on the noise. The hair on the back of her neck stood up. She looked into the shadows, straining her eyes to see further into the darkness. Suddenly, she realized she wasn't alone.

As she strained to see, there was a slight shuffle followed by a click. Music began to play, coming from within the darkness. The tune was familiar, but the peculiarity of it being played, added to her confusion. It was a song she'd heard all her life, played by her father at random times. He'd claim she was named after the Eric Clapton hit song.

The energy of the guitar had always stirred emotion in her, this time it was different. Everything was different. None of this was right and she grew even more frightened.

Layla had always loved the song, fantasizing it was written by a long-lost love just for her, but hearing it then as she sat tied to a chair in a dark, muculent dungeon made her loathe the words and hate whoever was playing it.

"Who's there? Why are you doing this to me? Please, just let me go!"

The song kept playing. Layla continued, "Please! I just want to go home. I didn't do anything to you, please. Just let me, go." She began to sob.

As the song ended, there was another click followed by silence. Layla peered into the shadowy corner, looking for answers, but her tears blurred her vision. The helplessness was too overwhelming.

"Please, whoever you are, just let me go." Anger boiled and erupted. "WHAT DO YOU WANT? JUST LET ME GO!" Her screeching voice quickly dissipated and the silence returned.

Through her watery eyes, a form began to materialize through the darkness. It slowly moved toward her until she could make out the evil eyes of her captor. Behind a pair of glasses, they burned with a lustful vigor that paralyzed Layla.

"No." The man hissed in a low, harsh tone. "Now, you belong to me."

Chapter 13

Using the back corner of the restaurant, the din of the main dining room was hushed enough so the team's conversation wasn't drowned out.

"Pass the chips," Louis ordered. Receiving another basket, he immediately grabbed a chip and scooped out a pile of salsa. With a mouth half full, he said, "I wuv dis stuhf."

"Slow down, Louis," Melinda said. "Seriously, that's like your third basket."

With another salsa-laden chip, he bit down in joyful disobedience and a smile.

Normally an advocate for Louis's peculiar levity, Rachel wasn't in the mood. She wanted to move the case forward. "Can we move on to what you guys found out about the house?"

"I did an archive's search in the local newspapers and came up empty for that address," Beth piped up while Louis finished chewing. "I broadened the search for that street and then the entire neighborhood and couldn't come up with anything but a house fire and a rash of burglaries."

"When were those?" Rachel asked, hoping to find a connection.

"The fire was in 2004, the burglaries..." Beth checked a notepad, "the burglaries were in the fall of 2008. So, well after your thing in '93. Hard to see anyway they could be connected."

Rachel was disappointed. But Beth continued, "I went back and reread the articles about you and your sister and tried to find anything else that may have stood out and cross referenced them with that address.

I still came up with nothing." She flipped her notepad close and grabbed a chip for herself.

Louis wiped his mouth and pulled his laptop from a bag under the table. He flipped it open and the screen lit up.

"Okay, I did everything humanly possible to find out about this family, the Sewell's. The dad, Marcus, worked in the oil business as some kind of plant manager, apparently like everyone else in Houston, while he lived here. When they moved to Michigan, he ditched the oil business for the car manufacturing business. It's all relative, I guess. According to his tax return last year, he's a Regional Plant Manager and still living in Brighton, Michigan."

After leaving the house, the team discussed the possibility that Marcus Sewell was the man responsible for the abduction of Rhonda and Rachel Goodwin and most likely countless other girls. But, he had no criminal record, and the only police involvement Louis could find was that he had been the at fault driver in a crash and the reporting person of an unruly employee while working at the oil refinery. Rachel insisted he be vetted closely, knowing the man who took her would easily be able to lead two different lives without detection.

"What about his credit card, anything else pop up on his financials?" she asked.

"No, I did a full work up. The dude has pretty good credit. His assets include the house in Michigan, two cars and a boat. His retirement accounts are in pretty good shape. He doesn't appear to gamble on anything substantial and gives to his church at least once a month."

"Maybe it's not him, Rachel?" Curt asked.

She shook her head. "That's the house. I know it."

"I believe you. But, that doesn't mean it's this guy."

"Louis, can you pull up a picture of him?"

"Sure, give me a second." Louis typed quickly, moved his mouse around a few times, clicked it and turned the laptop toward Rachel.

After twenty-two years, the curtain had lifted in her subconscious, revealing an image of her abductor, and she could finally give him a name. Her heart skipped a beat. As her eyes met the image of Marcus

Sewell, she knew instantly, that was not the man responsible. Rachel sulked in her chair, her disappointment was apparent.

"Not him?" Curt asked.

"No." She pouted. "Not even close. That guy's too chubby, too blond, and if that height is right on his drivers' license, too short." She looked away, frustrated. "Dammit!"

Rachel picked up her head as Melinda consoled her by rubbing her back. She looked around at the replica Spanish frescos painted on the wall of the restaurant giving it an authentic "old world" feel. She could tell the Spanish tiles on the awning that covered a row of booths against the wall were plastic, but they were a nice touch. A waiter walked by the table carrying a plate of sizzling steak, peppers, and onions to be wrapped in warm fajitas. But as the answers she'd gotten so close to started to dissipate, so did her appetite.

Their waiter came by with a tray of food and served each their dinner. Rachel just looked down at the dish, dejected.

"I feel like we're missing something." Beth said.

Instinctively, Rachel turned to Curt.

"She's right. What are we missing?"

Curt shook his head. "I'm not sure."

"Oh!" Louis shouted, spitting bits of chips and his burrito from his mouth. "Oh, I know." He finished chewing as he wildly waved his hands.

"What is it, Louis?" Rachel leaned forward in her chair.

He flailed his hands until he grabbed a napkin and wiped his hands. Rachel remembered Louis had a rule to never touch his "machine" with soiled fingers. Satisfied they were clean, Louis started typing.

Curt forced a cough in Louis' direction. Louis looked up at Curt, then at Rachel. "Oh, right. We never went back farther. Before the Sewell's. I remembered he was born in 1974 in Louisiana. He would've been nineteen in 1993. His marriage certificate is dated 1994 issued by the state of Louisiana, so obviously, they didn't move to Houston until after they married."

Rachel felt hope renew. All she needed was forward momentum. Living over two decades not knowing what truly happened to her and her sister created a void in her life. In the last eight hours, that void was nearly filled with the answers she always believed were out there. It was surreal to think about how close the team was to identifying the faceless man.

"So, what are you checking now?" Rachel asked.

"I'm trying to find out who the Sewell's bought the house from. But first..." Louis's fingers danced across the keyboard. Rachel wondered which operated faster, the machine or the mind of Louis Melton. "Yes! That's what I thought. They didn't move in until 1994. Seems they got the house on foreclosure. Apparently, the previous owner just abandoned the house."

"Really?" Rachel got up and was hovering just over Louis's shoulder.

"Yeah. I'm trying to get into the bank records to see who the deed belonged to."

Rachel tried to follow along on the screen, but her eyes went blurry, lost in thought.

Louis continued. "Dang it!"

"What?" Rachel whined.

"It's nothing." He answered, but Rachel saw his face contorted out of frustration.

"Then why the face?"

"No, it's just that the bank that foreclosed on the house has since been bought, and that bank has been bought, and that bank... you get the point. It's just buried further. It'll take some time, but I'll find it."

"Okay. If it's there, I know you'll find it," said Rachel.

"Oh, property tax records. That may have it. Hold on," Louis alerted.

Rachel sat back down and turned to her food. Unexpectedly, her appetite had returned.

On the other side of Rachel, Curt stirred in his seat. Anxious and bothered, she asked him, "What's wrong?"

"Nothing."

"Okay, looks like somethings bothering you? I'm over here on pins and needles, and you're huffing and puffing like some pissy little kid."

"Yeah, sorry. I don't know why the hell I didn't think of it. The house thing. Who was there before the Sewell family? It's so simple and obvious."

Rachel was taken aback. He was right. That's something the great Curt Walker would've keyed in on from the start. She had been too engrossed in everything that had happened to really notice Curt was having an off day. He usually leads the charge but had settled for a backseat role. It seemed very odd.

"It's okay. Everyone has an off day."

"Yeah, but still." Curt twitched and reached in his pocket for his cell phone. He scooted his chair back and stood up before answering. "It's Tracy. I'll be right back."

Curt answered and walked away from the table. Rachel thought about how Curt's absence was affecting his family. She was glad to have him with the team, but knowing what he'd been through for his family, it had to be difficult to balance.

The team finished up their dinners while Louis worked. He stayed focused, hunched over the keyboard, grunting and smirking to himself as he searched cyberspace for answers. The conversation turned superficial as they knew they just needed to wait until Louis worked his magic.

Curt returned from his phone call and sat down without saying anything.

"Everything all right?" Rachel asked.

Curt looked hesitant to answer, but replied, "Yeah, just some stuff Josh is having to work out."

Rachel didn't want to probe further, knowing that he would probably explain everything when the rest of the team wasn't around.

The fury of Louis' keyboard finger dance went silent. Rachel looked over and studied Louis' face, his eyes were fixed on the laptop's screen. There was something there.

"What is it? Did you find something?"

"Yeah." He said, without taking his eyes from the computer.

"Well?" Curt said. "What did you find?"

"I found him. I found the guy."

Chapter 14

Tracy Walker had been loosening boundaries set in place to protect her son, Josh. Against her better judgment as a mother, she was trying to adhere to advice given by Josh's therapist and give him some personal space. All she wanted to do was to hold him and never let go. Being missing for three years at the hands of a power-hungry rapist, tends to make a mother worry. But, for Josh's sake, she had allowed him to stay at the house unsupervised while she took care of a few errands. He usually stuck to video games or listened to music.

Josh was nearly thirteen, a tumultuous time regardless of his terrifying past, and Tracy struggled to get through to her son. Curt not being home didn't make things easier. She resented that he wanted to leave her and Josh for this team she wasn't allowed to talk about.

"I need to be out there, looking for more kids like Josh," Curt told her as he left for Texas. "I'm only a phone call away."

It didn't matter what Tracy said, Curt was going to leave anyway.

As Tracy pulled into the driveway, the fear of coming home to an empty house grew. It was a lasting echo of the three years when Josh was gone. She told herself he was safe, and that the nightmare was over, and if she wanted him to get better, she needed to relinquish some motherly control.

Walking in the door, she didn't hear the expected video game action coming from Josh's room. Ignoring her paranoia, Tracy went to her room, dropped her purse, keys and changed clothes. When Josh didn't come greet her, she called out to him.

"Josh, I'm home, honey."

There was no reply. The fear began to build.

"Josh?" She called. Tracy tried to calm down, reminding herself that loosening the boundaries was a good thing. She pushed open his bedroom door, hoping to find him listening to music. But, his room was empty. She searched the whole house, calling out for him.

When she came to the kitchen, something inside her mind made her account for all the knives. A month ago, Curt woke up and found Josh on the living room floor holding a knife. He explained to his father that he was just holding it and wasn't having any bad thoughts. Tracy's intuition told her otherwise, but the nurturer inside wanted desperately to believe him. She looked the knives over and saw they were all there. Relief settled, but only for a moment.

She reached for the house phone, ready to dial Curt when she saw a piece of paper with a handwritten note sitting on the counter. It was from Josh. *Went on a walk, be back soon.*

"A walk?" She asked the empty house. "That's new." Tracy's fear subsided, but there was still a concern that she couldn't shake. She grabbed her keys from the bedroom and began to drive around looking for him.

Ten minutes later, after circling the neighborhood, she branched out further to the feeder street that connected their neighborhood to a main artery of the city. The street ran down a hill and crossed over the interstate. From the distance up the hill, she saw a small figure standing on the side of the road near the overpass. Tracy felt a wave of relief, knowing that Josh hadn't done anything crazy, but she was reconsidering the loose boundaries.

Tracy pulled alongside of Josh and asked through the open window, "Hey buddy, what's going on?"

Josh turned slowly. She read in his eyes that he was overburdened by his past. She felt helpless because she didn't know how to help him.

"Hey, Mom."

"Pretty far for a walk, don't 'cha think?"

Josh looked around, clearly not realizing he had walked over a mile away from the house.

"Come on. Get in and I'll drive you home."

Josh got in, and Tracy turned the car around and headed home. She felt compelled to ask why the hell he wandered off so far from the house, but she knew he was in a delicate state of mind and she needed to be careful how she addressed him.

"So…" She felt as if he were a stranger and she was in a forced conversation. "What made you want to take a walk?"

"Dunno."

"Well, if you want, I'd be happy to go with you next time. I loved it when we all went on walks together."

"Okay, Mom," he said unenthusiastically. He was clearly still dealing with what drew him away from the safety of their home, so Tracy let the conversation fade.

"When's Dad coming home?" he asked.

"Uh, I don't know. I expect him to call later and check in. We can ask him then, okay?"

Josh nodded.

Tracy was not happy with Curt's absence. Before rejoining the team, he promised to leave instantly in the event she called. She thought, she would gladly call and say Josh needed him, just to get him home. "You want me to call him and tell him to come home?"

"No." He answered quickly.

"No? I mean, he said he would come right home if we called."

"No, I don't want him to come home right now."

She sensed Josh was getting irritated. "Okay, okay."

An awkward silence fell inside the car. They were almost home, but the quiet made it seem like they were miles away.

"It's not that I don't want him home, it's just that I know he's out looking for more kids, like me."

The rationale caught Tracy off guard. It actually made sense. It was a very mature way of thinking for the young boy.

"Oh, well, I'm sure that's exactly what he's doing."

"Good. I know he'll find them." Stunned, Tracy looked at Josh and saw a smile break across his face and lighten his spirits. *Whatever works*, she told herself.

After dinner, bath, and some reading with Josh—they were halfway through the second Harry Potter book—Tracy put Josh to bed and retired to her room to call Curt. Josh called earlier and they talked about where he was and what they were doing. Curt explained the team had hiked through miles of woods and found a house where a bad person once lived. Josh found solace in knowing that Curt and the team were going to stop the bad guy.

Tracy didn't want to talk to Curt in front of Josh, but she had to tell him about Josh wandering off.

"Hello?"

"Hey, you still at that restaurant?"

"Yeah, Louis is doing his thing. He said it might take a while."

"When I came home today, he'd left the house to go on a walk."

"A walk?" Curt sounded concerned.

"Yeah, he left a note saying he went on a walk. So, I left and went looking for him." Tracy didn't know how to translate what happened, so she just came out with it. "I found him standing on the overpass by the interstate."

"What?" Curt snapped. "What was he doing?"

"I'm not sure. He was just standing there with a blank look on his face. Have you ever taken him there before? I mean, why there?"

"I don't know. And he was just standing there?"

"Yes."

"Was the sun setting or something? Maybe he was admiring a cool view."

Tracy shook her head; she had been too panicked at the time to notice if the sun was setting or if there was anything else to capture his attention. "Yeah, maybe. It was about that time. I wasn't really paying attention to that. I was pretty freaked out, Curt. I don't know if he's getting any better."

"You want me to come home?"

She wanted to demand that he come straight home, but Josh had been so adamant Curt stay, looking for missing kids, that she was afraid to go against his wishes and agitate him further. "No. But, I feel like I can't leave him alone, now."

"Well, I agree we need to loosen boundaries, but maybe not that loose."

"Yeah, alright." Tracy wasn't sure what that meant.

They exchanged good-byes and hung up. Tracy felt uneasy. From Josh's therapeutic process, to her and Curt's marriage, and maintaining her own sanity, she felt overburdened.

Chapter 15

Rachel felt all eyes on her. Louis turned his laptop around for the second time to show her an image of a man. This time, hell returned in the image of the faceless man. His eyes were distant and uncaring, that of a sociopath with no moral compass. The panic that seized her from within, although she was surrounded by friends, told Rachel that this was the man from her nightmare. Finally, the faceless man had a name.

"Harold Stephen Moye," Louis said, presenting the screen. He had found a dated picture, stored away in the archives of the Texas DMV, showing a man in his late thirties, rigid jaw-line, pallid tone, dark cropped hair, and thick black rimmed glasses.

With her mouth agape, Rachel was stunned silent. Staring at the image, there was no doubt in her mind that this was the man responsible for turning her life into a tailspin she'd almost never recovered from. Often, she allowed herself to think about what would've been had darkness not found her. What kind of women she and Rhonda would've become? What kind of perfect husband she would have married? The fulfilling job, beautiful children, cute picket-fenced house, and caring circle of friends that would've made life easy, not the difficult hell she was left to endure.

"Well?" Curt asked gently. "Is that the guy?"

Rachel snapped to. She blinked herself back to reality and looked at Curt. He and the rest of the team waited for her response. "Um.... Yes. That's him."

There was no celebration, shouting, or high-fives, just a sense of relief that washed over the table. Identifying the perpetrator in any situation was the hardest part, but once that was done, the real work could begin.

"How'd you come up with him, Louis?" Curt asked.

"Well, I checked the foreclosure notice and traced the bank's holdings back until I got an original name on the lien. I double checked with archived property appraiser records as well as his driver's license history. It all matched back to Moye."

"Where is he now?" Rachel asked.

"Um, well…, okay. That's the problem currently. I'm not sure."

Beth stood up, "Give me the name one more time. I'll go see what I can dig up."

Louis repeated the name, and Beth walked out of the restaurant with Melinda.

"What do you mean, Louis? You're not sure?" Curt asked.

"Okay, well. I'm not done, but it's kind of like this guy disappeared in 1993."

"I wonder why?" Curt added, facetiously while looking at Rachel.

Louis went back to typing on the laptop. "Oh my God," he said.

"What?" Rachel asked, sensing the tension.

"On this census report, his profession is listed as teacher."

A moment of abhorrent realization fell on Rachel, Curt, and Louis. The access a serial pedophile would have as a teacher was unfathomable. His victim toll could be astronomical. For Rachel, she immediately thought of all her past teachers and how she could have come across Moye's path. Diving deep within her memory, she came up empty. "Where was he a teacher? I'm sure I never had him. I think I would've made that connection back then."

"It doesn't say where. So, no telling what kind of teacher and for what school. The census reports aren't that specific. I can find out by going through the school board directories, but that'll take time."

"No, we can always back track later. We need to find where he is now."

"If he's still alive," Louis added.

"True." Rachel thought about the possibility of Moye being dead. The thought of not having to face him gave her a sense of relief, then it turned to guilt, and she ignored the thought altogether.

Louis continued typing, letting his fingers glide across the keyboard with a harmonious gait. He was trying to amass information on Moye to give the team ammunition to go after him. At least, that's what Rachel believed.

Rachel turned to Curt, leaving Louis to his computer. "Are we rushing into this? I mean, I feel kind of foolish being at the center of all this."

"No, of course not."

Rachel shook her head. "I don't know."

"Listen, if this is the man that did those terrible things to you and your sister, he deserves to be caught first of all. Secondly, I don't believe for one moment y'all were his first and only victims. And lastly, if he wasn't caught, he could still be doing the same thing to God knows who else. So, us going after him isn't just justice for you, it's justice for any person he's ever hurt and stopping him before he hurts anyone else."

"Yeah, you're right."

"Of course, I am," Curt said with a confident smile. "What do you think we do on this team?"

"Well, I thought it was finding missing kids, but this seems a little different?"

"Not really. You were a kid when he grabbed you. Odds are, he hasn't changed his victim profile."

"Okay, I see your point."

"Good. Let us work. We'll find him."

Louis was making slow progress, but nothing revealed his current whereabouts.

"Excuse me, Senor?" A waiter from the restaurant was standing over Curt and Rachel. "We are closed, now," he said politely as he extended his hand toward the door.

"Oh, right. Sorry. Work stuff was keeping us late," Curt said. The waiter smiled, but clearly didn't care what the excuse was.

Louis begrudgingly packed up his computer and followed Rachel and Curt outside to the van. Rachel saw that Melinda had the van running, and Beth was engrossed in her laptop sitting in the passenger seat, bare feet propped up on the dash.

Only as a matter of conversation, Rachel asked Beth while climbing in the van, "Get any headway on where Moye might be?" She didn't expect an answer, it being such a tall order in a short time.

Beth ignored the question and Rachel sat down, miffed from the silent treatment. As Curt and Louis climbed in, Melinda craned her head around the seat. "She's on a roll. But to answer your question, yes. She's located him and stumbled onto something big."

"What?" Rachel asked incredulous. She could feel Louis leaning over her shoulder, also eager to know what Melinda meant by "big."

"Apparently, he's living in the Tampa, Florida, area and Beth thinks he's still actively hunting girls."

Beth took a second away from her work to look and acknowledge what Melinda had relayed. She nodded that her statement was true and then turned back to the screen.

"How the hell she does that, I don't know." Louis said with his customary whine. He plopped back down in his seat in the back. A silence fell inside the Mercedes Sprinter while the team waited for more information from Beth.

"So, now what?" Rachel asked.

"We go to Tampa," Melinda answered.

"When?"

Melinda searched the eyes of the other team members and replied, "Now."

Chapter 16

The Investigations Bureau was quiet, so it was easy for Sandra Benitez to hear her rotund partner, Sal Munroe, sauntering down toward her cubicle.

"The mother is downstairs. Can you talk to her?" he asked. The way he said "mother" made it seem like she was a repulsive nag that was contagious. "I got that thing, still."

She gave him a sideways look, knowing he asked only because he didn't want to deal with the woman, not because he was amidst something more important. "Sure," she said.

Detective Sandra Benitez was new to the Tampa Police Homicide Unit. Being new and being a woman, she had to endure a barrage of grunt work if she wanted respect among her mostly male peers. Reaching the homicide unit in under ten years on the job caused grumblings of tokenism being the reason she was picked, not for her merits. On their first homicide, Munroe had kept her restrained for most of the case, relegating her to the mundane tasks instead of being on the front line of the investigation. Stuck overseeing evidence collection, while he interviewed the suspect, hardly seemed like a good way to learn the job. However, being new, she had kept her mouth shut.

This was another time to stay quiet. The mother waiting downstairs wanted to know about her daughter's missing persons case. The girl disappeared after running away and showing up at a school dance. The mother reported her missing the same night after checking on her and noticing she was gone from her room. Patrol came up empty at the school after learning she went to the dance to meet up with her boyfriend. In the boy's statement, he said she ran off the dance floor for some unknown reason and that was the last anyone saw her.

The cause of Munroe's apprehension and the annoyance of Benitez, was that the mother believed the girl was the victim of foul play and not just another runaway. She explained that her daughter, "would not just run away," and insisted they treat the investigation as such. She had called the day after the girl's disappearance, trying to convince the detectives something was wrong, and they needed to do more.

The issue was the girl's history. Layla Bragden had a documented history of mental instability and irrational behavior. Benitez found several reports of disturbances at their house where Layla lashed out and became destructive following an argument with her mother. She smashed lamps, vases, and a few dishes out of anger. She blamed her parent's divorce and the mother's lack of understanding for her outbursts. Several weeks prior she had snuck out of the house and was found at her boyfriend's place several hours later by patrol officers. Everything about the girl screamed runaway.

"That little girl's shacked up with some new boy, Mom doesn't know about." Munroe offered callously. "I'm tellin' you, that's the case."

"Yeah, you're probably right."

Benitez hated agreeing with her seasoned partner. It felt contradictory to what she felt in her heart. Her compassion for the job and the victims she served burned brighter than her partner, but Munroe had the experience to back it up, and she had to respect that.

As Benitez pushed her way into the lobby, she saw Mrs. Bragden sitting there with a distant stare. She looked lost.

"Hi, Mrs. Bragden, I'm Detective Sandra Benitez, nice to meet you."

"Um, yeah. Hi, it's Emily."

"Yes, Emily. I'm sorry it's under these circumstances, but... You didn't have to come down here, you could have called."

"I don't know what else to do. I have to do something." Tears welled in the corner of her eyes.

"Okay."

Sandra Benitez had been a cop for ten years. She loved her job and strived to help those in need. Trying to steer away from the jaded cynicism born out of the frustrations of the job, she held on tight to her compassion, never letting it fade. It was what made her do the job each and every day.

In this instance, her compassion overruled her partner's callous assumption. It was the desperation that radiated from Emily Bragden's eyes. "C'mon. Let's go get some coffee."

Ten minutes later, they sat in the corner of a Starbucks two blocks down from the police station. Routinely visited by cops, it was dubbed an unofficial substation. Benitez used it as an excuse to get away from her partner and give Emily Bragden the attention she needed.

"Do you think she's just another troubled young girl acting out?" Emily asked. Benitez tried to shield her doubts, but Emily read it immediately. "You do, don't you?"

"It's not that. It's just that…" Benitez took a sip of her coffee while she formed a good answer. "It's that I have to go on facts. The facts are that there is plenty of documentation that Layla's had her fair share of troubles, ever since your divorce. And without anything else contradicting, I can't help but think that."

Emily set her cup down and wept. Benitez regretted being forward. But, she didn't want to give the mother, or any person in her position, false hope. It allows the harshness of reality, when it finally arrives, to not sting as much. She reached out and placed her hand gently on Emily's trying to console her.

"If I'm missing anything, Emily, please tell me."

"I just know. As a mother." Benitez hated the ensuing argument she knew was coming. "Are you a mother, Detective?"

Benitez withdrew her hand, "No, ma'am. I'm not." Her compassion ran deep for everyone and not being a parent made no difference.

"Okay. Well…" She could tell that Emily wanted to be hurtful in that moment but restrained herself. "A mother knows, Detective. I'm sorry that doesn't equate into your world of facts, but I know my daughter was going through some tough times, but she wouldn't run away. Not like this anyway. She's so much more strong-willed than that. She'd rather stand and fight than run away, trust me."

"Well, Emily…, she's done it before."

Mrs. Bragden gave a flat look back at Benitez. After an awkward silence, "Yes, Detective, you have a point. But, she left that time because of a boy and was found right afterward. This time was also because of a boy, but this time she disappeared."

Benitez felt as if Emily was proving her argument, not countering it. She decided not to point that out.

"So, what is it that I can help you with tonight?"

"Ugh, I don't know. I feel so damn helpless, and I don't feel like going home if I know she's not going to be there."

"That's understandable, but you should be there in case she comes home."

"Do you think that'll happen?"

Benitez wasn't going to make promises she couldn't deliver. "I tell you what. Tomorrow, I'll go back to the school where the dance was and take a look around. I'll go find this boy she was trying to meet up with and interview him further and talk to anyone else who saw her at the dance. How does that sound?"

"Tomorrow?" With the tone Emily used, Benitez translated that into, "*You're not going to do it now?*"

"Yes, ma'am. I've been up since early this morning working this case and another. If I'm to be worth a damn, I need some sleep."

Mrs. Bragden nodded and stood up to leave. "I guess you're right."

Benitez stood up and placed her hand on her shoulder, "Go home, wait for Layla to come back. Hopefully, I'll have some answers in the morning."

Walking back to the station, Benitez hung on to how Emily described her daughter as strong-willed and willing to fight. It reminded

106

her of herself as a young woman trying to find her place in the world. Being attracted to women instead of men, she learned to stand up and fight against the hatred toward homosexuals and not to back down. If Layla was the same way, maybe there was more to her disappearance than she thought.

Chapter 17

Rachel barely slept during the long overnight drive to Florida. She went over the research Beth had accumulated on Moye back at the Mexican restaurant. She discovered a pattern of girls who went missing over the past twenty years in the Tampa Bay area. The frequency was nearly every two to three months. Coincidentally, the M.O. started soon after Moye left the Houston area and relocated to Florida. Of course, a suspect was never caught or identified. The girls were all around the same age, and they were all remarkably similar in appearance. There was something familiar about the girls, but Rachel couldn't quite figure it out. Disturbingly, Rachel noticed, none of the girls in these cases had been found. Dead or alive.

Rachel put down Beth's laptop with all the research and leaned toward the passenger chair. Beth was curled up asleep in the seat. Rachel had a question and didn't want to wait until she woke up.

Nudging gently, "Hey, Beth…." She waited, "Beth? You awake?"

Rachel pushed a little harder and Beth shook awake. Groggy and with half-opened eyes, Beth looked at Rachel. "What?"

"I got a question about Moye."

Beth dropped her head back and closed her eyes. "Sure, what's up?"

"Did his M.O. change from Texas to Florida? I mean, surely someone noticed the cases were connected, right?"

"I just started putting together the stuff from Texas, so it's hard to say. But reading the Florida cases, I compared it to your specific case."

Beth yawned and kept her eyes closed. Rachel clung to her words. "There were *some* differences."

"Like what?"

Beth cracked her eyes open and looked at Rachel. "You were taken by force, on the street, out in the open."

Rachel shuddered. "Okay, how were the Florida girls taken?"

"That's the thing, the police never figured out how. They all went missing by either not returning from somewhere, or they were expected somewhere and never showed. It was like they were plucked out of thin air."

"Anything else?"

"Nothing glaring, but in your case, he grabbed two victims, you and Rhonda, at the same time. That, apparently, was an anomaly because best I can tell, he's never repeated that." Beth yawned again and adjusted in her seat. "He's always taken just one girl at a time."

Rachel thought to herself, "Hmmm." She wondered why Moye had decided to take both she and her sister that awful day. If that was not his M.O., what changed in his mind? She leaned back in the captain's chair and shut her eyes. She felt as if she were standing at the edge of a cliff, safe if she remained still, but moving forward could prove perilous.

She thought about the steps taken to get to this point. The images buried in her subconscious had come to her in vivid color. She recalled the memories again, making sure they weren't just figments of her imagination, created by her desire for answers. She remembered the dark room, the foretelling of that creaky floorboard of evil things to come, the mad dash through the woods, and the delirium that followed. The twenty-years of self-tortured recovery would forever remain in her consciousness. This was real, she thought. It was real and she would finally get her answers.

***

An odd noise, something similar to a coin dropping on a hard surface, stirred Tracy from her sleep. Her eyes flittered open, but there was no follow up sound or reaction. Her eyelids fell heavy and closed as she listened. Dawn was breaking, and the black of night was slowly being replaced by the blue-gray morning.

She inhaled and stretched her legs across the queen bed. Half-way expecting to bump into Curt sleeping next to her, she grew disappointed when he wasn't. Tracy peeked up at the alarm clock and saw that it was just after six a.m. It was too early to get up, so she adjusted in the bed and tried to get a little more sleep.

Another noise. Something metallic hit the floor.

"What the hell?"

Tracy's frustration at being roused from her sleep turned to slight panic as her thoughts instantly fell to Josh. Her fear was in the unknown. Finding him standing by the overpass scared her. Not knowing what he was thinking frightened her the most. She sat up and peeled back the covers. She tip-toed to her door and eased it open.

The noise came for a third time. It was coming from somewhere deep in the living room or the kitchen. She walked down the hall toward the noise. A light was on in the kitchen, and Josh's bedroom door was open. Tracy braced herself and turned the corner to see Josh sitting at the kitchen table. The peninsula counter sat tall and blocked her view of everything but his head which perked up once he realized she was there.

"Hey Josh. You're up early. Did you sleep okay?"

"Um..., yeah. It was okay, I guess."

He was hiding something. He stopped moving and just stared back at her. Something inside told her to move forward to see what he was doing, but she hesitated out of fear. As she took a few steps, the odd noise was explained, and she fought every urge to scream.

Stay calm, she told herself. *Stay calm.*

Moving closer to Josh, she saw he had removed several of the kitchen knives and was holding them up high and letting them fall, blade first so they would stick into the wood top of the table. The problem was that he held his left hand in the fall zone, letting chance decide if he would be impaled or not.

"Josh, baby?" She tried to rein in her excitement. "What are you doing?"

"I don't know," he replied in a pathetic whimper.

Tracy moved swiftly and collected up the knives before he did something else. She decided she would remove them from the house and anything else that was dangerous. Once she took them out of reach, she turned and looked at him, this time with a motherly look.

"No, Josh. Baby, that's not good enough. Please, I want to help you but you have to let me know what's going on. Tell me how you're feeling or why you think it's a good idea to play with knives."

Josh didn't react. He sulked in his chair and turned angry. "I told you. I. Don't. Know."

She could see the battle with his inner demons waging internally. *It's not fair*, she told herself. He should never have to know this level of pain. Tears began to fall from her eyes. Stepping over to Josh, she reached out and held him tight. He reached up, began to cry, and squeezed her back.

Later that morning, Tracy made the phone call to Curt, telling him he had to come home.

Chapter 18

After a grueling seventeen-hour trek across the southeastern United States, the team finally rolled into Tampa. It was early afternoon and the team was exhausted. However, Rachel felt a surge of energy; being this close to Moye, she wanted to keep the momentum.

"Okay, what do we do first?" Rachel asked.

"Um, we just drove all night straight through, so I say our first move is to find a nice hotel and get some rest," Melinda offered.

Rachel pouted at the thought of stopping. "Oh…, okay."

"C'mon!" Melinda turned around in her seat while stopped at a traffic light. "You can't expect everyone to be on top of their game without sleep. I know this is very personal to you, but I don't think one afternoon is going to make a difference."

"Yeah, you're right."

"Especially since now we're down Curt."

Before turning south on I-75, the team made a quick stop in Tallahassee and dropped Curt off at his house. He was vague as to why, but everyone knew it was for reasons surrounding Josh's well-being. For that, no one argued with the unfortunate timing, even though his absence was a painful void. Rachel hated that he wasn't there with them but having him by her side as they'd identified Moye gave her the confidence to continue.

The hotel that Beth and Melinda found was posh and a little above the grade they were accustomed to. The lobby floor was all marble and sitting in the middle was a huge glass wall with cascading water flowing down the front face. Smoothed stones and water ferns adorned the base of the center piece.

"Whoa!" Louis said, taking in the hotel's décor.

"You're welcome," Beth answered. "I think we're entitled to a little spoiling here and there."

Rachel watched as the other three dragged their suitcases toward the elevators. Standing next to Louis, she leaned close and spoke in a whisper.

"I'd like to keep working, Louis. At least get a location for where he might be living."

"Um…." Uneasy at the request, he glanced down at the laptop tucked under his arm, as if he were considering letting her borrow it to find him.

Rachel looked back toward the lobby and saw a sign that read, "vending," over an arrow pointing down a hallway. "I'll go get you an ice-cold Mountain Dew. How 'bout that?"

His uneasiness subsided, but he wasn't convinced.

"Okay, two sodas."

"And some salt and vinegar chips," he demanded.

Rachel smiled. "Fine. My room or yours?"

Louis Melton's body stiffened. The thought of having a woman in his hotel room was obviously very foreign. He stammered, "Um, well, uh."

"Relax. I'll go get your snacks and meet you in your room in five minutes."

Five minutes later, Louis opened the door to his room and let Rachel inside. The earlier awkwardness vanished as he keyed in on the caffeinated drinks and salty snack.

"First things, first." He popped the tab back and gulped down nearly half of the soda with the fervor of an alcoholic in need of a beer. "That hit the spot. Okay, so you want to find a devious killer who kidnaps young women, virtually leaving no trace behind and has managed to elude the cops for over a quarter century?"

It seemed daunting when put like that, Rachel thought, but nodded, hoping Louis was up for the challenge.

"Awesome. Let's get to it."

Louis sat at the desk in the corner of the room. He worked from the laptop but had a secondary one set off to the side, and Rachel noticed he was continuously checking his cell phone and responding to someone. He guzzled down the first soda while warming up the machines and quickly opening the second one. With more caution given to the chips, Rachel watched as Louis ceremoniously opened the bag so that the entire top was opened. He creased one side several times with his fingers giving it a neat edge and then pinched the bottom and slightly turn it up making the chips inside slide down the crease into his open mouth.

Rachel watched the nerdy genius with all his peculiarities in awe. There was so much effort in how he ate the chips, she was left baffled. Unable to concentrate on all of Beth's research, she kept watching Louis and his odd habits. Finally, he noticed.

"What?"

She broke from her trance and shook her head. "Nothing."

"It's so I don't get my fingers all greasy when I'm working. It's bad for the machines."

"Ahh, right."

Setting aside the spectacle that is Louis Melton, Rachel concentrated on Beth's research and tried to analyze what it all meant. Nearly sixty girls, around the age of fifteen, went missing over the last twenty years that seemed to fit a particular, albeit loose, modus operandi.

"Only their ages and the geographical proximity seem to be the obvious links to the girls," Rachel spoke out loud. "But, in reading all the articles, they range from constant runaways to the all-American girl next door."

"That's it?" Louis asked.

"Yeah, I mean, and this is really assuming that all these girls were actually victims, because we don't know how or where or when they were taken. This guy, and again, assuming it's Moye, has been very careful."

"What else do they have in common? Schools? Clubs? Boyfriends?"

"No, none of that. They are spread out in different school zones, only a few, that I could find, belong to the same organizations and none really had friends in common."

Rachel set aside the research and her notes and laid back on the bed. That energy surge had long since passed, and she wished she had gotten herself a Mountain Dew.

"How's it coming on your end?"

"Slow."

She blew out a breath and sat up on the bed. "I need some coffee. You need another drink?"

"No. I'm good for now."

Rachel started a cup brewing from the complimentary samples from the hotel. Her mind started wandering about the other girls that Moye could be responsible for taking. She then moved back to the research, knowing the answers might lie within. An idea came to her, thinking it would help her stay awake and give a visual outlook of the victims. "Do you have a printer up here?" she asked.

Louis didn't take his eyes off of his screen. "Yup."

Waiting for him to elaborate, Rachel stood by the coffee maker. After a long silence, she coughed to get his attention.

"Huh? What?"

"The printer, Louis."

"Oh, right."

Louis got up, but checked his cell phone first. He thumbed something quickly, smiled and dove into his luggage.

"You texting someone?"

"Um, no. Not really."

Hoping he wasn't getting outside help on their search for Moye, she gave him an expectant look.

"It's a strategy game I'm playing with..." Louis paused and smiled. "Someone."

"Someone, huh?"

"Yeah." Louis pulled a printer from a bag, plugged it in, and fed the paper tray with blank sheets. "Ready. What do you want to print?"

"Pictures of all the missing girls. I feel it'll give me a better sense of how they went missing if I can see them all together."

"Okay, I'm going to need another Dew. This isn't some high-speed printer I got, you know. That'll take a bit."

"Fine. I'll be back in a few."

Riding down in the elevator, Rachel caught her image staring back at her from the mirrored walls. She looked tired. Averting her eyes, she opted to watch the floor counter go down. She was very tired but hoped the effort to find Moye was worth the lack of sleep. He was a demon from her past now brought back into the present. She was much stronger and wiser than when she was a teenage girl, but that level of fear rarely goes away.

The elevator dinged opened and she stepped out toward the marble floor of the lobby. She traversed it to get Louis more caffeine. Loud talking and laughter pulled her attention toward the hotel bar. Seeing a few men dressed in unbuttoned dress shirts, abandoned ties, and popped collars, holding drinks in a cheer, reminded her that normal people do exist, not just monsters and those who chase them. It also reminded her of Curt. She missed him already.

Passing back through the lobby the businessmen had moved and encircled a few women at the other end of the bar. This time, she was reminded of her own past and the many nights she sought refuge from the darkness in the attention of drunken men. That was not her anymore, like Curt had told her back in Vail, after saving her life.

***

Louis was waiting for Rachel's return, first to hand her all the printed pictures, second to guzzle another Mountain Dew.

"Here. They're all printed out for you." She exchanged the drink for the pictures and got to work taping them up on the wall side by side.

"Okay, I think I got something," Louis announced.

"Let's hear it."

"Okay, so basically Harold Stephen Moye doesn't exist past 1993, but there's never been a death certificate or anything like that to suggest he died. So, moving along on what Beth found about the similar missing girls, puts him in the Tampa Bay area, I started searching for similar names with similar dates of birth, like Stephen Moye, Harold Stephens, Stephen Harold. You get the point. It took a while, but I narrowed it down by race, assuming that didn't change, and found several possibilities."

"How many? And can you be sure you found the right one?"

"Well, I'll let you decide that. I found about thirty possibilities in the area, but Harold Stephens," Louis spun the laptop screen around to show Rachel, "has the exact same social security number as Moye except for it's off one digit and all his records begin in 1994."

Rachel stopped taping up the pictures to study the screen. Harold Stephens was the same man, only he had aged twenty years since she last saw him standing over the heart shaped rock. Moye had simply dropped his last name in an attempt to change his identity. But he couldn't escape the virtual reach of Louis Melton.

"That's him," she said, a bit flatly.

"Damn right it's him." He sounded hurt.

Rachel was almost too tired to notice she hurt Louis's feelings. "I'm sorry. Thank you, Louis. I'm just tired. I'm going to go back to my room, now. We can pick this up in the morning."

Chapter 19

Rachel managed a few hours of sleep due to pure physical exhaustion. The emotional turmoil of the past twenty-four hours had left her on empty. She struggled with the sheer numbers of missing girls that Moye could be responsible for. As she woke, the girls were her first conscious thought. There was something oddly familiar about the lot, but she couldn't place it. After showering, she ordered room service and sent texts to the team to meet in Louis's room after breakfast. She wanted to show the team what they discovered the night before.

As Beth and Melinda walked in the room, they nearly stopped in place as all the eight-by-ten photos of the missing girls stared back from the wall. Rachel moved in behind them, letting them absorb the moment. For her, knowing that almost sixty girls were missing at the hands of Harold Stephen Moye was tough to accept, but seeing them staring back at her, waiting for justice, was overwhelming.

Rachel explained what Louis was able to uncover the night before about how Moye altered his identity. Louis was struggling to keep his eyes open for the early morning guests. He periodically dozed off while they talked.

"Damn. That's a lot of girls," Beth said. "Doing the research is one thing, but seeing all of them like this…" She let out a low whistle. "This is a lot of girls."

The mood turned dark, even as the morning sun pushed its way through the pulled drapes.

"So, what's the plan?" Beth asked.

All eyes turned to Rachel. She wondered if they looked to her because Curt went home or because of the personal connection she had to the case.

"Well, I was thinking we set up on the house and watch for a bit. You know, watch his habits and get an idea of his schedule. With any luck, we prove he's responsible for the missing girls and feed him to the cops."

Melinda nodded, Louis nodded off back to sleep, and Beth had a twisted look on her face.

"What's that look for, Beth?" Rachel was ready to defend her leadership decision.

"Oh, nothing. I'm reminded of a recent missing girl case I read about on the road trip here. I think Moye could be good for it."

"Recent?"

"Yeah, like, she disappeared two days ago." Beth pulled out her phone and scrolled with her thumbs. "Layla Bragden, fifteen, went missing after last being seen at a school dance." Beth kept the disgusted look on her face.

"What is it?"

"This article suggests she ran away and has a history of suicide attempts."

"Okay, you obviously don't think so?"

"No." Beth tapped her screen and presented it to the group. "The age fits, the area fits, and she could be these girl's sister."

Rachel compared the image on Beth's screen to the wall of images and agreed with Beth's assessment. The realization that there was a fresh case, not more than forty-eight hours old, fell on the room. They weren't chasing a ghost from Rachel's past anymore, they were hunting an active predator.

"Okay, we need more on the current missing girl. We should split up."

Melinda looked at Beth, then at Rachel. "We'll track down the missing girl case and see what the police have."

119

"Okay, me and…," Rachel looked over at the bed to see Louis had fallen back asleep. "Me and sleeping beauty will go set up on Moye's house and watch until you guys catch back up."

Before turning to leave, Beth pounced on Louis playfully, and he ripped awake.

"Huh? What the—"

Beth let out a loud cackle and left the room with Melinda giggling. Louis looked more dejected that he missed an up-close opportunity with Beth rather than disturbed he was roused from comfortable slumber. He looked up at Rachel who shot back a grin at his obvious tell.

***

Shaking off the incessant whining of a sleep-deprived Louis Melton, Rachel focused on the fact that they were getting close to the man responsible for her abduction and her sister's presumed death. She ignored barrel-rolling butterflies the size of jetliners in her stomach as Louis drove the Mercedes Sprinter through Moye's neighborhood. He found a good spot for surveillance at the end of the block.

"Think this is inconspicuous enough?" he asked, checking his mirrors and the surrounding area.

"Yeah, it's fine." Rachel knew she sounded absent, but her eyes were fixed on Moye's house. It had the same feel as the house in Texas, normal. That gave her great concern. Even in her little experience as a member of the team, a normal appearance often equated to the evil-doer's skill at concealment. In this case, it was high.

Louis put the van in park and jumped to the back to his work station. He fired up his machines and popped open a fresh Mountain Dew from the mini-fridge. Letting out an after-sip "ahhh," he cracked his knuckles in a ritualistic warm-up. Beth called and asked Louis to try and get the police report of Layla Bragden's disappearance. He promised to have it in full within the hour.

Rachel was fixed to her Captain's chair, staring out the large side window, waiting on a glimpse of a monster.

"It looks so—" Louis said from behind Rachel.

"Normal," she finished.

"Yeah. Exactly."

He saw it too, she thought. The house was an off-white, stucco one-story that sat on a descending slope. The front yard was well-manicured St. Augustine grass, neatly trimmed around the edges of the curb, driveway, and sidewalk. Symmetrical flower beds that were equally impressive, even in the winter months, sat on either side of the lawn. Tall shrubbery encased a privacy fence that shielded the back yard, but Rachel could tell a large body of water was at the bottom of the slope and ran the length of the neighboring houses. She recalled Louis crossing a bridge that ran over a small river opening up into a much larger lake. She figured Moye's house backed up to the body of water.

Her mind immediately began to devise a plan to break into the house and use the water to make a stealthy approach. She made a mental note.

Rachel grabbed a pair of binoculars and peered through them, studying the front of Moye's house like it held the answers to her twenty-two-year-old mystery. Who was this man? What made him take her and her sister and presumably sixty more young girls since? One thing she knew; she wasn't leaving until she had answers.

***

Deciding to wait until they had access to the police report, Beth and Melinda delayed talking with Layla's mother for more information. They decided to head toward the school where the dance was held to look around.

Beth was on the phone with Louis while Melinda drove.

"Yes, send all that stuff to me along with the police report... uh, huh... okay.... You said within the hour, Louis!" Beth giggled. "Okay, all I'm sayin' is, don't promise what you can't deliver."

Beth said goodbye and hung up.

"Were you flirting with him?" Melinda asked.

"Uh..., no. He's my friend."

121

"Right," she said, her tone laced with skepticism. "So, what did he say?"

"Layla was a social media posting demon. She updated all the time and last posted a picture at nine forty-five p.m. He's sending us everything he could get."

"And the police report?"

"He said he's almost got it." Beth checked her watch. "He's got exactly three minutes."

Two minutes later, Melinda parked a rental car across the street from East Tampa High School. She cut the engine and watched as a few students ran down a sidewalk and into the side of a building, no doubt late for class.

Beth's phone chimed, and she checked the notification.

"Well, I'll be damned. He did it."

Beth explained that Louis managed to send her the promised police report and all the recent pictures from Layla's social media account. She read through the bare bones report and understood why the newspaper article suggested she was a runaway in trouble and not a victim of foul play.

"She's got a history of suicide attempts and apparently ran away from home last week to hang out with the same boy she went looking for at this school dance," Beth summarized.

"What about the pictures, anything there?"

Beth flipped through them and held her iPad up so Melinda could see them as well.

When they came to the last picture uploaded, it was an angled selfie of a sad Layla sitting somewhere dark. Beth manipulated the picture with her index finger and thumb, zooming in on the image's corner and trying to identify where she was.

Grabbing for her phone, Beth quickly thumbed a message and sent it to Louis. She asked him to hack into her account and get access to the cloud storage.

"Asking him to get the rest of the pictures?" Melinda figured.

"Yep. Email and texts, too."

Ten minutes later, Louis provided Layla's cloud account password. Using her iPad, Beth signed on as Layla and accessed her texts, emails, and other photo's.

Scanning through, she immediately keyed in on the last thread with *Luke* when Layla sent several risqué pictures of herself topless with her arm covering the majority of her adolescent breasts.

"Whoa!" Beth said at the photos. "Girl wasn't playing around."

"Anything about that night?"

"No, not really. Just that sad looking selfie."

"If she was meeting up with this Luke kid, why was she alone and looking so sad in this picture?"

"Dunno."

"Did the cops ever talk to this Luke kid?"

Beth rescanned the police report. "It mentions a Lucas Millwood, assuming that's Luke, he told the responding officers that she left the dance a little after nine."

"She goes to meet up with this kid specifically, and she posts that picture alone thirty minutes later? He's holding back. We should talk to him."

Beth agreed and continued scanning through Layla's digital life. "You know, I'm getting the feeling that this girl isn't some screwed up little girl, but rather a normal, going-through-teenage-angst-like-the-rest-of-us kind of girl."

"Yeah, I think the cops took the lazy route on this one." Melinda sat up in her seat and stared toward the parking lot of the school. "Speaking of cops…"

Beth looked up from her iPad to see what Melinda was talking about. A tall Hispanic woman, dressed in a light gray pants suit, black flats, and with black hair tied up in a loose, bun strolled toward the office. The glint of her silver badge and bulge of her service weapon through her jacket made it obvious she was a detective.

"What was the name of the detectives on the case?" Melinda asked.

Beth tapped and swiped her iPad, then answered, "Detectives Munroe and Benitez."

"*Hello*, Detective Benitez."

"Now who's flirting?"

Chapter 20

Walking into the school's office, Sandra Benitez felt like an awkward freshman all over again, getting lost on her first day of high school and needing help from the office staff. Although, her school was across town at West Hillsborough, it still reminded her of that terrible day.

Remembering she was an adult, with a badge and a gun, she smiled and patiently waited for the woman on the other side of the counter to finish her phone conversation. Having lied to Sal, telling him she was following up on a shooting they had caught the week before Layla's disappearance, she wanted to look around the school. She wasn't being defiant to her partner, it's just that she promised Mrs. Bragden she would look further into the case.

"Yes Detective, may I help you?" The woman, a pleasant red-head wearing a name tag that read, "Kathy," asked.

Detective Benitez introduced herself in a low tone so as not to attract unwanted attention from others waiting in the office. She explained why she was at the school and that she wanted to look around.

"Oh right. I heard about that. Poor girl…, and her mother." Kathy gasped and put her hand to her chest. "I don't really know the girl but let me check with the principal and let him know you're here. I hope you guys find her."

Benitez waited several minutes, staving off probing stares from students noticing her badge and gun. She heard a few references to her being a part of *Charlie's Angel's* from a group of three boys who stopped in to say hello to Kathy. She was almost flattered, but she preferred Olivia Benson from *Law and Order: SVU*. She fashioned herself more like the New York detective as opposed to the international super spies.

Principal Locke came out of his office and introduced himself.

"Kathy said you're looking into the Layla Bragden case and wanted to look around?"

"Yes, sir."

"The uniformed officers came by that night to look around. Is there something new in the case?"

Benitez had read the reports and knew the patrol officers canvassed around the school, but she wasn't confident that they were as thorough as they could have been.

"I just wanted to look for myself, if that's okay?"

"Um, of course. We want to cooperate in any way we can, Detective." Principal Locke's face cringed.

"What is it?" Benitez prepared for a sparring contest. If he was about to demand a search warrant, she was going to give him hell. It's not that she wasn't confident she could get one; it was that going through the process would be a waste of time, because he could just grant her access in the spirit of this cooperation he mentioned.

"Do you mind waiting until the students get to first period? The bell will ring in about two minutes. That way, you'll be left to wander as needed without all the prying eyes and not to mention all the paranoid parents who would undoubtedly get text updates and then call me wanting to know everything."

"Ahh, yes. Good idea. I think we're on the same page."

After the bell rang, Benitez walked across the school to the gymnasium where the school dance had been held. She stepped inside, quietly in case a P.E. class had started. It was empty and quiet for her to look around. Some of the banners from the dance were still up, but all other remnants were gone. She walked out on the court floor and took in the cavernous gym, focusing on the case at hand and not her own memories of playing basketball on the junior varsity team. Unable to get a feel for the gym, she stepped outside and studied the available avenues, considering where Layla might have gone.

There were two nearby access points to the main school building, one close to the gym and one a bit further away. If there had been any loiterers outside of the dance, she figured Layla would have chosen the further one for its seclusion.

Benitez headed toward the farther hallway access and saw a painted sign above the door had a picture of liquid-filled beakers, orbiting planets, and molecule configurations on it. She pulled the door and walked through, letting it close behind her. As it clanked shut, the metallic echo bounced off the walls, and she got embarrassed at the loud noise, praying it didn't invite unwanted attention. She froze in place, half-way expecting some sweater-vest and glasses teacher to step out of a classroom and shush her.

The faux pas went unchecked and Benitez continued her canvass. She walked down the hallway, passing several classroom doors. A staircase sat at the far end, and a set of bathroom doors split the hallway in half. Benitez walked to the other end of the hallway and stopped just inside the double doors, peering outside the glass inlays. It led to a courtyard with an identical brick building across the way. She wasn't getting any fuzzy feelings and felt like this was an exercise in futility. Her thoughts turned to Emily Bragden, Layla's mom. She did not want to call her back and tell her that she came up empty. Not yet, anyway.

Turning to head back the way she came, the small item immediately caught her attention. She wondered why she missed it on her first pass. Unsure of what it was from the distance, but as Benitez got closer, she recognized it as a shoe. For some reason, it was wedged between the wall and iron piping that ran along the base of the walls. Kneeling down to look closer, it looked clean, free of dust and grime that would be expected on something wedged that low to the floor. She knew it had been left recently.

She stood up, leaving the shoe in place, holding back her excitement and focused on its importance. Thinking hard, she didn't realize she was looking out of a window. A thought occurred and she looked up to the top frame of the bottom pane. The latch was pulled out halfway. Benitez stepped up on the piping and got a closer look at the clasp, but nothing stood out. It was just a dingy old catch. Stepping back down, she noticed blemishes in the glass. They caught the sun at just the right angle. She could see them because she was mere inches away from the glass. When she stepped back, they were unnoticeable.

"That's weird." Benitez stood abnormally close to the window, examining the blemishes. They were random but had a distinct shape to them. Her attention immediately moved back to the shoe, then back to the window, up to the latch, and then it made sense.

Benitez once read somewhere that preparedness is a virtue of a great detective. Part of that preparation, specifically, is having evidence bags and rubber gloves handy at all times. This now made all those foolish times she received a ribbing while she stuffed her pockets with plastic bags and rubber gloves before leaving the station worth it. Pulling a baggie and gloves from her jacket pocket, she knelt and carefully pulled the shoe from between the wall and pipe so as not to disturb any potential evidence. Holding it by the toe, she looked closely at the short two-inch heel. She moved the short spike up to the glass and matched it perfectly to the blemishes.

"You tried to escape, didn't you, Layla?" she asked the empty hallway. She was almost disappointed when no answer came.

"But, what were you trying to escape from? And why was this an option?"

Benitez studied the window again and looked to her left and then to her right. She stared down the long hallway letting her mind process everything. "Why not the doors?" She asked the empty hallway. Benitez went to the door and examined them closely. Not finding anything glaring, she knelt for a closer look. Nothing there.

She re-entered the hallway, trying to force the puzzle pieces together. What did the pock marks on the window mean? Why was her shoe there?

Benitez focused on the glass, transporting her consciousness back to the night of the dance. She needed to put herself in the shoes of Layla

Bragden. Letting her mind wander into the unknown, she glared at the end of the hallway. Back to the glass, then to the other end of the hallway. A picture began to materialize. She reached inside her jacket pocket and pulled out a notebook, flipped through a few pages and read something.

Doors locked, janitor unlocked on scene.

Benitez had summarized the officer's report for reference. The picture was now clear.

"She was trapped. That's why she wanted to bust out the window."

She removed her cell phone and with her camera application snapped pictures, some from afar and some close up, of the pock marks in the glass. She gave the scene a once-over and headed back to the car, satisfied she had more answers. Putting the sequence of events together, Benitez surmised that Layla tried to unlock the window, and when that didn't work, she gave it a few whacks with her shoe. Benitez could see why Emily Bragden would describe her daughter as a fighter.

Back at the front office, Benitez got Kathy's attention.

"Excuse me, do they always lock the science wing doors at night?"

"Usually, yeah."

"That doesn't make a lot of sense. How'd she get in?"

With a confused look, Kathy asked, "How did who'd get in?"

"Nothing. Trying to figure something out is all."

"Oh right, Layla." Kathy bit her bottom lip in an earnest attempt to help. "Well…," she offered. "Actually, now that I think about it, I don't believe they keep them locked during events so there is access to extra bathrooms."

"Really?" Benitez grew excited. "Can we confirm that?"

"Um, sure. I think so." Kathy picked up her phone and ran her finger down a list. She punched in a number and waited.

A minute later, Kathy had confirmed from the head maintenance man that during the dance, he had left the doors unlocked. He heard the man's voice add commentary about how weird it was that he had to unlock it later for the police. Convinced Layla was the victim of a violent crime and not some mixed up runaway, Benitez left the school with a new sense of direction.

***

Perking up in the passenger seat, Beth saw Detective Benitez walking back to the parking lot with purpose. "She's moving a lot faster than when she walked up."

Melinda sat up and found the detective with her eyes. "And she's carrying something."

"Maybe she found something. A lead?"

Melinda placed a pair of binoculars to her eyes and followed Benitez. "It's a shoe. A girl's shoe. Pull up those pictures from her cloud account, from the night of the dance."

Beth did as instructed and found a full-size mirrored selfie of Layla in her stored photos. Beth zoomed in on her feet and showed Melinda. "Does it look like those?"

Melinda pulled the binoculars away from her face to look at the picture. Showing no reaction, she moved the binoculars back. "Yes, that's gotta be her shoe."

"Looks like Detective Benitez found a lead."

Melinda continued to watch the female detective until she got into her unmarked car and drove away.

"Pretty, *and* a good detective, huh?" Beth taunted.

Melinda shot her sideways look, but a guilty grin creased her face. "Let's go talk to the boyfriend."

"Don't want to follow the detective?"

"Stop it," Beth giggled at Melinda's discomfort. "C'mon. Let her run that lead down while we talk to the boy."

"Just callin' it like I see it."

***

Spending the next few morning hours exploring the city, Melinda and Beth took a detour through Ybor City. The historic neighborhood with its own identity impressed the pair of women. The bright neon lights

130

of the night clubs were turned off, but the streets that cut through the old brick buildings were lined with people, tourists and locals hunting for lunch.

"That looks good." Melinda spied a small Cuban sandwich shop wedged between a restaurant and nightclub on 7th Avenue. A small sign above the door read, Cedro's, in the color scheme of the Cuban national flag.

"It looks like a dump. Are you serious?" Beth complained.

"C'mon. Be adventurous. Some of the best food comes from places that don't look like much."

"So does dysentery."

"Hush, girl," Melinda snapped, playfully. She found a pay-parking lot down the street, and the two walked back to the deli.

They ordered, Beth begrudgingly, and took their sandwiches to a high-top table that over looked the sidewalk.

"So," Melinda started, "what's going on with you and Louis?"

Beth prolonged her chewing to ignore answering. "Nuffin," she replied with a shrug and a full mouth.

"Fine. I'll leave it alone. For now." She smiled and took a bite of her side order of fried plantains. A serious thought came to her and she glanced around for any unwanted ears. In a hushed voice she asked, "Somethings been bothering me about this guy, Moye."

This time with her food swallowed, Beth responded. "Oh yeah, like what?"

"It seems too clean. These girls that are taken. What's happening to them?"

"I don't know." Beth thought for a moment. "But you're right. That's unusual."

"Right. Some of them should have turned up dead or even alive and able to give some type of account of what happened, but you didn't find anything like that?"

Beth took in a pinch of French fries and then pulled out her laptop from her backpack. "I hope they have wi-fi here." She wiped her hands and turned on her machine.

131

"You know, I never did a search for any murdered girls that fit the profile, I just did missing persons cases." Beth typed in a few key words and awaited a response.

Melinda finished a few more bites of her Cuban sandwich and took in the décor of the charming little restaurant. She mused when she spotted a few actual holes in the wall behind the deli counter. She watched a short, dark, tan-skinned man with a prominent black mustache barking orders and wondered if he was Cedro himself. She had been right about the place having good food.

"Okay, wow. I think I got something," Beth said. "From 1994 to 1996 there were three murders of young girls, ages eighteen, fifteen and sixteen. All were found within a mile of each other along the Hillsborough River."

"Eighteen? That's a little old, but the other ages fit. What else?"

"Well, okay. According to this article, the police were able to determine they're all related, and they gave the killer the nickname of the Hillsborough River killer. There's never been an arrest even though multiple suspects have been interviewed." Beth clicked and typed a few more times and then stopped to read the screen, Melinda waited. "This article details the girls. Ahh, that's interesting."

"What?"

"The first victim had an arrest for prostitution."

Melinda's face turned serious. "You have a picture of her?"

"Yeah, the article included her mug shot." Beth turned her laptop so Melinda could see. The victim looked like a strung-out cherub. So young, yet so tainted by the harshness of the world. Melinda had seen dozens of girls like her, and she immediately reminded her of Holly Maitland from New Orleans.

"And the others, prostitutes too?"

"No," Beth stated. "Number two was a chronic runaway that had her fair share of trouble, but apparently, things got serious when number three, Laura Diaz, went missing after tennis practice and was found three days later on the banks of the Hillsborough River."

"Why did she make it serious? Was she a *real* victim?"

"Yeah, All-American girl, varsity tennis player, and ideal student who was last seen walking home from practice. When she didn't turn up at home, her parents reported her missing."

"And no leads?"

"Article says the typical boilerplate stuff. The police are looking into all leads, talking to all witnesses, blah, blah, blah. The Diaz's put up a reward of ten grand for any information, but there haven't been any arrests."

The women let the information absorb into their minds while they ate. The din of the small dining area was loud enough to mask their macabre conversation.

Melinda perked up with a thought. "How close does Moye live to this river?"

Beth went back to the computer and a moment later, "Well. Imagine that. He lives on a lake that is fed by the Hillsborough River. He's about three miles from where they found Laura Diaz."

"And the murders, they just stopped?"

"Looks like it." Beth shoved her laptop to the side and finished her chicken sandwich and fries. "Why would they just stop like that?"

"Um, normally it's because they get caught or die. Or are caught for something else and go to prison."

"Okay, but we know that Moye didn't get caught…, or die. What the hell?"

"Well, shit. I don't know," Melinda said. "We have almost sixty other girls that says he didn't stop."

"Where the hell did all those girls go?"

Chapter 21

The smile on Joshua Walker's face was priceless. A few laughs escaped his normally brooding temperament. Curt had tried everything the psychiatrist suggested, most unsuccessful, but humoring his son one afternoon, he discovered the boy responded well to hearing about the exploits of his team of crusaders.

"And then what happened, Dad?" Josh was sitting on the edge of the deck chair. Curt's idea of playing catch was short-lived and so, he brought up what happened in Houston with the Sheridans.

"So, Rachel tells me, 'I've got this,' and to take both kids to the van. I look back and she pops out the business end of a collapsible baton."

"What?" Josh's voice rose with incredulousness.

"Yeah, so the guy comes at her ready to fight and she ducks and moves and sticks the guy in the knee. He gets soooo angry and tries to grab her, but she's too quick. She pops him again and again until he goes down to the ground."

"She kicked his butt?"

"Well, she went to hit him one more time and she missed." Curt went silent, letting the twist in the story hang in the air.

"Whaaaaat?"

"He was able to get up and throw her to the ground. He started kicking at her and yelling at her, so I made sure the kids were in the van and went back to help."

"You kick his butt, dad?"

"Well…" Curt smiled, wearing the admiration for a bit. "I ran up behind him so he didn't see me coming. I reared back and kicked him as hard as I could in the same spot where Rachel had hit him with the baton. Before he could realize what was going on, I gave him a hard punch. Pow!" Curt pantomimed the vicious uppercut he gave Zeke Sheridan. "And he fell like a sack of potatoes."

Josh laughed at the story and beamed with pride because his father was once again able to save the day. Curt loved how it brought Josh to life, giving him a way out of his depressive state. Josh had started asking Curt to tell him about his "adventures." Calling it that seemed odd, Curt thought. In the three years when Josh was missing, he would not have categorized them as adventurous. It sounded too whimsical and clean with endings where everyone lived happily ever after. They came across so much evil out there, it left a stain on the happy endings. But to make his son happy, Curt was fine calling them adventures.

With his mood brightened at the end of the tale, Curt saw Josh appeared happier. It gave him hope that the boy's future was unwritten and full with promise.

"You don't think those stories of yours are too… adult… and graphic for him?" Tracy had joined Curt out on the deck as they watched Josh throw the ball up in the air to himself. "I'd like to think you are cleaning it up a bit, but I'm not sure."

"I don't want to come off as coddling him. He's twelve, almost thirteen. I think he'd see through it if I made them all G-rated."

"I don't know." She let out a frustrated sigh. "Letting him know how much bad is out there in the world, he might not see that there is good, too."

"He knows more than us how much evil is out there. It's no secret. But, I found something that he finds joy in, Tracy. It's not like I'm making this stuff up. He knows what I did to find him. I think he finds solace in knowing that we're out there saving other kids like him."

Curt could feel the tension emanating from Tracy. She wasn't satisfied with his answer, but he was done defending it. The boy liked it, responded well, and was in a better mood because of his stories. That was all that mattered.

Leaving Tracy on the deck, Curt got up and joined Josh in the yard to pick up their game of catch.

***

The nightmares never stopped. Curt was ripped awake, startling Tracy next to him as they bolted upright in bed. Josh was screaming, again.

Whipping the covers off, he sprinted down the hallway and into Josh's room, hitting the light switch on the way into the bedroom. The lamp next to the bed blinked on and shone a dull light, softly illuminating the room. Curt sat next to Josh on his bed.

"Hey, buddy. It's okay, it's okay. It's just a dream." Curt reached out to console his son.

"No, stay away from me." Josh violently pushed Curt away and sprang from the bed. His face looked tortured as he cowered in the corner.

"It's me, Dad. Josh, you're home, safe. Look?" Curt stood up, arms out, palms up in the most submissive and non-threatening posture he could manage.

"Daddy?" He squeaked, between pants.

"It's me. You're home, Joshua. With your mom and dad, safe."

These nightmares were constant. Curt wished he could just reach into the boys' brain and rip them out so they would no longer haunt him. He knew those pathetic excuses for humans, Glenn Gregory and Tobias Helton, continued their assault on Josh in the dream world. For that, Curt also wished he could somehow enter the nightmare and kill them both. He had to find satisfaction knowing that Helton no longer existed in the real world and Gregory was safely behind bars. It was the former Senator, Thomas Pittman, that he wished he could get into a jail cell with. He's the one who created all of the chaos.

Josh snapped out of whatever trance had hold of him and walked back to his bed. Curt relaxed, hoping the storm was weathered, but Josh began to cry.

"I'm sorry, Dad."

"No, Josh. It's not your fault, buddy." Curt moved in, putting his arms around his son, bringing him close.

Josh said it again and kept repeating it softly until it was just a whisper, then nothing. Curt didn't know what Josh could be sorry about, leaving him at a loss for words. Rubbing his back, trying to console him, the only thing he could think of to say was, "Everything will be okay."

After a minute, Josh's head perked up from Curt's chest. "Tell me about the first kid again, the one from California you saved?"

It was Curt's first mission after joining the team. It made headlines up and down the west coast, leaving a myriad of questions about how this kid, the son of a wealthy manufacturing CEO, suddenly turned up one day after being missing for years. It proved to be a favorite of Josh's.

"Sure." Curt settled him back into the bed under covers and sat beside him. "We had stopped at this fruit stand on the side of the road when these two boys came up to us, trying to recruit people to join their cult, the Order of the Heavens."

"That's when you saw him?"

"Yep. We locked eyes, and something inside told me, this kid was lost. Turns out, I was right."

Curt retold the story about how they had to break into the high-tech cult compound that had kidnapped and brainwashed the boy followed, by a daring escape down the mountains of Northern California. Josh's eyes shut half-way through, but Curt knew he was still listening. He noticed Josh held his hand throughout the story, keeping him in place, like an anchor of security.

Finally, after Curt finished the part of the reunion with the boy's parents, Josh fell asleep. Curt eased away from his grip and slipped out of his room, praying that the nightmare was over.

Chapter 22

After a long morning of uneventful surveillance, Rachel noticed the front door shudder, then push open. A small black and gray yorkie eagerly stepped out onto the small porch. Rachel's eyes followed the attached leash up to a hand, then an arm, torso, and the full form of Harold Stephen Moye. No matter his name change or geographical relocation, it was him. Rachel knew by the same black-rimmed glasses that hung on the end of his nose. He pushed them up to his bridge before leading the dog down the steps. Watching him sent shivers down Rachel's spine.

Bewildered that a monster could be capable of such evil and at the same time do something so benign and normal as walking a dog, Rachel sat there stunned. She watched him walk down the block and past the Mercedes Sprinter. He looked old, moving slow and gingerly, his prowess diminished. Rachel didn't let his appearance assuage her focus, rather she seethed in hatred as he walked by, sizing him up, formulating a plan to expose him for the villain he is. *He is still dangerous*, she reminded herself.

"So, that's him in real life, huh?" Louis's voice broke the awkward silence inside the van. Startled, Rachel registered the comment and realized she had been holding her breath as he passed.

Clearing her throat, she replied, "Yeah. That's him."

"Looks kind of like Mr. Rodgers," Louis said, unimpressed.

Moye slowly made the end of the block and turned out of sight. Louis went back to his computer, and Rachel leaned back in the captain's chair. She let out a long sigh, filled with anxiety about her chosen mission.

"I believe in you, ya know," Louis broke the silence again.

"Huh?"

"I believe in you," He repeated. "This... *thing*... we do, it's not easy. Matter of fact, in terms of emotional difficulty, it's probably the hardest thing we could ever do."

Rachel cocked her head, curious as to Louis's rationale.

"Think about it," Louis continued. "Facing our fears is one of mankind's toughest challenges. Hell, it's easier to send people to the moon than cure them of their darkest fears. Most people never face their fears, running away from them as fast as they can. Now, take us for example. We do the very opposite. We're like a bright light that goes into the darkest trenches, searching for hope. And then there's you. Not only are you facing your darkest fear, which isn't heights or public speaking, it happens to be exposing a serial killer who's gone undetected for over two decades."

Rachel smiled, letting the perspective register.

"Also, this guy is responsible for your own personal hell and possibly the unconfirmed death of your sister."

The smile went away, returning the mood back to serious.

"So, like I said, with all that going on, I believe in you. You can do this, and we've got your back."

It was the most mature thing she'd ever heard come from Louis Melton. "Thank you, Louis."

Moye returned ten minutes later and went back inside. Rachel noted the time, hoping it was a part of his routine, something they could exploit. Thoughts of sneaking in from the back waterway came to mind.

"Louis, can you do a little research on the water that's behind the house?"

"Um, like what it's made of? Cuz, I don't need to research that. Two parts hydrogen, one p—"

"No, smartass." All the sensitivity from a moment ago had vaporized. "Like, how big is it? Is it part of the bay? Where does it go or come from? How many public access points are there? Stuff like that."

"Oh, right," he answered. "Sorry."

Five minutes of quiet passed when Louis spoke. "It's a forty-acre lake that's squeezed between Moye's neighborhood and another one. It's fed by an off-shoot of the Hillsborough river, which actually dumps into the bay. Looks like during the spring and summer months it's used as a local recreational spot with skiing and other water sports. Lots of wildlife in and around the water. Whoa..., even gators!" Louis sounded shocked. "Seriously, alligators?"

"Oh yeah?"

"Looks like there was an attack about three years ago on the lake." Louis said, reading from his monitor. "Florida Wildlife Commission and Tampa PD responded and killed the alligator. They measured it at eleven feet long. That's like practically a dinosaur!"

"C'mon Louis, it *is* Florida. The state's pretty much crawling with them."

"Well, all the more reason for me to stay in the van."

Rachel shot him a sideways look. He responded with a shoulder shrug and an impish look before turning back to his computer screen.

"Well, maybe I won't sneak in through the water after all."

"Didn't know you were thinking of doing that. I would say you're smart to reconsider."

Rachel peered out through the side window toward Moye's house again. There hadn't been any movement since the dog walk.

"So, what are you thinking? I mean, about going in."

"Not sure. I want to watch a bit more and see if a routine develops."

"Okay, but just warning you now, that Mountain Dew I drank earlier was only rented, F-Y-I! Gonna hav'ta pee soon, and there ain't no bathroom in here."

Rachel rolled her eyes and kept watching the house.

***

The Circle K convenience store was the impromptu meeting place for the popular sophomores from East Tampa High. Lucas Millwood, showing off a black Mustang GT, was parked in the epicenter of the activity, sporting a personalized license tag that read: *Lucile*. Millwood stood leaned up against the hood, surrounded by a half-dozen other teenagers doing what they do best, loitering.

"I don't get it," Beth said.

"Get what?" Melinda asked. They were watching from across the parking lot. Beth had been busy wading through the virtual life of Lucas Millwood.

"Who is Lucile? Is that the cars name? I don't get it." Beth was obviously frustrated.

Melinda laughed. "You are young."

"I don't see anywhere where he has a relative or a friend by that name."

"It's from *Cool Hand Luke*?"

"Who?"

"It's a movie from the sixties."

"Oh, well no wonder."

Beth put away her laptop and sat quietly, watching the teenagers interact. It was a change from hunting the lost to spying on the normal.

"I don't get that either."

"What?"

"Hanging out at a gas station? I don't see the fun in that."

"They're just kids. You never just hung out with your friends?"

"No. I didn't really have any friends, growing up in foster care."

"Well, this is normal, in case you were wondering."

"I don't think I'm missing anything."

Beth zeroed in on Luke, studying his mannerisms. The kid played it cool for the most part, trying to maintain a nonchalant persona.

"Oh, so he thinks he's this *Luke*, cool hand?"

"Something like that."

Millwood's friends began to peel off and leave, whittling down the group to just him. Before leaving, he walked inside the store, and Beth and Melinda took this opportunity to talk to him.

As Millwood walked outside, he noticed Beth standing by his prized automobile. A lustful grin came across his face.

"Hey beautiful. Wanna go for a ride?"

Beth turned and scoffed in the face of Luke Millwood, then broke out into uncontrollable laughter. "Oh, that was pathetic." She said between laughs. "No, I don't want a ride. Thanks for the laugh, though."

Offended, Luke scowled at Beth. "Okay, whatever. Excuse me, then."

Melinda appeared from behind a gas pump and stood in front of the high schooler. "We need to talk to you for a second, Luke."

Confused, he addressed Melinda, but backed up defensively. "How'd you know my name?"

"Not important, Luke. We want to ask you about Layla Bragden."

"Layla? Why? Are ya'll cops are something?"

"No, we just want to help find her. Did you know she was coming to the dance that night?"

Luke hesitated before answering, unsure of the two strange women. "Um, yeah. I knew."

"And you told the police that you last saw her leaving the gym close to nine o'clock?"

"Yeah, I did."

With irritation in her voice, Beth asked the next question. "What happened when she got there to make her want to leave so soon?" Luke immediately looked away. Beth continued. "I mean, she was all set to see you there. Apparently, it was her sole purpose for sneaking out that night."

"I don't know. I guess she just changed her mind."

"Bullshit," Beth spat.

"Hey!" Luke volleyed. "If you're not cops, I know I don't have to talk to you, so if you don't mind, I'd like to leave now."

"Luke?" Melinda asked in a calming manner. "We're just worried about Layla and want to make sure the cops aren't missing anything." After consideration, Luke bowed his head with shame. "What is it?"

"Okay, it's not my fault though."

Beth scoffed again.

"Ignore her," Melinda said, keeping Luke's focus on her. "What's not your fault? The fact she ran off?"

"Well, kinda. I mean…, I didn't think she'd actually come and we were sort of…" Luke trailed off.

"Sort of what, Luke?"

"I thought we were broken up."

"But she didn't think the same, I take it?"

"I guess not. But how the hell was I supposed to know?"

Beth stepped back up, still angry at the boy. "Um, she sent you racy pictures, hello?"

An incredulous look froze Luke. "How'd you know?"

Melinda took back control. "Don't worry about that. Tell us what happened Luke? What didn't you tell the cops?"

"I was with someone else. She came in the dance, and I was dancing with Sarah. I saw her and she saw me, but…" His head fell with guilt.

"You kept dancing with Sarah, huh?" Melinda helped him finish the sentence.

He nodded.

"Is that it?" Melinda asked with a motherly tone.

"Yes, ma'am," Luke said. "I guess she got upset and ran off."

"So what do you think happened to her, Luke? You think she's off hiding in embarrassment?" Beth snapped. Luke straightened up and shook his head. "No, that's right, lover boy. While you were off chasing some other girl, she was getting kidnapped by some sadistic killer, doing God knows what to her."

"What? What do you mean, kidnapped? The cops never said that."

"Well, that's what happened, *Cool Hand*! So instead of dancing with you that night, she ran off alone, making it easier for this guy to grab her. So, you drive off in your little Lucile here and think about that."

143

Chapter 23

The damp air seeping in through the bottom floorboards made Layla shiver, but the humid conditions of the basement kept her moist with sweat. The exhaustion from her imprisonment had worn her down. She teetered on the brink of sleep, but the fear of death kept her awake. She was stuck in a hellish limbo. She heard the slithering of something frightful coming from below, fueling her half-naked body with adrenaline. She couldn't fathom the monsters that lurked underneath.

She tugged at her bonds, moving her wrists out and in, over and over trying to stretch the bindings out enough to slip one free. At the expense of her shoulders, Layla pulled awkwardly behind her back and felt like she was getting close. She managed to get it just to the knuckle of her thumb, needing a mere half-inch before freeing herself.

Steadily working on the ropes, a hurried step approached the door and it swung open. The man pounced down the stairs and over into the far dark corner. Something was different. Layla eased up work on the binding as he fiddled with something in the corner. The light bulb hovering above her head flickered on, bathing her in the dim yellow light.

Brushing past Layla, the man walked to a counter in the opposite corner. He carried a small wrapped package and plopped it down. With his back to her, Layla watched him manipulate the package contents. Unaware of what it could be, she skipped a breath when the metal glint of a meat cleaver was raised above his head and slammed down hard against the counter top. After a few more chopping motions, slices and collecting, he turned to face Layla. His face was expressionless, flat and void of emotion which made her even more nervous.

Stepping to Layla's left, the man knelt down to the floor and lifted the small metal flap on the floor. He held out the contents he was chopping. Layla could see they were small brownish-pink chunks of meat, and he let them slide off a plate down the hole in the floor.

"What are you doing?" she asked.

Met with an angry stare, the man didn't answer. Moving back to the dark corner, she heard the creak of a chair taking on weight. The man hmphed, between heavy breaths. Suddenly, he stormed back over to Layla and stood in front of her with a printed picture extended out to show Layla. Her eyes went wide with rage when she saw the image. "Don't you go near her!"

"What are you going to do about it?" the man challenged.

It was the same question, with an anticipatory tone. Layla grew confused, thinking the man was looking for a certain answer.

"Untie my hands and I'll show you!" Layla spat. She glared at the man, ready to fight if he harmed her little sister. If a fight is what he wanted, she was ready.

"Do you know what I'll do to her?" the man yelled. His glasses slid to the end of his nose, and with an aged bony finger, he fixed them back in place.

Still confused, his anger sent her into a spiraling fear that was paralyzing. The courage she had built up was draining fast. Tears leaked from her eyes.

"Do you?" He demanded an answer. "So, what are you going to do about it?"

She sobbed, but again, with the last ounce of courage, she yelled back, "Don't go near her. I swear if you do—" Another sob came mitigating her bravado.

The man leaned in, putting him face to face with Layla. The stench of his body odor and foul breath attacked her nostrils. Repulsed by the man, she continued to sob, hoping this nightmare would end quickly.

Storming back to his shadowy corner, he growled, "Damn, you..." The man yelled out something that sounded like a name, but it wasn't hers. A sense of urgency came to Layla. Something was off about the man. He seemed desperate. Her instincts told her that something bad was about to happen. She began to pull at the ropes behind her back while he busied himself in that dark corner. Pulling tight, the rope stopped at the base of her right thumb. She pulled as hard as she could, ignoring the searing pain in her shoulders, but it didn't budge. She needed it to slide only a little bit. Sobbing frantically, she feared she was about to take her last breath. Her body flashed hot and broke out into a sweat.

Stomping back to the center of the basement, the man knelt down at her feet and freed her ankles from the legs of the chair. She flailed wildly, but he leaned forward, pressing his heavy weight against her body. His strong hand gripped her throat tight, pushing her back against the chair. Layla gasped and stopped kicking. His demon eyes bore into Layla as she submitted and stopped resisting. He flicked off the bare light bulb and released Layla, leaving her in the darkness. He turned for the stairs. The urgency grew into panic and she pulled again at her bindings. She felt progress, but no matter how hard she pulled, she couldn't get the rope over the thumb knuckle.

Stopping at the base of the stairs, the man rested his hand on the random lever that protruded up from the floor. Instantly, she realized its purpose.

"No, no, please." She begged.

The man stopped. He turned and looked at Layla's vulnerability and nakedness. Finality mixed with lust shone in his eyes as he anticipated a specific reaction from Layla. She was ignorant to what this could be other than pure torture. When nothing happened, he glowered a look of disgust.

"Nooooooo!" Layla shouted pulling violently at her restraints.

With little effort by Moye, the lever sprung forward. The square line in the floor suddenly opened up, swallowing her whole. Layla felt the pull of gravity take her through the opening and send her face down straight toward the slithering monsters.

Chapter 24

Watching Moye's house for the better part of the afternoon and evening proved to be anything but exciting. The adrenaline from finding out answers to a twenty-two-year-old mystery of who the faceless man had worn out hours before, and the day drudged on tirelessly. Rachel pulled herself away from the window and binoculars to stretch out her legs on the bench seat of the Mercedes Sprinter. She checked her notes again, there was no change from the hour before. She sighed, which caught the attention of the equally bored Louis Melton.

"Who would've thought tracking a serial killer would be so boring, huh?" he said.

Rachel chuckled, "Yeah, I know, right." She tossed down her note pad and bent over to touch her toes, stretching her back. "The only thing he's come out for today are the dog walks. Four times, roughly two hours apart."

"Wouldn't think a dog that size would need to poop so often either."

Rachel laughed again. *It feels good to laugh*, she thought. She'd been dealing with so much in the last few days, that when she was this close to how the nightmare began, she could remain normal and surround herself with normal people. Not the superficial "normal" that psychopaths used as camouflage, but the genuine version of everyday people. She glanced back at Louis, who had creased the underside of a bag of chips and slid the remnants down into his mouth making exaggerated chomping noises. *Normal enough.*

A call from Melinda came in, and Louis put it on the van's speaker.

"Hey Melinda, what were you able to find out about the girl?" Rachel asked.

"I think it's safe to say that Layla Bragden was kidnapped. Both Beth and I agree that Moye is good for it as well as at least three murders back in the late nineties."

"Really?"

Melinda filled Rachel in on the research she and Beth came upon while at lunch, detailing how the first two girls didn't fit in Moye's desired victims, but the third was spot on.

Inexplicably, Rachel immediately felt responsible for those girl's deaths as well as Layla's disappearance. She turned to look back at Moye's house. The porch light flicked on simultaneously as did two other flood lights, one at each corner of the house.

"Let's try and focus on the current case and hope we find something on the others. Any evidence that ties him directly to Layla's kidnapping? Any witnesses?" asked Rachel.

"No evidence, not yet anyway. And no witnesses," Melinda said.

"Especially not shit-for-brains Layla calls a boyfriend," Beth added with venom.

"Damn," Rachel said, frustrated. "I hate the fact she could be trapped in that house, but we have no evidence, except for...," she paused, "Except for these memories of mine."

"Well, we didn't come all the way back to Florida because we thought you were making those up, Rachel." Melinda sounded sincere, even over the van's speaker.

Trust your instincts.

Curt's words echoed inside of Rachel's head. It gave her confidence to move forward. There was no way she was going to let another innocent girl die at the hands of Harold Stephen Moye. A plan came to her, giving her foresight on how to take this monster down.

"What's our next move, Rachel?" Melinda asked.

An expectant silence came over the van. Rachel analyzed her plan in her head and reassured herself it was a good idea. "You guys make your way to us. I'll need help with an operation."

"Operation?" Beth asked.

"I'm going in."

Rachel pinned her hair back in a ponytail and changed into a button-up blouse, making Louis look the other way, to give her a slightly professional look. Running with her idea to get inside the house, she grew anxious.

"Are you sure about this?" The worry in Louis's voice was evident. "I mean, this guy tried to kill you before, what makes you think he won't try again once he sees you?"

"First of all, I'm all grown up now," Rachel answered. "Secondly, I've hated this guy most of my life. I mean, it's a hate that sends me over the edge every time I think about what he did to me, to Rhonda, and if he so much as tries anything, I'll be ready, and I'll kill him myself."

Louis didn't respond. Finished putting her hair up, Rachel looked over and read fear on Louis's face. He rebutted, "Okay, but just remember, there's a reason why this guy has gone undetected for all these years. He clearly knows what he's doing."

"That's why I got you, dear!" Rachel took an earbud from his workstation and fixed it snuggly in her left ear. Louis rolled back and after a few strokes on the keyboard, an airy echo sounded in her ear.

"Check, check. Can you hear me?"

"Loud and clear."

Rachel pulled out her cell phone and hit the back-facing camera angle. Using it as a mirror, she considered the slight alteration and addition of makeup to her disguise. It lacked something and she looked around the van for the missing piece.

"What are you looking for?" asked Louis.

Staring back at him, she smiled. She reached over toward him and gently removed his black, squared-rimmed glasses. She put them on, her eyes watered as the thick lenses enlarged and blurred everything.

"That won't work," she said, then removed them and set them on top of her pulled back hair. Looking at her phone screen for final approval, she was satisfied with her look.

"You do look like a reporter," Louis stated.

Rachel let out a nervous sigh and closed her eyes. She ran through her plan once more. Use the ruse of a reporter in search of an interview to gain access to the house, then have Beth and Melinda come by and distract him as lost motorists while she searches the house for any sign of Layla or any of the other missing girls. Louis will be support in the van, monitoring what he can on the virtual side of things. She saw the plan go smoothly and was satisfied with the details, hoping it would make Curt proud. Rachel allowed the scenario to go awry in her mind, feeding the fantasy of having an excuse to beat Moye into submission before dragging his bruised, unconscious body to the police station.

"You ready?" Louis asked.

With an unsteady confidence, she replied, "Yes."

***

Moments after Melinda and Beth arrived, Rachel briefed them on their parts of the operation. After they were ready, Rachel slid out of the Mercedes Sprinter, walked the opposite direction of Moye's house, and circled around the parallel block. She used the walking time to rehearse what to say. This would be her first *under-cover* mission.

Beth stepped up to Rachel with apprehension on her face. "Are you sure about this?"

It was the second time she had been asked that in the last hour. "Yeah, I'm sure." As soon as the words left her mouth, doubt filled her mind.

"Going after dead-beat dads and runaways strung out by their pimps is one thing. This guy's a dangerous killer. Not to sound pessimistic, but don't you think this guy is out of our league? Especially without Curt."

Rachel nodded, validating Beth's concerns. She had a point. However, the need for answers and the thought of Layla trapped in a hell Rachel knew all too well, her mind was made up.

"I wish Curt was here, but he's got other responsibilities in his life. And I'm not going to let Layla stay in hell one minute more than she has to."

"Okay." Rachel could see that didn't satisfy Beth, but she returned with a helpful smile that let her know she would support her decision. Beth turned and stepped into the van.

"Hey?" Rachel called out to her.

"Yeah?"

"Thanks. I know you asked because you're worried." Beth gave her a smile and climbed up to the front passenger seat.

As Rachel approached Moye's house from the opposite direction of the van, she tried to quiet her nerves. She stopped, took another deep breath and moved forward. She checked her props, a fountain pen, notepad, and a generic ID card that read, "Media," dangling from a lanyard. She stowed the pen behind her right ear to draw unwanted attention from the earbud in her left.

"I got this," she said.

"Yeah, you do," said Louis via the comms. The voice surprised her as she forgot she was tethered to the team by the earbuds.

Finally, she was about to face the monster who stalked her nightmares. Rachel knocked on the door. She peered through the side window but saw nothing horrific. She knocked again. Apprehension began to take over her thoughts as she waited impatiently on the front porch. She wondered if something was wrong. She wondered if she should abort and come up with a new plan, or even call Curt and have him do his thing to see if Layla was inside. The anxiety was getting unbearable.

Suddenly, the door cracked open and Moye's face poked through. "Can I help you?"

Rachel froze, stammering over what to say, trying not to stray from the ruse. Moye opened up the door wider and stepped forward. His face appeared gentle and inviting. It was him, the monster, only older, she thought. Instinctively, Moye pushed his glasses up to the bridge of his nose sending a shockwave of horrifying nostalgia through her body. For

151

an instant, she was fifteen and terrified. "Yes, can I help you? Are you a reporter or something?"

"Rachel!" Louis buzzed in her ear, ripping her out of her trance.

"Um, yes. Sorry, sorry about that. Yes, I am a reporter with Channel 6 news. I was wondering if you might be willing to do an interview regarding the recent changes in your neighborhood and the future development plans for the lake?"

Rachel prayed that she came off legit. Louis had been able to find a recent news article about another development being planned on the other side of the lake that backed up to Moye's house. It was causing controversy with the environmental activists who claimed it was displacing native animals and would cause unnecessary pollution to the contributing Hillsborough River. It seemed like good fodder for a ruse.

"Oh?" Moye responded. "I didn't know there were any plans, so I'm not sure I have much to say."

"Well, sir, to be honest, any thoughts and opinions would be welcomed."

"Where's your camera guy? Don't you have a camera guy to do TV news interviews?"

Rachel kept her poker face, but she was screaming on the inside. She heard Louis swear over the comms, but quickly, an answer came.

"Well, nowadays, sir, we do pretty much everything on our cell phones." Rachel pulled her phone out of her pocket to show Moye she was prepared. "It's all about a thirty second or minute clip of video once it's all edited down."

"Oh, okay. Well, in that case. Come in."

Moye let the door open all the way and then walked into the living room. Rachel stepped in and shut the door behind her. She sized up Moye while his back was turned. He was much shorter than she remembered, however she was much younger and smaller back then. He moved slowly and his upper back was starting to hunch over. She felt power surge through her body, ensuring that her strength could easily overpower him if the time came. *Stick to the plan*, she reminded herself.

Moye invited her to sit as he found comfort in a well-worn Barcalounger. Rachel sat on the other side of a glass-top coffee table, on a matching sofa opposite Moye.

"What news channel did you say again?"

"Channel 6," Rachel said without hesitation. Now that she was inside the house she was more focused.

"Ah, and you're a reporter? I don't recall seeing you on the news?"

"Yeah, I'm a new hire. I was over at Channel 49 up in Tallahassee. This is actually my first assignment. I'm using it to try and get to know some of the local people."

"Oh, alrighty. Welcome to Tampa, then…."

Rachel realized she had failed to introduce herself, and worse yet, she failed to think of an alternate name for the ruse. She blurted the first name that came to her, "Marie. Marie Fitzpatrick." Marie was her middle name, and she surprised herself with Fitzpatrick. She didn't know anyone by that name.

"Welcome, Marie."

"Thanks. And your name, sir?"

"Oh, it's Harold."

"Nice to meet you, Harold." Rachel said holding back every impulse to attack him and demand to know what he did with Layla.

"Nice to meet you." Moye then jerked upright in his seat. "Oh shoot! I forgot I just put some tea on. Let me get to it before I burn the place down."

"Oh, by all means," Rachel answered.

"I'll be right back. Would you like a cup?"

"Sure." Rachel gave in, for the sake of the ruse.

Moye returned a moment later. "So, what did you want to ask me?"

"Well, sir…"

***

Melinda and Beth listened as Rachel began her phony interview of Moye and the issues surrounding the urban development in the area. Beth picked up where she left off with her research on the missing girls while Melinda kept watch on the house.

The crackle of a police radio played in the background. Louis turned it on in the event that their ruse made any of the neighbors suspicious. They had been hanging out in the area for the better part of the day and were bound to attract some unwanted attention.

"Louis?" Beth summoned from the front seat without looking. "Did we ever go back and find out what Moye did back in Texas? You know, like for a job?"

"Um, not really. The census report stated he was a teacher, but nothing specific beyond that."

"Can you narrow that down now? It may shed some light on a few things I found."

"Yeah, of course."

"Oh, and can you pull up Rachel's original report? I want to compare it to the missing girls here and see what overlap I can find with those murders from the nineties. I think it may help out as well."

With a macho grunt, Louis said, "You know I can."

With Beth and Louis pecking away at their respective laptops, Melinda stayed tuned to the conversation Rachel was having with Moye while watching the front of the house through a pair of binoculars.

Ten minutes passed and Melinda checked her watch. She and Beth were to set to knock on the front door in the next five.

"You ready, Beth?" Melinda asked. "She'll need the distraction so she can start searching for Layla."

Beth remained glued to her laptop. She was typing, clicking and rechecking some physical files stacked on the center console. Her feet were firmly planted on the floorboard instead of propped up on the dash.

"Beth?" Melinda called again.

"What?" Beth didn't bother to look away.

"We need to go."

"Okay, but I just found something weird. I found a connection and I think I know why Moye changed his M.O."

Louis chimed in with equal enthusiasm. "I got something too. On him, though."

Melinda let out a fretful sigh. "What did you find?" She checked her watch and added, "Make it fast."

Beth went first. "All the girls, I'm pretty sure, have little sisters. I mean, I haven't gone back and checked all fifty-seven files, but all of the ones from this decade have little sisters."

"What about the three murdered girls?"

"Not sure about the first two, but Laura Diaz sure did. Lilly Diaz, age four at the time."

"What does that mean?" Melinda asked.

Beth shrugged, "Not exactly sure, but Rachel was abducted with her sister, so that can't be a coincidence."

"No, it can't." Melinda agreed. She turned to Louis, "What did you find?"

"Moye was a Business Education instructor at the high school in Sweetland, and after a little digging and the coaxing of a certain school board's firewall, Harold Stephens is a district supervisor over the campus's site security. He basically does IT work for the schools."

"So basically, he has untethered access to all of the Tampa Bay area schools?" Melinda concluded with disappointment. "Jesus, doesn't anyone do real background checks anymore?"

A moment of silence followed while the trio let the new information soak in.

"You guys need to get going!" Louis said with urgency.

Melinda and Beth scrambled out of the van. They hurried down the block to the rental car, needing it as a required prop to be stranded motorists. Louis had given them two smoke-bombs strung together to be placed under the hood. When lit, they would create the illusion of a real breakdown giving Rachel as much time as possible.

Louis watched as they drove passed the van in the rental sedan and stopped in front of Moye's house. Beth got out and lit the fuse to the smoke-bomb and slid it between the front grill slats. Soon, thick white smoke began seeping out of the hood's outline.

A ding on Louis' computer went off, pulling his attention back to his work station. He checked the screen. Rachel's missing person's file finally downloaded. He clicked it open to make sure he pilfered the right file from the police department's archives. He scanned the officer's report and saw the names, dates, and other known information were correct. It was the right file.

"They all had little sisters?" Louis asked the empty van, heavy with suspicion. He scrolled down the contents of the scanned file and clicked on a link that said, "image."

When the file opened, Louis' eyes widened in shock. He clambered for the front seat of the van and snatched up Beth's research. He frantically searched for something within the files, discarding papers without regard, until he found what he was looking for. Returning to his seat in a panic, he held up the photographs of the missing girls and compared them to the screen.

"Rachel?" Louis screamed over the earbud comms. "Rachel? You gotta get out of there, now!"

***

Moye made a return trip to the kitchen and came back with a tray of tea. "It's my special blend. I hope you like it."

Rachel smiled, but knew there was no way in hell she was going to drink anything prepared by a serial killer. She grew anxious and fidgety waiting on Beth and Melinda to create the distraction. As Moye poured the tea, Rachel carefully scanned the room. Sofa, television, television stand, curio filled with knickknacks, a chair, side table, and another chair was all she saw. No easily accessible weapons or restraint devices she could see. Moye held out the cup of tea and she accepted it. Rachel held it to her nose as if to smell it, and then set it down.

"Going to let that cool, but it does smell good."

Moye gave her a pleased look. He picked up a remote, sitting on the small table next to his chair and aimed it at the television. "Are there any more questions you have for me, Ms. Fitzpatrick?"

"Um, well?" Rachel considered her notes of the fake interview. She needed to stall until the distraction came. "No, I think that covers it. But, while I'm here, are there any concerns about the community you wish to discuss? Maybe there's something else I could do a story on later."

"Oh, well...," Moye paused to think. "not real—"

Moye's doorbell rang. It sent a tremendous wave of relief through Rachel's body. She hid her excitement as Moye stared across the room at her.

"Busy night. I wasn't expecting anyone."

"Don't let me keep you," Rachel said.

"Okay, one moment please. Excuse me."

Moye got out of the Barcalounger and walked over toward the door. Rachel eyed the hallway that went behind Moye's chair. That led to the back of the house and hopefully to where he was keeping Layla. Her head began to feel heavy and she grew dizzy. Her eyelids weighed a ton, and her limbs suddenly buzzed and felt detached. The room began to spin as she heard Louis Melton's voice calling her name. She tried to answer, but she couldn't speak. Her thoughts raced as she was awake and alert, but her body was failing her, like someone else was in control. Louis's voice trailed off and sounded like he was yelling from the end of a very long tunnel. Panicked, she willed herself to stand, but it only made her woozier, and the room spin faster. Suddenly, she lost control and fell flat on the floor.

Glancing at the full cup of tea, she couldn't understand why this was happening to her. She was careful and didn't take a sip. On the ground, she heard a slight hum and hiss of air coming from somewhere behind her.

Rachel's eyes were wide with fear. She could only see ankle high in the direction of the front door. She gave her body the command to scream as loud as she could, but she wasn't sure that her mouth even opened. She watched, helplessly from the floor of Moye's living room as she was once again trapped.

Moye's shoes appeared from around the corner and walked toward her. His gait was purposeful and strong, not feeble like it was while he walked the dog. He stopped a few feet away and picked up a cordless phone from the side table, the height of her view. Moye spoke, but his voice was muffled. After setting the phone down, Moye knelt down so that his face was inches away from Rachel's.

"Didn't think I'd know it was you, huh Rachel?" His grin went wide as his gaze turned to evil. "I never forget a face, especially the one that got away." Moye sucked in a deep satisfying breath and added, "I've been waiting for this moment for so long. You have no idea."

Rachel sent commands for her body to fight, claw, scrape, grab, and punch, whatever it took to escape, but her body ignored direction and was limp on the floor. All that managed to come out of her mouth was a pitiful, strained whine. The nightmare had restarted.

"Now, we get to finish what we started."

Chapter 26

Melinda and Beth heard Louis cry out over the comms for Rachel to get out. He added, "It's a trap, get out, Rachel!" But there was no response. Melinda cupped her ear to try and hear anything useful but was met with airy silence.

"What is it, Louis?" Melinda asked.

"It's a trap. All the girls, they look just like Rachel. It's all about Rachel. Get her out of there!"

Standing on the porch after ringing the doorbell, they began to beat on the door. "Open up, now!"

Beth tried to look through the windows to see what was happening, but the curtains blocked everything out. Melinda began kicking at the door. She shouldered it a few times, but the decorative wood door proved to be more solid than it appeared. Melinda backed up and gave it a mighty kick, only to see it not budge at her efforts.

"Might as well be a damned brick wall," Melinda said in defeat.

"Get back to the van before he does something to you," Louis screamed over the comms.

Melinda and Beth ran off the porch, jumped in the rental and pulled down the street. The smoldering smoke-bomb had pin-balled through the engine compartment until it fell to the street. Racing up to the back of the Sprinter van, both women jumped in, just as frantic as Louis.

"What the hell is happening?" Melinda asked between pants.

"It's about Rachel. Since Texas, it's been all about her," Louis answered.

"I don't understand. What do you mean, 'it's about her'?"

Louis expanded the picture of fifteen-year-old Rachel. "She's a natural brunette, straight hair, classic features....". Louis grabbed a handful of the fifty-seven other images and held up the first few. "Just like these girls. We never saw it because we've only known Rachel as a blonde, not as a fifteen-year-old brown-haired girl."

"What do we do?" Beth asked.

"Uh," Louis stuttered. "I don't know."

"Should we call the police?" Beth suggested. Melinda and Louis looked at her, then to each other, considering the idea, but with heavy skepticism. Calling the police and explaining the situation would mean they would have to explain why they were there and who they were. There were legal ramifications if they were to reveal their true mission.

"No, we can't do that without exposing ourselves. There has to be another way," Louis decided.

"We need to do something." Melinda stated.

Louis forced himself to think. He stared out the window toward Moye's house, willing a plan to formulate. His eyes scanned the area, looking for a way for his virtual touch to get inside the house. Suddenly, he found an entry by way of a tiny octagonal sign in the front yard.

"He has an alarm system!" Louis dove between the women and got behind his laptop. He began typing furiously on the keyboard. "If I can get into the alarm company's server, I can activate his alarm where it would warrant a police response. That way they'll come and check it out, find her, and hopefully Layla, too, leaving us in the background."

"That's brilliant. Do it!" Melinda cheered.

Unable to sit idle, Beth grabbed her cell phone and made a call. "I'm going to let Alexis know."

Louis Melton let out an excited cackle, then announced, "I'm in," and refocused on his computer screen. "Now, to pinpoint his account."

"Okay, let's hurry. He could be doing God-knows-what to her in there." Melinda was hovering over Louis' shoulder, unable to interpret the action on the monitor.

160

"Wait…. No!" Louis suddenly shouted. "Shit…. Shit…. No!" He backed away from his work station. "What the—"

"What is it, Louis?" Melinda became scared, not used to seeing Louis fail in this arena.

"It's not possible," he muttered.

"What?" Melinda grew angry as well as fearful.

"It's Moye, he's managed to intercept me and kick me out of the system. It's like he knew I was coming." As an afterthought, Louis sprang forward and ripped the power plug out of the socket and the Ethernet connection to the wire-less router. "Shit!"

"Now what?"

"He was about to infiltrate my system. First, he blocked me once I pinpointed his account, then turned it around and was about to climb through my system."

"What?" Beth asked incredulously. She had just hung up with Alexis and overheard Louis.

"Yeah…. We're floating in the dark right no—"

The crackle of the police radio interrupted Louis as the words, "Large black van," came across the channel. Louis turned up the volume to listen closer.

"Complainant says there are three suspects sitting in a Mercedes van, black in color, who just tried to scam him out of money. Complainant advises that he's seen the van before and knows of a neighbor who was recently scammed out of ten thousand dollars by the same suspects."

"Oh shit!" Beth stated. "That's not good."

"The suspects are described as a white male, white female, and a black female. They are still on scene in the van parked down the street from the complainant's address."

"We've got to get out of here," Louis whined.

"No, we can't leave Rachel." Melinda countered.

"If we stay, those cops are going to come around here, and we'll probably get arrested, then we'll be of no help to Rachel." Louis summarized. "We're the only ones who knows she's in there."

"Shit!" Melinda yelled out. "Okay, okay. I've got an idea, but it's kind of a Hail Mary." Melinda got into the driver's seat and hurried out of the area before the patrol units showed up.

Beth picked up the phone and made another call.

"What are you doing?" Melinda asked Beth.

"I'm setting up plan B."

***

The fading light of dusk was almost done giving way to nightfall. Melinda parked the bulky Mercedes Sprinter van next to the curb, in an open space downtown. She put the van in gear and looked up at the behemoth glass structure just beyond the windshield. In glowing white letters, the words "Tampa Police" sprawled across the face of the building.

"Here?" Louis questioned. "I thought we agreed to not go to the police."

"Well, yes and no," she answered.

Beth realized Melinda's intentions and interjected. "You think you can trust her?"

"I think we have no other option," Melinda replied.

"Then let's make it happen. We're losing time."

As Melinda fished out her phone, found the number for the homicide unit and dialed, Louis cried out in confusion. "Wait. Who is she? Why do we not think she's trustworthy and again, I thought we weren't involving the cops?"

The other end answered and Melinda asked for Detective Benitez and added it was about the Layla Bragden kidnapping.

"Hello?" Louis waited for an answer with the patience of a toddler.

Benitez answered the phone at the same time Melinda turned in her seat and glared menacingly at Louis. He knew to drop the petulance and took a seat.

"This is Benitez, how can I help you?"

"Yes, Detective. I have valuable information on Layla Bragden and it's crucial that you meet me at once."

"And who are you?"

Melinda hesitated, then spoke, "That's not important. But my information is."

"Okay, fine." Benitez sounded skeptical. "But if it's important, tell me over the phone, and then I'll decided if I want to meet."

"We are wasting time. She is in danger now, we have to hurry. Please?"

Silence came on Detective Benitez's end. Then, eagerly she asked, "Wait, my secretary said you had information on Layla's kidnapping. She's only listed as a missing person, but how do you know—"

"Let's just say we have common interests, Detective. Please, does that buy me at least a face-to-face? If I don't convince you inside of three minutes, you walk away."

"Fine. We can meet, but I'll be with my partn—"

"No!" Melinda snapped. "No, you need to come alone."

A long pause followed. Finally, Benitez answered, "Fine. There's a Starbucks two blocks from the Police Station, how long will it take you to get there?"

Melinda checked the rear mirror and saw the familiar green logo of the coffee shop down the street. "I'll be there waiting."

***

Beth and Louis sat opposing each other in the table next to the corner booth, he with his laptop open and she nervously finger-tapping a small stack of files. Melinda anxiously stirred in the booth, waiting for the Detective to show up. Counting each minute that went by sent waves of panic radiating through the group, fearing the worst about Rachel.

Detective Benitez stepped inside the coffee shop and looked around, studying each person who was paying her attention and trying to identify her anonymous caller. When she made it to the corner booth, Melinda offered a worried, but gentle smile and a wave to confirm it was her that she spoke to on the phone. The detective walked around Louis and Beth and sat down in the booth with Melinda.

"Thank you for coming, Detective." Melinda said in a hushed tone.

"You've got three minutes, make it count," she said with indifference.

"I know who took Layla and where she is."

The detective's eyes narrowed as she processed the statement. After a moment, she asked, "Okay, who and where?"

"His name is Harold Stephen Moye. He changed his name to Harold Stephens when he moved from Texas to Florida back in '93. There he was suspected in the kidnapping of at least two young girls and probably the death of one of them. Once in Florida, we believe he's responsible for almost sixty missing teenage girls taken from the Tampa Bay area. He's living in an east side neighborhood where we think he's got Layla."

"You think?"

"Well, we don't know for sure, but everything we know about him tells us that he's got her."

Benitez leaned back in the booth and crossed her arms. Never looking away from Melinda, she narrowed her eyes again while in thought.

"So, you don't know for sure, but you have a hunch. Is that right?"

"Well...." Melinda struggled for an answer and responded cryptically. "Yes, but it's stronger than a hunch."

Detective Benitez sprang forward in the booth, placed both hands on the table, and leaned in toward Melinda. The move startled her. "Listen, I believe you're telling the truth about Layla, and I want to find her and bring her home safe, but there is something else you're not telling me. Stop wasting my time and tell me what you're hiding. Your three minutes is almost up."

Scorned, Melinda looked helplessly over at Louis and Beth for help. Benitez shot a look to the neighboring table and sized up the two. Louis gave Melinda a "go ahead" nod.

For the next ten minutes, Detective Benitez was brought up to speed on how they zeroed in on Moye's residence after learning his identity back in Texas. Beth briefly detailed the Texas cases and then summarized most of the Florida cases and how each girl has an uncanny resemblance to Rachel at the age when she was kidnapped. She added the circumstantial possibility Moye could be the Hillsborough River Killer from the late nineteen-nineties.

Benitez didn't bother hiding her doubts that the team had just happened to stumble across one of Tampa's most notorious and unsolved murders. She scoffed and returned a stoic expression with her arms still crossed.

Melinda continued and explained they stumbled across Moye at roughly the same time Layla disappeared. She admitted following the detective to the school and seeing her walk out with the dress shoe, confirming a kidnapping. Louis added that after setting up surveillance, Rachel decided to go in and is now being held captive, but only after they realized it was a trap.

Benitez listened attentively as Melinda explained everything. Having digested it all, it was her time to respond. "Okay, so...," she started, but then paused. "So, we're not going to touch on how illegal some of what you told me is, but the gist of it is that your friend, Rachel, went inside to try and find where he's keeping Layla? Now, she's being held captive because of something that happened between her and this guy, Moye, twenty years ago?"

"More or less. You can see why we need to hurry?"

"And you think this guy is also the Hillsborough River Killer? Who went dormant after killing three girls twenty years ago?"

Having heard the spin Benitez put on the assessment gave Melinda pause. It did have an air of absurdity.

Weighing the options as presented, Benitez slid back in the vinyl booth making a rubbing noise. Peering across the table she scrutinized the three team members carefully. With hasty consideration, she replied. "Okay, we have a few legal issues but... fine. I'll take any lead at this point, and if it helps me find Layla, then let's do it. We'll just table the idea that this guy is a serial killer from the nineties and focus on the missing girl, okay?"

"Yes, thank you, Detective," Melinda said shaking her hand.

"But, if this isn't what you say it is…," she paused while removing something from the inside of her blazer. She held up a small audio recorder, "I'm using all of that illegal stuff you just admitted to arrest all three of you."

***

Arriving back at Moye's house, the team gave a collective sigh, seeing the lights still on and Moye's car in the driveway. It felt as if nothing had changed and Rachel was still alive. They'd been gone nearly an hour trying to find and convince Detective Benitez to help them. Melinda rode over with Benitez while Louis and Beth followed in the Sprinter. During the car ride, Melinda explained that she used to be a police officer in Atlanta before she quit following her involvement in a police shooting that resulted in the death of a drug dealer. The dealer just happened to be the one who gave her sister the fatal dose of crack cocaine. A sense of respect formed between the current and former cop.

Exiting the unmarked car, Melinda made sure her ear comms were on. Louis verified it was working and continued to spot-check Rachel's to see if he could hear anything, but only static registered on her end.

"So, you know I don't have cause to go in, right?" Benitez clarified. "I mean, what you have at this point is all circumstantial about Moye being this serial kidnapper/killer."

"But Rachel is in there, right now," Melinda countered. "We saw her go in."

"Right, but are you going to be a witness if this goes south, or would you like to stay anonymous?"

"Shit," Louis answered for her over the comms.

"Let her play it her way for now," Beth offered.

Melinda nodded to the detective, letting her proceed.

"But trust me, I won't just let it go. I'm on your side." Benitez offered a quick smile to Melinda before she walked up to Moye's porch. Melinda stopped at the base of the stairs.

After a hefty, purposeful knock, Moye came to the door. He gave a superficial smile and a quick scan of Benitez. All traces of his evil exploits from the hour prior had vanished as he displayed a version of an unsuspecting elderly gentleman.

"May I help you, Detective?"

Benitez was seemed to be thrown off by his non-threatening demeanor. "Um, yes, sir. I'm Detective Benitez with the Tampa Police Department, I'm here following up on a missing persons case." She held out her badge for inspection.

"Hold on, I don't see too good without my glasses." Moye removed a pair of black-rimmed glasses and put them on and read the inscription of the detective's badge. Appearing satisfied, he asked, "Missing persons?"

"Yes, I have information that you may know something about the whereabouts of that missing person."

"Oh, I don't think so, Detective. You have the wrong house."

"So, my witnesses..." Detective Benitez turned slightly so that Melinda was in Moye's line of sight, "... are lying?"

Moye's brows raised with an absent look. "I guess so. Sorry to waste your time." He started to shove away from the door to close it, but Benitez continued.

"Oh, there's no waste of time, sir. Not when it comes to missing children." A subliminal cat and mouse game of warfare had begun. "Do you have any children, sir?"

Moye paused with the door and maintained his gentle façade. "Me, any children? No, ma'am, I never had the pleasure."

"No nieces or nephews, anything like that?"

A slight sense of irritation flashed across Moye's face, but only for an instant before the friendly neighbor returned. "No, ma'am. I was an only child."

"Oh, that's too bad. So, why is there a young girl's barrette laying on the floor underneath your buffet?"

Moye kept up the charade, but there was a hint of worry. Without looking back, "There isn't one, detective. Like I said, you have the wrong house."

"No, I'm sure that's what it is, I used to wear them all the time. It's a young girl's hair clip, but you said that you don't have children, which means no grandchildren and no nieces, yet there it is, plain as day."

"I'm sure you are mistaken," he refused to look.

"No, sir. I'm not. How could you possibly be sure of every little item in your house. You said yourself, 'you don't see too good without those glasses'."

Moye didn't answer. His welcoming demeanor waned into the beginning of an irritated scowl. Detective Benitez continued, "So, like I said, sir. I have information that you may know something about the girl I'm looking for. If I have the wrong house, wouldn't it be better for me to just settle that here and now and not let these rumors, if you will, fester and go unanswered? You know, set the record straight? Just let me come in, take a look around and hey, maybe that silly little clip accidentally wound up in here by the cable repair man or someone like that. Then, I can go back to the witnesses and let them know that you... You know, I didn't even catch your name, sir?"

Moye answered, "Mr. Stephens. Harold."

"Right," Benitez said doubtfully. "I would let the witnesses know that they were wrong about Mr. Stephens and request they stop making up such outlandish accusations."

Moye paused, seeming to mull over the cop's suggestion like identifying a bad taste in his mouth. Finally, he pushed open the front door, allowing the detective to walk through.

"Thank you, sir. It'll only take a minute."

"No back up, Detective?"

Without missing a beat, she answered, "They're in the car waiting with machine guns."

Before Moye could close the door, Benitez bent over to reach under a hutch in the hallway. Blocked from anyone's view, she let a small pink barrette fall from inside her sleeve. She pretended to pick it up and without comment, held it up for Moye to see.

***

The team watched as Detective Benitez entered the house, incredulous at her lightning quick wit and power of persuasion. They steadied themselves; they knew as soon as Benitez found Rachel, all hell would break loose.

"Damn, she's good," Melinda said over the radio.

"Holy shit, that was fantastic," Beth added.

"Wait!" Louis shouted. "I'm confused, is there a barrette or not?"

A moment later Melinda answered, "I don't really know." She was more than impressed, she was infatuated.

Chapter 27

"I don't understand why you have to go?"

Curt stopped packing his bag to address Tracy who stood in the bedroom doorway. With a pout on her face, he explained, "Rachel's in trouble. This guy has her held captive in his house. They need me."

"So why don't they call the police?"

"They did."

"And what are you going to do that's so different?" The venom in Tracy's tone was apparent.

"You know we operate… *differently*, Tracy. Please, I need to get going. Can we talk about this later?"

Tracy shook her head in pained disgust and walked away. Curt let her go. The ever-present strain in their marriage resurfaced, but as duty beckoned, Curt would have to make it up to her later.

Beth called Curt in a panic, explaining that Rachel had decided to go in Moye's house to look for Layla Bragden, using subterfuge. Once Louis compared Rachel's picture from twenty-two years ago to those of the recently kidnapped girls, he noticed there were uncanny similarities. He tried to warn Rachel, but it was too late, and Rachel was already inside with Moye. Curt stopped what he was doing to make the drive down to Tampa.

"Are you going to save her, Dad?"

Curt looked back to the door and saw Josh standing where Tracy was just a moment ago. He smiled and zipped up his bag. "Yeah, buddy. I am."

Where Light Cannot Reach |William Mark

Josh gave a proud smile and a head nod of approval.

"I'll be back as soon as I can, okay buddy?"

"Okay, Dad."

"Good. I'll have another good story for you." Curt shouldered the bag and headed out. Tracy waited by the kitchen door, arms folded, head bowed.

"I'll be back as soon as I can." Curt said.

"Okay." She lifted her head. Tears pooled at the corners of her eyes.

There wasn't anything he could say or do to make her understand why he needed to leave. To say anything would worsen the tension. Curt leaned in, kissed his wife, and walked out.

The Walker home was eerily silent, much like the horrific three years Josh was missing. There wasn't a harmonious balance to the home and a strained tension hung in the air. Draped over the back of a kitchen chair, Curt's trench coat went unnoticed. He had forgotten it as he left for Tampa.

Josh walked down the hallway toward his room and noticed his dad's coat. He went over to it and picked it up. It was heavier than he had figured. He picked it up by the shoulders to examine it as if it were an extension of his father. He looked at the rips and tears on the back, the thin wear marks on the elbows and the barely noticeable blood stains, faded from the wash.

He remembered that he wore it that day to the softball field and then again when he rescued him from his captors. He set the jacket down, smoothed it out over the chair back and walked away.

***

Det. Benitez slowly moved through the house, with Moye following closely. He shuffled his feet and struggled to keep up with the younger detective. Benitez kept a dialogue with him as she searched each room, careful to maintain the illusion of consent. With most of the house checked and no sign of the girl or this Rachel person, she was growing skeptical that she would find anything. She wondered if she was being played by these self-proclaimed "do-gooders" who were just trying to harass an old man.

Playing back the conversation from Starbucks in her head, she had been convinced by Melinda's conviction's believing that they were bona fide and that both Layla and Rachel were being held prisoners. There had been an instant connection between them. Melinda was attractive with a subtle beauty which Benitez found distracting. But, continuing the search, the house was proving void of evidence. She began to feel foolish and wondered if coming without her experienced partner was a mistake.

Aside from his master bedroom, there were two other bedrooms. In one of them, there was a computer and some above-grade technical equipment Benitez was unfamiliar with. They didn't pass as being nefarious, but she questioned the abstract mural of photographs on the wall. Dozens and dozens of pictures of seemingly common places. Sidewalks, driveways, park trails, parking lots and other conspicuous places. She studied them for a moment as she read Moye's body language as agitated.

"What's up with these?"

"Just random photography. I find beauty in common places."

Benitez disagreed with his definition of beauty. Giving them a moment more of her attention, one image registered as familiar, but it was from a distant past. Studying the picture closely, recognition came. It was an overall shot of a park bench that sat on the far side of the tennis courts at a rival school, Northlake High. She had gotten trounced in her first match on the varsity squad at that school and questioned if she even wanted to continue playing tennis. Embarrassed by her poor performance, she cried on that bench until everyone left the courts. Passing on the coincidence and the memory, she moved on, not finding anything criminally suspicious about the images.

The other bedroom was empty except a single twin bed and a matching dresser. His unusual art taste was displayed in another collage of photographs. This time the images were of the forest floor, open fields, vacant lots, river banks, and other naturistic images. There were fewer images than in the other room. The only one that stood out to Benitez was an older picture of a large rock that looked like a sideways shaped heart. It was in the center of all the pictures which drew her eye, but again, nothing seemed suspicious. She only questioned his taste in art.

Benitez glanced at Moye when she thought he wasn't looking, trying to gauge his comfort level as she moved through his house. Not once did he waver as she checked the closets, under the beds and even within a stand-up dresser. Benitez had learned the hard way that a grown man could easily conceal himself by hollowing out a few drawers and hunkering down.

Without a single twitch or even a hint of nervousness, she watched Moye closely. With only the kitchen left to search, Benitez stiffened her gait, preparing to react in case Moye tried something before finding a clue.

"Pretty clean house, Mr. Stephens."

"Thank you, Detective."

"Most houses we search are filthy and disgusting."

"Glad I could oblige."

As Benitez passed the hallway leading back to the front door, she shrugged toward Melinda, who was standing in the threshold. The detective held her palms upward to signify she hadn't found anything yet. Melinda's face held a concerned look that cleared Benitez's doubts that she was being anything less than truthful.

The kitchen was dark and the late evening hour offered no outside lighting. An eerie chill washed over Benitez, causing her to hesitate before entering. She wondered if it was her instincts trying to tell her danger was near. Suddenly stopping, she looked at Moye, a few steps behind her. Her abrupt reaction to the dark caught him off guard, and for a split second, before he realized she was looking at him, Moye's face crinkled with worry, as if she were getting close to something he wanted to stay hidden.

Reaching into the darkness, she felt the wall for a light switch and flicked it on. As the light hit Moye's face, the worry vanished, but it was too late. Benitez's instincts were firing off like a battleship sending a hailstorm of cannonballs towards the enemy.

Turning to face the kitchen, Benitez was greeted with an aesthetic picture of a normal functioning kitchen. A stove, sink, refrigerator, and a small table for two pushed up against the wall. The only short-coming was that the appliances held an outdated almond color. Benitez scanned the small galley kitchen with her eyes. It had a lonely feel to it, but it was still on the normal side of the spectrum. She opened a few cabinets, but only for show, knowing that like the rest of the house, this room didn't hold any sign of either Layla or Rachel.

There was a shut door on the far wall. Benitez knew that whatever was behind that door was the last possible hiding place. An idea came to her.

With a bold bluntness she asked, "That where you keep your victims?" It was said in earnest, but with a hint of absurdity in case she needed to play it off as an insult. But in that instance, Benitez knew she was in the presence of a killer, just as Melinda had suggested, because the question found Moye off balance and he had a look of confirmation instead of denial.

Moye quickly corrected his expression and answered, "Of course not, detective."

"Good." She said, moving fast toward the door. In a swift move, Benitez flung the right side of her jacket exposing her holstered gun for quick access, twisted the doorknob and shoved open the door. She flicked on the light as her right hand rested on the grip of her service weapon. Her eyes wide and ready to react, she took in the contents of the room, looking for threats or clues. However, she was met with disappointment. It was just a utility room with a washer and dryer on one side and a deep freeze on the other. Holding on to one last shred of a possibility, she lifted the deep freeze lid, in case it hid past horrors in a long-awaited frozen state. Peaking inside, it contained a sad picture of single-serving frozen pizzas and microwave meals.

Benitez sighed and questioned her ability to read people. She stood in the middle of the room and felt a draft, but realized it was from the cold air that escaped from the freezer. She looked up at the ceiling and accepted that there was nothing there, except for an odd smell of dank air that she couldn't place. She concluded, she had been wrong. Melinda had been wrong. *I better not have been played,* she thought.

Leaving the laundry room and returning back through the kitchen, Benitez saw the back door. A thin veil of a curtain covered the glass encased door. She peeled back an edge to look outside. It led to a small deck. Not waiting for permission, Benitez unlocked the door and stepped out on the deck. It looked out onto an arm of the lake that reached to Moye's corner of the neighborhood. The moonlight danced over the undulating water below. *It's quite peaceful*, she thought. Benitez stepped to the edge of the deck and looked down. The backyard sloped sharply down to the water which ran underneath Moye's house. She glanced back and through her peripheral vision and saw Moye standing in the doorway. His body stood relaxed. Benitez had no idea what she was looking for but gave the backyard another look.

"Satisfied, Detective?" Moye asked from the doorway.

She gave him a crooked smile, "No."

"Would you care to look again?"

Defeated, she replied, "No."

Benitez made her way back to the front door. Before leaving she turned to look into Moye's eyes one last time. Her athletic build and height let her meet him almost at eye level. The earlier concern she read was gone. In its place was a confidence that when the time came, she might never break. She held his stare in an awkward standoff. Moye stood there in silence.

"Have a nice night, Mr. Stephens." She said with an edge of contempt.

"Good night, Detective."

Benitez walked over to the Sprinter van to address Melinda.

"I looked everywhere and I mean everywhere. Short of taking a wrecking ball to the place, I'm afraid the girl and your friend are not in there."

Stunned, all three stared back incredulously at the detective.

175

Benitez defended herself and said, "Listen, there's something not right with that guy, and I give you that, but I get the feeling you're wasting my time."

"No, I swear we've been up front about everything," Melinda said. "She's in there, detective. I promise."

Benitez muddled around with the thought of Moye being responsible for Layla's disappearance. He gave her the creeps, no doubt, but there wasn't any hard evidence. More was needed if she was to make a solid case. The pleas of some strange do-gooders weren't going to convince her.

"Well, I've put myself out there plenty for you. If he complains about me searching his house, it's my ass that'll get chewed." Benitez softened her stern expression. "But, in the end, it's still a lead. I'll start looking over the case files and comparing what I can to this guy and see if anything sticks. Short of that, I can't help you. And just so were clear, don't go harassing this guy."

"Thanks for your help, Detective." Melinda sounded hurt.

Benitez looked up at Melinda. There was a connection towards her since Starbucks, and she felt bad for not being able to do more. "Listen, if you guys find anything else, call me."

As the detective turned to walk away, Melinda called out, "Wait?"

"What is it?"

"The barrette?" Melinda asked with a curious smirk. "What was that about?"

Benitez smiled from ear to ear. She pulled out the small hair clip from her pocket and flipped it in the air as if it were a coin.

"Like I said, I'm on your side."

***

"Now what?" Louis asked. He, Beth and Melinda were huddled inside the Sprinter van.

"If not in the house, she's got to be somewhere," Melinda said. Turning to Louis, she asked, "Can you see if Moye owns any property

176

nearby. An office, storage shed, empty lot…, anywhere he could have taken in her in such a short time."

"On it." Louis jumped to the back of the van eager to get busy.

"What else can we do in the mean time?" Melinda asked blankly.

Beth spoke up, "We go to plan B."

Chapter 28

Rachel gasped for air as the weight of the fog lifted, but her intake of breath was stifled by a taught rag wrapped around her head like a horse's bridle. She clamped down on the fabric with her teeth and strained to pull air through her nose. Her eyes shot wide, but slowly came into focus. It was dark. She moved her head around searching her surroundings, but there was nothing definitive. It was all a black void.

A muted yelp was all she could muster with the gag in her mouth. Instinctively, she reached to yank it out, but her arms failed to respond. She looked to see what the problem was, but they were wrapped behind her. Thin lines of faint, light gray light came from underneath her like a faded spotlight. She was seated in a wooden chair. She wiggled her hands only to realize they were bound together with some type of rope. She kicked just the same and figured her ankles were bound in the same fashion.

Recalling her last thoughts, she remembered being in Moye's living room and suddenly falling to the floor. He stood over her and said something, but it was like he was at the other end of a long tunnel. Wait, the words came to her. He spoke her name. He had picked her up and dragged her to the other side of the house. At one point, he stopped and propped her up like a doll while he moved something out of her peripheral vision. She tried to make an escape, but although her mind was alert, her body was paralyzed and remained still like she was already dead. Finally, he dragged her down a set of stairs and sat her in a chair.

He said something to her, but it echoed to the point of incoherence. Everything began to blur until she succumbed to the darkness.

But I didn't drink the tea, she thought. Confused, she played back the interaction she had while pretending to be a reporter. *The tea,* she thought again, mystified. It had to have been drugged or poisoned. But she didn't drink any? How could she be in this state? She was so careful, or so she thought.

He knew it was me, she realized incredulously. *But how? It was like he had been waiting for me all this time.* Rachel grew angry with herself. *How could I have been so stupid?*

Rachel's breathing increased and a hot sensation enveloped her body. A layer of sweat formed on her skin as panic gripped her tight. Not again, she whimpered. Not this nightmare.

A light breeze wafted up from underneath her chair, causing her damp skin to gooseflesh. She tried to shake it off, but the confinement restricted her efforts. She struggled against the bindings, tiring herself out with no real results.

As her eyes adjusted to the dark, the ambient light illuminated her immediate surroundings. Just then she noticed that she had been stripped down to just her bra and underwear. Images of her fifteen-year-old version fighting helplessly against the faceless monster flooded her consciousness. She had been so afraid back then that she would never see her sister or mother again, she had lost all hope and just wanted everything to end. If not for the rage he caused by taking her sister instead of her that final time, she wouldn't have had the strength to escape. Rachel had to find that rage again.

A sloshing wet noise broke the silence of the darkened room, causing an added fear in Rachel. It came from underneath her, somewhere below the floor. Something moved. She looked down for an answer, straining to see through the dim light. Her nostrils flared working hard on taking in breath after breath. She realized the thin lines of light were slits between the floorboards beneath her. She figured she must be in some type of basement or hidden room attached to Moye's house.

A light flicked on in the room and Rachel saw it illuminating a horizontal line revealing of a set of stairs. Fearing it's meaning, she remained silent, listening. There were two sets of footsteps moving, one fast, one slow. The fast-moving steps moved to one side of the room, then the other, and then stopped somewhere in the middle. Moye's voice spoke and the other person reacted. It was a softer but stern voice. A woman's, she realized. Melinda?

Rachel yelled as loud as she could, trying to break through the rag stuffed in her mouth. It was muted, but in her head, it was deafening. Please let them hear me, she prayed. She screamed for help and then stopped to listen for a reaction. Again, she cried, "I'm dow heer-ah. Peese, hep!"

There was no reaction. She widened her mouth hoping her words would move around the gag, but it only pulled tighter at the edges of her mouth, causing her to dry heave. She fought back the urge to vomit, knowing that if she did, it would be clogged by the gag and could cause her to drown. She had seen it a few times before in severe child abuse cases while working with DCF. She clamped down on the rag with her teeth, lifted her head up, and breathed through her nose. As the feeling subsided, she looked to the top of the stairs to see the light blink off, sending that section of the room back into the black. Whoever it was, was now gone.

Further away, she heard a door open and footsteps slowly move from high above her. She tried to make a loud enough noise but looking up caused the choking feeling to return. She coughed again, keeping the urge to vomit quelled.

Despair engulfed Rachel Goodwin's soul. The strong-willed woman she perceived herself to be was now reduced to a helpless prisoner, held by the same monster who ruined her life as a teenager. How could this have happened? How could he have realized it was her? And after so many years.

What seemed an eternity had passed since the light on the top of the stairs came on and went off. Her eyes were fully adjusted to the dark, using the little bit of gray light that came in between the floorboards. She couldn't see into the far corners of the room, but she could make out the area around her and the base of the stairs. A long stick jutted out from the floor next to the stair railing. Rachel stared at this, wondering at its purpose since it didn't seem to fit in or have any functional use. She constantly pulled at her bindings, trying to loosen the tight hold, but nothing seemed to budge.

Calmed, focused on slowing her breathing, Rachel worked on one problem at a time. The immediate problem was to get free from the ropes. Her wrists were bound and the backs of her hands were almost touching. She pulled apart, but there wasn't enough strength in her arms to make a difference. Straining to stretch out the ropes sent piercing aches resonating through her shoulders. She had to think of something else. Twisting her seat, she realized that she could rotate her elbows slightly without restriction from her shoulders. She leaned forward and moved them inward, toward her body, causing her wrists to twist around to where they were touching palms. Progress, she thought. Now she could grab something if needed.

Her ankles were bound to separate legs of the chair. She had the ability to stand, if not for being anchored to the seat by the wrist ropes. She kicked each foot, gauging the tension of the knots. Realizing there was no amount of flexibility that would guarantee release, they would have to be untied to set her free.

Purposeful footsteps neared. She looked up toward the top of the stairs to see the light flick on. Straining to see through the dark, she saw thin shadows dancing on the other side of the door. She heard something heavy move before the doorknob twisted and the door swung open. Moye filled the doorway, the light from the room behind him silhouetted his frame as he slowly descended the stairs. He moved with fluidity and ease, not like the old man he portrayed before.

Without realizing it, Rachel started to pant, taking short breaths though the damp fabric of her gag. She watched frozen as the devil she knew came toward her.

"Now, we can finish what we started, Rachel."

His dark shadow stood before her. She could smell his body odor, a mix of sweat and aftershave. The scent transported her back twenty-two years when she tried to fight him off before he took Rhonda. He had grabbed her and thrown her to the floor, and in that encounter, some of his stink had rubbed off on her. She shuddered at the memory.

Moye's form moved closer and then around the chair. He ran his fingertips softly across her back, around her shoulders, and across her chest. Rachel cringed at his touch. His fingers might as well be the deadly tentacles of a poisonous jellyfish.

"No more interruptions, now. It's just me and you." Rachel didn't respond, not wanting to give him any satisfaction. Moye continued to run his hands around her body, groping her neck, breasts, and stomach. "My, my. You have grown into such..." He inhaled as if the air gave him arousal, "... a woman. Haven't you?" His hands caressed her face, then he gently rubbed her cheek with the back of his hand. The endearment and tenderness brought back the sick feeling in her stomach. Again, she was on the verge of retching. Defiantly, she whipped her head away.

"Go wuck yosell!" she managed.

"Tsk, tsk. Such language is not fit for a lady."

"Leh me go."

Moye stopped in front of her. A grind and click sound came from directly overhead. A light flickered on in the center of the room, directly above Rachel. Now illuminated, Moye bent down and stopped only inches away from Rachel's face. Even through the same black-rimmed glasses he wore years earlier, she could see his eyes were black, soulless pits, void of humanity.

"Let you go?" Moye scoffed and stood erect. "Why, I've been waiting twenty-two years for this." He smiled a cocky grin. "I'll bet you have, too."

Rachel rolled her eyes.

"Oh, don't act coy." Moye said. "You don't have to admit it, but I know that I am a part of you, just like you are a part of me."

Seething at his words, Rachel felt her eyes burning hot with rage. Moye reached for her face again. She dodged his touch, but he leaned in and forcefully grabbed her face. She pulled against him, but he was too strong. Hooking his finger down the side of her cheek, he grabbed the mouth gag and pulled it out of her mouth. Rachel moved her jaw back and forth and sucked in a deep breath now that she could. She didn't say it, but her eyes gave Moye thanks.

"You're welcome."

Moye stepped back and then moved over to Rachel's right, disappearing into a darkened corner. She followed him with her eyes but couldn't see what he was doing.

"Why are you doing this?" Her voice was soft and sounded pathetic. She was hiding the rage inside.

"Why does anyone do anything? Why do we live false pretenses? Why do we ignore our most basic desires?"

Rachel kept silent. She wasn't going to play his game.

"Why did you knock on my door after twenty-two years?"

"You have to be stopped."

"And you thought you could do that?" Moye let out a conceited laugh. "You and those other misfits in the van? Not even that cop they sent had a clue. I'm sorry my dear." Moye paused and added in a low morbid tone, "I am what I am. There's no stopping that."

"Where's Layla? What did you do with her?" Rachel twisted as much as she could, hoping to see where he was keeping Layla. There were a few darkened spots in the far corners and underneath the stairs that she couldn't penetrate with her eyes, but there were no signs of Layla.

"Ah, yes. Layla." His cocksure attitude returned. "She was a pretty little candidate, wasn't she?"

"What did you do to her?"

"I'm sorry to tell you this, but she's no longer with us, Rachel. Plus, she was what the profilers call a surrogate anyway."

Rachel's heart sank. She and the team were too late to save Layla, and now she had become ensnared in the same trap. She flexed her arms pulling at the wrists again. She felt them loosen, albeit only millimeters, but progress was progress.

"A surrogate?" Rachel asked.

"Yes." Moye stood up and stepped in front of Rachel eager to explain. "They all were. Imposters, really."

"They?" Rachel asked, innocently.

"Stop acting coy, its unbecoming." Moye snapped. "You know who I'm talking about. All of them, the beauties who would never be; they were all pitiful substitutes."

"The fifty-seven girls that have gone missing since you moved to Florida?"

A wide grin spread across his face. "Has it been that many?"

"Now who's being coy?"

"Touché, my dear. Touché."

"What happened to them?"

"That's not important." Moye answered. "But find solace in knowing that *none of them* lived up to you, the real thing."

"Are they all dead?"

Moye shrugged absently, as if he'd been asked if he knew the weather forecast.

"You killed them all? Because of me?" The revelation hit Rachel hard. It felt as if her heart withered away like ash in a strong breeze.

"Well…, not because of you, per se. But, because they weren't you."

"Weren't me? I don't understand." Flashes of her offering herself to him as a young girl came to her. "Back then, instead of me, you…"

Moye grew silent. He lowered his head in shame. "Back then I was disgusted by you. Offering yourself to me like a little harlot, it was shameful. I immediately regretted taking you along with your sister. Now, *she* was the real deal beauty back then. But something happened. You happened. You changed everything."

"What do you mean?"

"You changed the game."

Her face contorted out of confusion. "I still don't understand."

"You escaped!"

"Okay?"

"Don't you see. No one had ever escaped before. I had my way of doing things, the right way, and you changed it. But, chasing you through those woods, that was invigorating. It was thrilling, God, I wanted you more than anything after that."

Rachel began to see a clearer picture. "Because you couldn't have me, your desires changed?"

"Yes!" Moye beamed. "Yes, that's it. Oh, this is exhilarating, Rachel. Can't you feel it?"

She shook her head.

"Oh, yes you can. It's the connection we share. A true bond. I've waited so long for this moment that I am just beside myself now that you're here. We are a part of each other and you know it."

"I'm nothing like you."

The elation in Moye's face disappeared. The soulless pits he called eyes were dull and black. Her words had struck a chord. He looked hurt.

"Let me show you something." Moye turned and walked back to Rachel's right. He vanished somewhere in the shadows and returned, carrying something in his hand. Standing in front of her, she saw a non-descript book. She thought it might be a journal of sorts.

Moye's face was flush as he debated something. He strummed the outside of the book with his fingers, clearly trying to decide whether to share it with Rachel or not.

"I've…" He stopped, almost as if he were embarrassed. "I've kept up with you over the years."

Rachel was shocked. Moye opened up the book revealing newspaper clippings from when she went missing in 1993. Her picture, yellowed from the years of exposure, had a worn mark on the face. Moye answered her question about why there was a wear mark, as he instinctively reached down and rubbed the picture with his finger. He turned the page, displaying other newspaper clippings about the investigation and showed a picture of Rachel and her mother standing together at a news conference asking the public for help finding Rhonda. Rachel's face was blanked out by another wear mark. Her stomach began to turn, and she was thankful the gag had been removed.

185

"See, I followed you, wherever you went." Moye continued to flip the pages past a few articles about the anniversary of Rhonda's disappearance, her graduating class picture, and her few minor arrests for drunk and disorderly. At the back of the book, Moye paused, "This is my favorite." He turned the page slowly and Rachel saw a picture of her standing next to Alexis Vanderhill. It was at a fundraiser in San Francisco. She remembered that was when Alexis had recruited Rachel to the team.

"Not sure I prefer you as a blonde, Rachel, but you looked so grown up and beautiful."

Blood rushed to Rachel's head. It was Moye's comment about her being a blonde that made her light-headed. She had dyed her hair blonde and kept it that way since leaving the hospital after having been found black-out drunk, with her underwear missing. She'd been a brunette up until that point, and now everything made perfect sense as Moye had told her she was his demented focus. All those poor girls, Layla and before, were his pathetic and brutal attempt to be with her. She began to weep.

"Oh, no. Don't do that. Don't cry. Not tonight. Tonight is a joyous occasion."

"Oh, go fuck yourself," she blurted between sobs. "I'm half-naked, tied to a fucking chair and you tell me you've killed sixty innocent girls because they weren't me? Excuse me if I find this anything but joyous."

Moye looked dumbfounded by her outburst. He snapped shut the journal and returned to the shadowy corner. Stomping back in front of her, Moye grabbed her head with both hands. She pulled away, thrashing away from his grip. Rearing back, Moye sent a blow crashing down against Rachel's left cheek, ending the struggle and knocking her loopy. He pulled up her face with both hands while she was still dazed and replaced the gag back in her mouth. She tried to fight, but with her arms and feet bound to the chair, she offered little resistance.

Standing above Rachel, Moye huffed out of frustration, as if the perfect date wasn't going as planned. Rachel found pleasure in his discomfort. "I'll let you calm down a bit, but sooner or later, you will show me gratitude." Moye clicked off the basement light and ascended the staircase, leaving Rachel alone in the dark. As Moye shut the door, moved something around and the light flicked off, the silence of the dungeon-like room returned. Before Rachel could calm down, knowing that she was away from Moye, a wet flop and slither came from beneath the floorboard, sending her back into a panic.

Chapter 29

After passing Ocala on I-75, Curt called the team and put his phone on speaker. He listened as the team explained how the case unfolded and then went sideways once Rachel tried to gain access to Moye's house under the guise of a reporter. They told him how all the missing girls from Florida struck an uncanny resemblance to Rachel and how they believed Moye had longed for her ever since she had escaped. Providing the details surrounding the deaths back in the late nineties, Curt listened to the prospect that Moye was the Hillsborough River Killer. The update ended as they explained how they entrusted Detective Benitez who searched the house but came up empty.

"What do you mean, she didn't find anything?" Curt asked, angrily.

"Moye let her in and she said she looked everywhere," Melinda answered.

"He just *let* her in?"

"Yeah. I mean, she used some kind of wicked Jedi mind trick and he let her in," Louis added.

"That doesn't make sense. He's got to be hiding her somewhere close."

"We thought the same thing. We have Louis trying to dig up any properties Moye owns in the area," Melinda added.

A moment of silent thought passed. Curt spoke, "Are you guys still watching the house?"

"As best we can."

Curt grunted. The answer wasn't good enough.

"*He* actually called the cops on us," Louis said defensively. "He almost counter-hacked my machine when I tried to activate his alarm from the van. I'm telling you, this guy is smart, Curt. He's had an answer for us every step of the way, man. Like three steps ahead of us."

Curt's tone eased. "So, where are you, if you are still watching?"

"About two blocks down. We're not on top of him, but through the binos we can see if he leaves," Melinda answered.

Curt thought about how to approach Moye once he arrived. Since the police came and went with no luck, it was time to side-step the law and go in uninvited. Beyond that, Curt's thoughts felt clouded and unclear. He knew the threat was Moye, but something was different, as if he couldn't feel the pulse of the situation. Something he had developed a knack for in the two years prior. Nearing the area, he tried to focus on Moye and listen to his instincts, but there was only silence. This worried him.

Glancing at the digital clock in the dash of his Crown Vic, he noted the time. He would be there in less than twenty minutes.

***

Whatever lurked beneath the floorboards remained below. That gave Rachel a small amount of comfort, leaving her to concentrate on her immediate problems. Flexing and pulling her wrists apart, she managed to stretch out the rope's tight grip, what she imagined, was a few more millimeters. The humidity that seeped up through the floor kept her skin at a constant level of dampness from sweat. This worked toward her advantage with the expansion of her bindings. She was able to slip them further down her hands, but she was far from free.

With no concept of time, other than the feel of night and her own exhaustion, Rachel saw the light turn on at the top of the stairs. The sound of something heavy rolling followed, then Moye pushed open the door and walked down the stairs. He was only a dark shadow, but Rachel felt his eyes bore into hers as he took each step down and stood in front of her. The floorboard creaked under his weight as he took a deep breath.

Moye expelled a lustful breath, then said, "I brought you something to drink." The overhead light flicked on, blinding Rachel's eyes as she looked up. Through squinted eyes, she noticed he was holding a glass of water. She was thirsty but resisted the thought of accepting anything to drink for fear it would only serve to incapacitate her.

She bulged her eyes with expectation and glanced down. Moye understood this and removed the wet fabric from her mouth.

"I'm fine," she said, rejecting the offer of water.

"Oh, come on." Moye whined. "It's just water. I know you're thirsty. Would you rather have the tea from earlier? I can go make some."

Rachel heard the genuineness in his voice but remained skeptic. "Did you give the other girls water?"

A flat look crossed Moye's face. "Do you want the damn water or not?"

"Fine. But can you untie me so I can hold the glass."

Moye smiled. "No, Rachel. I don't think so. Not yet anyway." He brought the glass up to her lips and lifted. She took in the water. As soon as the water hit her mouth, she realized that she was thirsty. She gulped the water, spilling some down her mouth and onto her chest. The cool touch of the water was refreshing in an otherwise horrific situation.

"Let me go, please," she pleaded, calmly.

"You just got here. And like I said earlier. We have unfinished business."

Rachel wept. "Please, you don't have to do this."

"No!" Moye yelled. "You ran away from me, Rachel. You left me, remember. I had to move to another part of the country, you obviously know I had to change my name, but it was you who left, not me." Moye steadied himself, taking a calming breath. "And, it was you who came back. You knocked on my door, Rachel. You are a part of me, like I am a part of you. We are like one."

"No, I'm nothing like you," she said. Summoning an inner strength, she spoke, "I came here to stop you and find Layla Bragden. I came here because you are a despicable human being."

Moye sneered down at Rachel. "You didn't think so when I chose your little sister over you."

The tears dried and the rage became renewed.

"Fuck you!"

"You know…," Moye sneered, no longer hiding the evil in his eyes. "she cried out for you when I was with her."

Rachel sobbed, "Stop it!"

"She begged for her big sister to help her."

"Please, stop!"

"No!" Moye said. "Your sister just gave in and waited for you to come, but you never did, did you?"

Rachel shook her head, trying to ward off his words. Her sobbing continued to an uncontrollable bawl. The nightmare she had lived with for the last two decades had always been twofold. There was the man who was responsible for her hell, which she had chosen to focus on, because it was easier to deal with than the other. It was too terrible to fathom but it was the root of all her psychological trauma. *Guilt.* It was guilt for leaving her sister. Although it was a conscious decision she made, it haunted her daily. She hated Moye even more for preying upon that guilt. It made her feel weak.

Moye stood close and ran the back of his hand down her tear-streaked cheeks. "Such pain," he said. "Such a burden, carrying around that guilt for so long." Moye moved around to her other side. He pushed her matted hair back over her ear. He drew circles around her naked shoulder. His touch sent a venomous shock wave through her body. "Maybe you can still help your sister?"

"What?" The sobbing had slowed and she now looked up toward Moye. He had a pleased look on his face.

"You shouldn't be carrying all that guilt, Rachel. Maybe there's a way you can still help her?"

Confused by the tinge of hope in his voice, she wondered, *what was he talking about*. Was Rhonda still alive?

"What do you mean, still help her?"

191

Moye feigned being bashful. He circled back around her, running his hand across her back.

"Tell me, dammit? What do you mean?"

"I think you know what I mean. Don't you see, Rachel, we're connected. We're a part of each other. Always have been, since the day we met. It took me a while to understand that."

"No, I don't know what you mean."

"Ugh. You know what I mean, Rachel. It's who you are. It's in your nature."

"No, I don't understand. Please, tell me how to help her?"

"I can't tell you." Moye became frustrated and started pacing around the basement. "If I tell you, it will ruin everything and then…." His face grew saddened, and he glanced toward the base of the stairs.

Following his glance, Rachel noticed the wooden stick by the base of the stairs again. With the overhead light on, she could see it more clearly. It looked like a lever, but to what she didn't know and Moye looking at it added to her fear.

"Fine," she said. "I don't want to ruin things."

Moye spun with a renewed excitement.

"But, tell me. Is my sister alive?"

Moye studied Rachel first, then moved closer. "Not yet."

Rachel closed her eyes, squeezing more tears from under her eyelids. She didn't want to play his game and didn't understand the meaning of any of this. Her anger grew and manifested into a rage. The rage she needed. With a calm façade, she pulled at the ropes with all her strength.

"Are you ready to help her, Rachel? She's waiting."

"Yes." She replied. "But, how can I with these ropes around my wrists?"

Moye pushed up his glasses to the bridge of his nose. He licked his lips in anticipation. He was contemplating something. "So, you're ready, then?" He looked as if he were a drunk, and Rachel's promise was the alcohol needed to feed his addiction.

Willing to say anything to get her hands loose, she answered, "Yes."

Moye moved quickly to the dark corner. His pace was with purpose, almost over eager and anxious. He moved back and stood in front of Rachel.

"You see it now, don't you? That we're connected."

"That we're a part of each other," she mimicked back to Moye.

"Yes." His face lit up with validation. Moye moved to the back of the chair and knelt down. She felt him tug at the ropes behind her back.

Suddenly he stopped.

"What was that?" Moye asked.

Rachel hadn't heard anything, but Moye was spooked.

"No, I heard something." He stood up and moved to the base of the stairs. Looking up, he tried to hone in on this phantom noise.

A slight rub and creak came from elsewhere in the house. Someone was upstairs. Rachel grew excited, hoping it was someone coming to her rescue. She inhaled to scream as loud as she could, alarming the would-be rescuer, but with lightning quick reflexes, Moye stuffed the rag back in her mouth before she let loose a siren's wail. She tried anyway, but the gag muted her efforts to a loud whisper. Moye clamped his hand tight over her mouth.

"No one is going to interrupt us again. I've waited too long for this to have someone interfere. I'm sorry, Rachel, if it's one of your friends from the van, I'm going to kill them."

Rachel gave him a pleading look not to harm her friends, but he turned his back to her and climbed up the stairs. He moved stealthily and disappeared through the door.

Hoping it was help in search of her, Rachel prayed they were ready for Moye and his cunningness. Knowing her team, she didn't believe it was one of them, but if not her team, then who?

Outfitted with an ear bud from Louis, Curt stalked up to the side of Moye's house, found concealment behind a hedge grouping, and watched for any movement. Studying the side of the house, he spied a side door and decided that would be the best point of entry. He needed something easy and quick, minimal noise where he could hopefully use

193

stealth to get inside. The possibility of a confrontation was high. He pulled the Glock from his holster, squeezed the grip tight, rolled it and press-checked the slide, ensuring there was a round in the chamber.

"How long has she been in there now?" Curt asked, talking barely above a whisper.

"Going on six hours now," Louis answered.

"Okay," Curt said. "I'm heading in."

"Be careful, Curtis."

Curt sprung forward from the hedges and crept up to the side door. Listening carefully, there was nothing audible coming from inside the house. The intermittent cricket chirp and the quiet slosh of the water's edge were the only sounds he heard. He removed his lock pick set and pulled out two thin metal picks. Shoving one in the bottom of the key hole, he slid the other on top and carefully moved it back and forth, scrubbing the inside of the lock. With steady effort and a twist of the knob, the door opened. Pausing for a reaction, Curt held the door still. After a few seconds, he pulled the door open slowly until he could squeeze inside.

The air inside was stale and cooler. An odd odor greeted him as he let his eyes adjust to the dim lighting. It was astringent and clinical. With light footsteps, he moved past the front door, hallway, and into the living room. The strange smell was more apparent, but he still couldn't identify it.

In a hushed tone Curt asked, "He didn't leave, did he?"

"No, he hasn't," Beth answered. "Not that we've seen from our position."

"Something doesn't feel right. It seems too quiet."

Curt reached up to his waistline and rested his hand on the grip of his pistol. After another moment of listening, the house was still. He should have heard something, a television, a cough, Moye moving around the house, anything but the silence.

Moving on with the mission, Curt took slow steps down the hallway to the other side of the house. He anticipated finding bedrooms and hopefully a clue to where Rachel was being held prisoner, something the

194

detective missed or couldn't further probe. Melinda told him about the detective searching the entire house and not finding anything. He didn't want to pass harsh judgement on another detective, but he questioned her thoroughness.

Peeking around the corner of the hallway, Curt was met with four white interior doors. Two were cracked open, one closed, and one pushed completely open. The room with the open door was a bathroom with the light off. Curt glanced inside, but there was nothing of note. To the closed door, he noticed the light was off as well by checking the crack under the door. Curt stood next to the door and listened intently. There was nothing. Curt withdrew his Glock with his right hand as he slowly twisted the knob with his left. With the lock disengaged, he slowly pushed the door open, revealing a darkened room. The light from the hallway slowly spilled in, lighting up the bed and the middle of the room. Curt raised up his Glock ready to address Moye or whatever evils lurked. With a quick step inside followed by a side step, Curt scanned the room. It was empty. He moved to the master bathroom, but it was empty as well.

"Something is off. I don't think he's here guys."

"She's got to be there somewhere, Curt," Melinda said.

Louis added, "Yeah, I've looked pretty extensively, and Moye, Stephens or any other possible aliases he's using, doesn't own any other property but this house."

"Damn." Curt fought away a twinge of frustration. "Keep looking."

Curt moved just as silently back to the other cracked doors. Following the same routine as before by slowly pushing the door open and leading with his Glock, he found the first room just as empty as everything else. Curious as to the all the pictures on the wall, he turned on the light. The images were sporadic and in no particular order. They were all of empty patches of earth, grassy fields, vacant lots and wide angled nature images. Curt studied them, brow furrowed, wondering if they held meaning or if they were they just some terrible photography Moye was proud of. *Beauty being in the eye of beholder*, he thought, but this wasn't beauty, just randomness captured on camera. Not getting any sense of meaning from the room, he shut the light off and went on to the next.

After entering and clearing the room, he wasn't surprised by a second collection of pictures adorning an entire wall. He flicked the light on and studied these images as well. Whereas the other room had the half-assed nature theme, the motif in this room was public places. Trails, streets, sidewalks, and other odd scenes. The beauty, if there was any, had been lost on Curt. He shook his head, unable to discern it's meaning. Glancing around the wall, there was little on specifics about where they were taken, telling Curt that they must serve some type of purpose.

"Mel?" he asked, still using the hushed tone.

"Yeah?" she answered.

"What was the detectives take on these photographs? She make any sense of them?"

"Um, no. Actually, she never really mentioned any photographs, so I guess they didn't seem relevant."

Curt nodded in acknowledgement even though no one was around.

"I can call her and ask? See what she thinks?" Melinda added. Curt detected a little extra enthusiasm in her tone. He turned his focus back to the wall. Out of the sea of random pictures, stood something familiar. Obvious and intentional, it was positioned in the center of the collage as if all others revolved around this particular image. It called out to Curt.

"What the hell?" Curt leaned in close, trying to decipher its meaning. It was a picture of the heart-shaped rock. There was no doubt it was the same rock Rachel hid under during her escape from Moye over two decades ago. Having seen the rock in person, Curt was certain the image was of the same rock. The picture had a thin layer of clouding, dating the photograph.

Curt took a step back, taking in the rest of the pictures, seeing them with a new perspective. He figured there were close to sixty images.

"Guys," Curt spoke. "I think I figured out what the pictures mean." Curt stared at the heart-shaped rock again. An awful feeling grew in the pit of his stomach.

"Well?" Louis whined. "What?"

A *thwack* sounded behind Curt. Before he could turn, a pain exploded in the back of his head. Mired in a near unconscious sandpit, Curt couldn't move, and his world fell fast to the ground. Realizing he was face down on the floor, he tried to push up and look behind him for whatever caused this, but another crushing blow was delivered and everything blinked to black.

Chapter 30

"C'mon, don't go home yet. It's still early!" Lucas Millwood begged the last of his friends to stay. They had nearly drained a case of Natural Light beer they had bribed some random guy to buy for them outside of a convenient store. After being turned down several times, Luke's persistence paid off, and he scored the beer for himself and his friends.

"It's late, dude. I got to get home. My parents will freak if I'm late again."

"Ahh. You suck!" Luke waved him off, as the friend sneered back at him. Luke grabbed another beer, sat down in the Mustang and turned up the can, letting his mouth fill with beer. Slowly, he let the frothy liquid down his throat, not yet perfecting the ability to chug a full can. Something the college boys he often hung out with had mastered. Letting the taste of beer linger, his face cringed at the bitterness. He was still getting used to drinking alcohol.

Embracing his inebriation, Luke cranked up the classic rock song playing on the radio and sang along in drunken harmony with "Pour Some Sugar on Me" Being alone, he needed a distraction. The beer wasn't enough. Anything to keep the thoughts of Layla out of his head. But, she somehow managed to creep back inside.

The song faded and the effects of the cold beer lost its edge. He couldn't shake the feeling that bogged him down. It all centered on Layla and what that woman told him earlier that day. The way she just laughed at him, it was insulting and he hated her for that, but, it was her parting words that bothered him the most. He couldn't shake her harsh words.

They echoed in his head as if she were standing next to him, repeating herself.

"So instead of dancing with you that night, she ran off alone, making it easier for this guy to grab her."

Luke shook his head, trying to muffle her voice. He hated the words and although she didn't come out and say it, her message was clear. *This is your fault.*

"No, it's not!" he yelled to the empty car. His own voice, burdened with guilt, startled him. He sat up in his leather bucket seat and looked around to see if anyone noticed. The back parking lot of the shopping center was empty except for a few parked cars belonging to employee's closing up the store. His outburst went unwitnessed, and his cool persona remained intact.

Luke laughed. He climbed out of the Mustang and kicked open the lid of the cooler. He drained his current beer, crushed the aluminum can, tossed it into the wood line that edged the back of the parking lot, and grabbed another from the cooler. As he popped the top, the sudsy liquid squirted out, spilling some on his hands. He put the can to his mouth and took in another mouthful and slowly let it pour down his throat gulp by gulp. Stepping back to the car, he nearly lost his balance and hopped a few times on his right foot to gain stability.

"Whoa!" Using his beer and outstretched hand for counter balance, he added, "Gotta get my shit together." Luke whipped his head back and forth like a wet dog drying its fur, trying to stave off the drunken shroud settling over him. Feeling a bit more alert, he sat back down in the Mustang.

Unhappy with the song selection, he rolled through the stations until he found something fast paced with energy. Finding a Metallica song halfway into a guitar solo, he leaned back in his seat and continued on the beer. The heavy metal wasn't loud enough to drown out the returning thoughts of Layla and the fact that she was missing. Another drink didn't work either. Luke cranked up the volume of the song's final crescendo, letting the fury of the drum beat drown out the resonance of his guilt.

As the song ended, silence took over, leaving his thoughts to reinvade his consciousness. This time, he gave in. He set the beer down in the cup holder and reached for his phone. He zig-zagged his thumb over the screen, unlocking it, bringing it to life. He opened his Facebook app and scrolled down to see what had been posted. Normally absorbed into the social happenings of his friends, Luke didn't actually bother reading anything. He looked at the empty search bar on the top of the screen. It beckoned him for only a moment before he gave in to his guilt. He typed in Layla's name, and when it appeared as the obvious search destination, he clicked on her image. Her page refreshed on the screen, and he looked at her wall. A wave of depression hit him hard as he saw her last post the night of the dance and looked at a picture of her sitting in the science wing hallway, crying. Suddenly, he wished he could have been there in that moment, maybe she wouldn't have gone missing. He would have fought off her kidnapper and saved her.

A tear welled up and before it could break the lip of his eyelid, he wiped it away. When he heard the news that she had been reported missing, he thought she had just runaway like she'd talked about doing several times before. It was surreal to think about her being kidnapped, especially after leaving the dance. After seeing him dancing with Sarah McGill. Another tear formed, but this time he let it roll down his cheek. *Maybe it was my fault*, he thought.

Luke closed the app and checked to see if he had any text messages. None. He was getting tired but didn't want to go home. Plus, drinking with an emotional catalyst began making the world spin and blur at the same time. He needed to experience something good, something pure, but wanted it to be about Layla. Then he remembered. He touched the cell phone screen and opened up his photo gallery. He scrolled through a few days' worth of pictures to find the one he wanted to see. Easily spotting the bare skin in the thumbnail size, he clicked open the image and the full screen picture appeared. A twinge of excitement assuaged the guilt and shame. This was a moment they shared, together.

Staring at her image, he longed for Layla. Her beautiful smile and that sexy look she gave him through the picture made him want to be with her. Keying in on her young cleavage, pushed up by her arm laying across her bare chest, he began to get aroused. Her lacy black panties hugged her small narrow hips, and Luke imagined what might have happened had he been there with her in that moment. As the tears returned, he ran his fingers across the tiny screen as if Layla would feel his soft touch.

"I miss you, Layla."

Grabbing his beer out of the cup holder, Luke finished it off. His eyelids grew heavy, but he fought the urge to leave. He stepped out and checked the cooler for anymore beers. A silver and blue label was apparent from under a sheet of ice and Luke fished it out, popped the top and took another starter sip. He looked up at the low crescent moon hanging crooked in the night sky, raised up his beer on unsteady legs, and took another drink.

Luke returned to the driver's seat of the Mustang and reclined his chair. He peeled back the moon roof cover and stared up into the sky, something he had done with Layla on one of the nights she snuck out. He had enjoyed the peace and amazement it brought and hoped he would find it amongst the blame and beer. The world spun in an inebriating haze as his mind swirled with thoughts of Layla. After a moment, he could no longer fight the dead weight of his eyelids.

Chapter 31

Instead of going home, Sandra Benitez grabbed sushi from the seafood department at a Publix grocery store before it closed. The late hour left few options, but she grabbed a California roll with spicy sauce drizzled in a crisscross. It was a go-to meal when she wanted to avoid the fattening temptation of a fast-food drive-thru. But, giving in to her sweet tooth, she grabbed a few cookies from the bakery on her way up to the check-out.

Carrying her late-night dinner up to the Criminal Investigations Bureau, she wasn't surprised to find the office empty. She flicked on the light switch that activated the section of the bureau where her desk was situated. She sat down, turned on her computer, and ate a few sauce laden bites of sushi while it booted up. Sifting through a small stack of folders, she pulled Layla Bragden's case file and opened it up. She'd read it several times before, but this time she read it with Moye figured in as a suspect. She liked to reread the report, putting it through a suspect filter and see what stuck out.

Nothing did. There was still nothing solid to act on, however, as she placed Moye in the suspect role, her instincts told her something was there. She glanced at the property receipt from where she'd impounded the shoe she had found stuck between the pipe and floor at Layla's school. She sent off an email request to have it processed for DNA at FDLE's biology lab. That reminded her of something.

Benitez removed her phone and pulled up the image of the blemished window from Layla's school. Convinced that was the abduction site, she emailed the picture to her friend in the Forensics Unit and requested she compare the marks to the heel of the shoe she found. Confident it would match, Benitez realized that this evidence only served to better prove she was taken by force, not necessarily point to her abductor. *It's still better than nothing*, she thought.

After finishing off a few more bites of sushi, Benitez rolled her mouse, waking her computer out of its slumber. After the screen blinked on, she entered multiple passwords to access the myriad of databases needed for modern police work. Old school had its place, for sure, but information was the new school smoking gun. Setting aside Layla's file, she ran the criminal history on Harold Stephens. Nothing came back. She opened up another page and ran the same name in a national database for criminal history. Several hits came back, but as she quickly scrutinized them, they were "near hits" and not actually Stephens. The system provided names that are similar with close date of births to the actual target as a way to eliminate human error or suspects providing fictitious information. Given what she did know about Stephens, she was able to eliminate all the "near hits".

Thinking about Melinda and her friends, she cleared Stephens' name and reentered Harold S. Moye. She clicked on the search tab and excitement grew in the pit of her stomach as the hourglass twirled in place. She could only imagine the computers hesitation was due to so much hidden information about to surface.

No records found.

She stared flatly back at the screen. She ran Moye's name in the national database. The icon reacted in the same way, but she wasn't hopeful. When the page refreshed, there was a hit. It looked like a "near hit" but the estimated percentage of a match was ninety-seven. Experience told her that was usually who she was looking for.

"Looky here!" she read out loud. "Mr. Moye was charged with disorderly conduct in nineteen-eighty-six and adjudicated guilty." She scanned the charge information and found the jurisdiction. "Harris County, Texas. Where's that?" Benitez opened up another internet page and googled Harris County, Texas. It was the county that incorporated most of Houston. She sat back and found this revelation somewhat satisfying, but then again, the menial charge of disorderly conduct is not the gateway to serial abduction and murder. That part didn't fit. Plus, that charge is so vague it encompasses a wide spectrum of illegal behavior from the devious to the childish. She wrote down the case number and made a note to call Harris County to get more details of his arrest.

"Well, shit." Benitez ate the last piece of sushi and opened up the Department of Highway Safety and Motor Vehicles database. If someone has or ever has had a driver's license in the state, this database would have access to the information. She entered Moye's name and there were no matching records. After she entered Stephens' name, his image and information came on the screen. It was an image dated at least ten years as his short-cropped hair wasn't as gray as it was today. She noticed he still sported the same black-rimmed glasses for his license picture. But like his introductory facial expression, in his picture he looked harmless. Benitez clicked on his driving history. If he had any tickets throughout the state, this is where she'd find them. Stephens had one listed. She clicked on the corresponding link and a scanned image of the actual ticket popped up. There was nothing of note on the citation. Stephens had been pulled over three years prior in a small town east of Tampa for failing to obey a traffic control device. Benitez translated that into rolling through a stop sign when some cop happened to be watching. Scrutinizing the ticket for any minutia of information that could be helpful, she noticed an optional link at the bottom of the page that, on past searches, wasn't normally there. Her curiosity didn't stall and she clicked on the link. An information box popped up with a handwritten narrative that had been scanned along with the ticket. It was submitted by the citing officer. Stephens had a three-foot alligator in his backseat and claimed he had trapped it and was taking the animal to a wildlife refuge.

"A gator?" Benitez wondered. "What the hell are you doing with a gator?" Something was off, she thought. She clicked back on the ticket and on the location section, noticed that Stephens was going eastbound when he was pulled over.

Thinking out loud, she said, "But you were west of your home heading east. You were on your way home, not the other way around."

She pondered the significance of Stephen's having an alligator and possibly lying to the small-town cop but came up empty. She googled reptile refuge places in the area and was surprised how many there were. *Then again*, she thought, *it was south Florida where alligators are aplenty.*

Letting her mind wander on the case, the fact that Moye lived on water came to her. Seeing his back-yard slope down and give way to the water's edge, she wondered how that piece of the puzzle fit. She had always liked the idea of living on water, especially the beach. When her thoughts turned to water, she suddenly remembered Melinda Dalton had offered the possibility that Moye was the Hillsborough River Killer. Benitez had fantasized about making a career collar of a serial killer. It would be the ultimate catch. Her name would be hoisted up to legend status within the department. Snapping out of her reverie, she leaned back in her chair and eyed the bulky, gray metal cabinets that lined the back wall of the bureau. They held all the department's cold cases as well as the files from the unsolved serial murders.

Moving on, Benitez looked back toward her sushi to find the plastic tray empty. "Damn." She was still hungry. Undeterred, she dove deeper into Stephens's life. She pulled up another database. It was the Tampa PD's record management system. If Stephens had any official contact with the police, it would be recorded in this database.

Typing Harold Stephens into the query sections, she hit send and waited for the cyber search to finish. The page refreshed, and she was actually surprised to see Stephens's name pop up. He was one of four names with the same spelling. Surprised again, she saw an entry associated with the address of the person she had spoken to earlier in the night, confirming it was the right person.

Scrolling down, she bypassed his physical description, phone numbers, addresses, and related identification numbers. She wanted to see what kind of police interaction he'd been a part of.

In the latest contact, Stephens was listed as a "reporting person." This meant *he* had called the police. The report was titled as a burglary, and Benitez clicked on the report link. Stephens had reported a break-in at the school district headquarters where a few laptops and some loose change were stolen in the middle of the night. The officers suspected juveniles were responsible based on the small size shoe prints found on scene.

"He works for the school board?" An unsettling feeling crawled up her spine. Stephens's job title was listed as regional supervisor for information services. Benitez knew that was the long way of saying IT work. Another chill seized her body because she realized Stephens's reach into the school system was virtually boundless. He had access to every child in the county.

The burglary report briefly described Stephens as notifying the police of the break-in as it was reported to him by one of his subordinates. Otherwise, he was not involved in the case. Benitez backed out of that page and back to the list of contacts. There were three more, but all were substantially far apart from each other. The first encounter was at the inception of the database in 2002. The second was six years later in 2008 and the last 2011. Benitez was unsure how to check for any contacts prior to 2002, short of a physical search of over a hundred thousand records per year. She was unfamiliar with how these records were kept and managed prior to her joining the force. Relegated to the last fifteen years of records, she looked at the other three contacts with Stephens.

Benitez shot straight up in her swivel chair. She stared at the other three contacts, unsure if her eyes were lying. This couldn't be a coincidence, she thought. All three contacts were for the same type of cases. Missing person cases. In her short career, she had learned that coincidences didn't equal proof. It was the smoke to flame, not necessarily a three-alarm fire. Proceeding, careful not to get ahead of herself, she read through the first case. A missing girl, seemingly vanished while in transition from an after-school activity to home. Benitez sifted through the report until she found how exactly Stephens name was involved. Finding his name in a supplemental report, Stephens was contacted as a general canvass of school officials on scene during the time frame the girl went missing. He was among a list of seven names, five teachers, a janitor, and Stephens. Benitez read the summary from his interview where Stephens claimed to be running diagnostics on the school's network until after the time frame. Putting this through the suspect filter, Benitez noticed that his alibi wasn't confirmed.

She moved onto the other two missing persons cases. Both were of young, high-school-age girls from a second and third school, different from the first. The reason for his contact was something seemingly benign, but Benitez was no longer convinced. Her suspect filter was catching all the bullshit.

Benitez leaned back in her chair. She felt as if she were at a crossroads in the case. She had reason to suspect Stephens was her culprit, but these were all coincidences. Damming coincidences that screamed guilt, but she needed something more immediate to take action. Contemplating how to make this work for her, the large gray cabinets housing the cold cases in the far corner of the bureau caught her eye.

The voice of Melinda Dalton reminded her that she and her friends in the black van thought Stephens was the Hillsborough River Killer. At the moment, that didn't seem so far-fetched, she thought.

Not many times in her career had Benitez had an "ah ha" moment. Being a detective, she learned that finding out the identity of a suspect wasn't terribly challenging. It was the requisite proof and subsequent chase that always proved difficult. Rarely did an investigation come down do a single moment of convergence where the mystery puzzle piece was revealed. But when it did, there was an "ah ha" moment

Benitez grabbed a key ring off of Munroe's desk and ran over to the cold case files. She scanned the outside tabs looking for the right set of years. Finding the one that read 1995-1999, she fed the corresponding key into the lock and twisted. Pulling open the cabinet, she scanned each shelf for the Hillsborough River Killer cases. The files were all categorized by the victim's name, but when she saw *HRK* marked on the spine of several thick binders, she had found what she was looking for.

Pulling them out, she flipped open the first of twelve murder books and scanned the table of contents. She needed to check one reference to satisfy her theory. There, she read, book three contained a list of everyone ever interviewed, witness, suspect or otherwise in the case.

"Book three." She said, reading the numbers printed on the outside. Finding book three, she ripped it open, looking for the detailed list. Taking a moment, she realized she was near giddy, like a kid about to get the keys to a Porshe. Reading the list, she slid her finger down the yellowed, worn page scanning the names until one stuck out.

"Holy shit!" Benitez said. She ran back to her desk, picked up the phone and called her partner. She just had an "ah ha" moment.

***

The digital clock on the Sprinter's dash read three thirty-five a.m. Louis, Melinda and Beth listened intently as Curt stealthily moved through Harold Moye's house. Room by room Curt searched for any sign of Rachel and Layla Bragden. Louis pecked away at his keyboard while Beth kept watch down the street with the binoculars. Melinda twitched in her seat, staring at her cellular phone as if it were the missing linchpin that the success of the operation depended on.

Louis asked Curt for a second time, "Well, what did you figure out about the pictures, Curt?"

There was no answer and worry added to the already thick anxiety inside the van. They waited a minute for a response.

"He probably needed to go silent." Louis justified to the others, although his face contradicted his words.

"Dammit," Melinda said out of frustration. "She's not answering her cell and her desk phone keeps going to voice mail." She looked back at Louis. "Tell Curt I'm trying to get through to the detective, but she's not answering."

"It's late. She could've called it a night, Mel," Beth offered.

"Shit, you're right." She read the dash. "We're running out of time."

"Curt? Can you talk?" Louis asked.

Still nothing. The three exchanged apprehensive looks.

"Cough if you need comm silence?"

Nothing but silence.

"Somethings wrong," Beth stated. "This isn't like Curt at all."

"Have faith in the big guy," Louis said. "He'll come through. He has to."

Chapter 32

The surrealistic shock of her predicament began to lessen its harsh sting. Her thoughts became more rational instead of sporadic and fear laden. Moye had been cryptic when explaining his motivation, much to her displeasure, but Rachel began to understand that he needed to fulfill some sick fantasy that had been culminating over the last twenty years. He called Layla and all the other girls surrogates. They were substitutes for Rachel, meaning she was the one he truly desired. The more she tried to wrap her mind around that fact, the more she questioned why. He had shunned her advances when she was held captive the first time. Back then, Moye didn't even give her a second glance. She was an unwanted mistake. So, what changed?

Rachel listened for the potential rescuer to find her in the basement. She tried to follow Moye's footsteps as he investigated the noise, but it was as if he floated throughout the house like a wraith. Rachel couldn't hear anything after the door at the top of the stairs shut. All she heard was a slow slosh of water coming from below the floorboards and what she thought was a clicking sound that didn't make sense. It sounded organic, but she ignored it to focus on Moye and the rescuer.

A loud thud resonated from somewhere in the house down to the basement. Rachel couldn't make sense of that noise either, but her best guess was that Moye and the rescuer found one another, and the sound was a body hitting the floor. She hoped it was Moye.

Not waiting to find out who won or lost the confrontation, Rachel pulled vehemently at her bindings. Surprised, something came loose.

However, it wasn't the ropes around her wrists, but suddenly she was able to move her arms vertically. With no ability to see, she imagined Moye had her wrists anchored to the chair to limit her mobility. Now, with a little give at the ankle ropes, she was able to stand up enough to lift her arms over the chair back and have them flush against her back, giving her a small sense of relief in her shoulders. Without hesitation, she managed to slide her wrists around her bottom, against the back of her thighs and down to her feet. The ankle bindings stopped any further progress, but now she was able to manipulate the ropes around her legs. Bent over awkwardly on top of her own lap, Rachel rubbed her face against the top of her thighs until friction pulled the gag out of her mouth. Once free, she sucked in air freely and was able to concentrate more on freeing the rest of her. Furiously she began to pick at the knots, digging her fingernails into the tight folds until it hurt. Then, despite the pain, she pressed harder.

First her right leg kicked free, and she moved on to her left, again digging into the knots. Hunched over and concentrating on the bindings, Rachel's body was covered in sweat. She felt light-headed from the exertion and the awkward position, but she continued unabated. Her fingertips quickly rubbed raw against the scratchy twine of the ropes. Glancing down, she saw blood seeping from blisters formed around her fingernails.

The light from atop the stairs came on, pulling her attention away from her ankles. Forced to remain hunched over, she craned her neck up to see who was coming. Whoever was coming was almost at the door. Rachel could hear the sound of something heavy rolling away from the door. Looking down, the knot was taut and she had lost feeling in her fingertips. There was less than twenty seconds to free herself. She needed to think fast.

Rachel wrapped the loose rope back around her right leg, stood up in the chair enough to scoot her arms back up around her butt giving her the illusion of still being bound. The door cracked open and Rachel realized her arms were still flush against her back and not behind the chair. As the shadowy figure took the first step, Rachel popped up and reached her arms back to the other side of the chair. Remembering the gag, she wrenched her head to the right trying to use her shoulder to reinsert it into her mouth. It hung too low on her neck and had to shrug her shoulders repeatedly to inch the rag upward. She began to panic.

The shadowy figure stopped at the stop of the stairs. He twisted around turning his back to Rachel. She used the reprieve to get the gag back in her mouth. After a pause, she saw Moye coming down the stairs backward. He was pulling something through the door. Something large. An audible thud followed. He stepped backward to the next step down, then came another thud. This continued until Moye was at the bottom of the stairs dragging what looked like a body behind him. Rachel's eyes widened with fear knowing that her would-be rescuer failed. She tried to see around Moye's body as he dragged the latest victim into the far corner, to the left of the stairs.

Unconscious and barely breathing, Rachel noticed the person was dressed as a man, blue jeans and a buttoned up white shirt. She eliminated it being Beth or Melinda. He was too big to be Louis. Was it a neighbor? A burglar? A cop sent to investigate?

Moye hovered over the unconscious man while he bound his wrists and ankles together. Rachel watched in revolted horror as the man lay helpless, imprisoned in the same dungeon of hell as herself.

Stepping away from the lifeless body, Moye was stiff and agitated. He huffed, smoothed over his buttoned-down shirt and fixed his black-rimmed glasses back to the bridge of his nose, attempting to maintain his desired façade. Turning to Rachel, his glare cut right through her as if the man's presence was her fault. With it not being any of the three from the van, she felt bad, but not responsible for the rescue attempt. Moye disappeared in his dark corner and Rachel turned back to the heap of a body on the other side of the stairs.

A twitch and body-stiffening told Rachel the person was coming out of the stupor. A muffled moan came from the man as he began to roll around on the floor. Rachel watched, as his back still faced her. The man reached his bound hands up to the back of his head, touching a tender spot, feeling for what she assumed was for blood. As the man moved, a sense of familiarity crawled over Rachel sending a corresponding sick feeling to the pit of her stomach.

No, please God, no. Don't let it be, she prayed.

The man rolled over and his face came into the reach of the bare light bulb that hung above Rachel. They locked eyes and Rachel's heart sank to somewhere beneath the wood planks of the floor as she recognized him. Her eyes watered as she cursed the fact Curt Walker had been condemned to her hell.

Curt attempted to sit, but his bindings prevented him from doing so. Gagged in the same fashion as Rachel had been, he rolled over to face her, trying to convey strength in his eyes. But with his capture, the hopelessness was overwhelming and tears began to streak down her face.

"Do you know him?" Moye barked from the dark corner. Rachel didn't answer and tried to recall her tears, but they had already stained her cheeks. Moye stood up and moved in front of her. "Answer me?" he boomed, angrily.

Rachel shook her head. Moye's eyes narrowed. He turned and stood next to Curt, studying Rachel. With a violence she'd not yet seen from Moye, he stepped back and let loose a brutal kick to the lower back of Curt. His body torqued and winced in pain and after Moye delivered another, Rachel gave a sympathetic gasp through the gag.

"You sure about that?" Moye asked, his eyes glaring red with hate. "Do you know him, yes or no?"

Rachel wanted to admit it but was afraid Moye would only kill him a moment later. If she didn't, he would continue the relentless torture. He looked at Curt's face, his eyes told her not to give in to the tormentor, but her heart wanted desperately for the pain to stop. Again, ignoring her heart, she shook her head.

Moye delivered two more solid kicks to the back and stomach of Curt, each one just as vicious as the first. His guttural groans sent shockwaves through her soul, knowing she couldn't bear to watch much more. Moye knelt down and grabbed his head, forcing him to look at her.

"You were going to try and take her from me, weren't you?"

Curt remained insolently silent.

213

Moye looked up at Rachel with contempt. He pushed Curt forward while he stood up and turned to the work bench behind the stairs. He grabbed something from the bench and knelt back down behind Curt. Dread caused chills to run up Rachel's spine, knowing whatever Moye grabbed, it was to further torment Curt.

Moye placed his left arm under Curt's neck holding his head up. Then, he slowly slid the blade of a K-bar knife to Curt's throat, pressing the razor-sharp steel against the soft skin of his neck. "I told you if one of your friends from the van got in my way, I'd kill them. I hope you didn't think I was kidding, Rachel."

"No, pweese. Doan do it." She begged Moye through the gag.

"No, Rachel. You don't understand. You're a part of me." Moye steadied the knife. "Just like I am a part of you."

Curt struggled, but with the combination of his bindings and Moye's chokehold, he was powerless to defend himself. Rachel pulled at her own bonds, but the rage wasn't enough, and she couldn't break free. She began to sob and begged Moye not to hurt him.

"If this will make you understand, Rachel, then that's the way it has to be." Moye braced himself against Curt's tensed body. Curt's nostrils flared, his eyes went wide with fear. Moye flexed the arm holding the knife to make the kill go quick and efficiently.

In a moment of clarity, Rachel's world slowed to a crawl. The moments ticked by as if caught on a slow-motion reel, everything except her thoughts which fired in rapid succession. Refusing to watch her friend die before her, she had to act fast. Her thoughts turned to Rhonda. Visions of Moye carrying her away that final time flashed where Rhonda had a look of defeat. She had lost her will. The anguish on Curt's face spoke to the reasons he wanted to live, his son being the main one. He was yet to be defeated. Rachel couldn't let that happen. Rhonda might be lost, but Curt was not. She knew what needed to be done.

"I'm ready," Rachel said in a low, calm tone.

Moye heard the statement and froze, the blade had already sliced the outer layer of skin, causing blood to trickle out. He looked at Rachel and then down at Curt as if asking what he should do. She spoke again. "I'm ready."

Moye shoved Curt away like refuse and stepped over to Rachel, studying her closely. "Is this a trick?"

She shook her head again, holding his stare.

His breathing grew excited, his eyes gleamed bright with an evil lust. He cut the gag off with the K-bar letting it fall to the floor.

"I'm ready. I'm ready to be a part of you again," she said, calmly. Fighting against every instinct in her body, she resolved to return to that hollowness from her tormented past. To climb into the familiar emptiness she found when she took on another lover—novice or seasoned—and hid until they finished. She would give him the illusion of desire.

Curt moaned in the corner, but it went ignored.

"The ropes. Cut them off," she said with assertiveness.

Moye hesitated. She could see his psychotic desire battling with his self-preservation. She didn't have his complete trust. She held his stare and seductively bit her bottom lip. After a moment, the desire proved to be victor, and Moye sliced off the ropes from her wrists. Rachel stood vulnerable and exposed, standing face to face with Moye.

"This is what you've wanted all these years, isn't it? For me to give myself to you."

Moye shuddered in ecstasy. "Yes, finally." He reached up and ran his fingers down her naked side. "I've waited so long for this."

"Well, here I am." She said, offering herself to Moye. "I'm ready."

Chapter 33

After several rings, a tired and groggy voice answered. "Munroe."

"Sal, it's Sandy. I got something and I'm not sure it can wait."

An exhaustive sigh blew through the phone's receiver. Benitez was sure she heard her partners head hit the pillow. "What time is it?"

"It's like three in the morning."

"You caught a case? We're not up for another week and a half." His confusion was obvious.

"No, it's the Layla Bragden case. I got something."

"The runaway?"

Benitez instantly grew angry at her senior partner. "No, Goddammit," she snapped. "She's not a fucking runaway. She was kidnapped and I got a suspect lead, and I need your help."

Only silence was heard on the other end. Benitez regretted her attitude, but she wasn't going to let it slide. She was right about Layla being a victim, and it was time to make her partner see it the same way. She had found something on Moye and needed Monroe's guidance to make a move.

"Alright, alright," Munroe grunted. She could tell he was getting out of bed so he wouldn't bother his wife any further. "Let me go to the office."

Benitez waited. Her eyes bounced from her computer screen to Book Three of the HRK case file opened to the interview list, making sure what she read made sense and that she wasn't getting her hopes up.

"Alright, Sandy. What'cha got?"

Benitez filled her sleepy partner in on finding the shoe at the school along with the pock-marked window glass. When Munroe didn't react, she added that she came up with a suspect, Harold Stephens, but had reason to believe he was lying about his name.

"Where'd you get his name from?"

"Cross referencing school officials with access to Layla's school the night of the dance and looking for those who fit the profile, you know, unsuspecting white guys who live alone." Benitez lied. She didn't know how Munroe would take the truth of being approached by a secret team in search of a kidnapped teammate, but she decided to play it as is for now.

Thick with skepticism, Munroe asked, "And you corroborated his name with something?"

"Well, that's where it gets interesting."

"Dammit, Sandy. It's fucking late. You should've started with interesting, get to it or I'm hanging up."

"Sorry." Benitez took a deep breath, ready to share her "ah ha" moment. "I think he's the Hillsborough River Killer."

Benitez waited for her partner's reaction. During the silence, she envisioned her partner finally seeing her as an equal and the accolades were loading up.

"Jesus Christ, Sandy. You called me for that shit?"

"What?" she said, incredulous.

Sal Munroe moaned. By the sound tailing off, she knew he had moved the phone away from his face in frustration.

"Sal, I'm serious," she countered.

"If I had a nickel for every time some enterprising rookie asshole came to me with the latest discovery of the serial killer that got away, I'd have sailed off in the sunset on a friggin yacht. Do you have anything of substance on the girl or not?"

"Sal, I'm serious. Stop being a fucking ass, right now. I know it's late. But this guy Stephens, listen to this: He was interviewed three times, the first in '02, the others in '08 and '11. All three cases were of missing girls, just like Layla. *All* are still considered missing. That's not a coincidence, Sal. That's a suspect!"

Benitez paused to let her sluggish partner register all of the information.

"And Sal, this guy Stephens…," Benitez paused for effect, "he's on the witness list from HRK. You talked to him about Laura Diaz."

"Get the fuck out!"

"Nope. I'm looking at the wit-list from the cold case file. His name's right here." She said modestly, but had a proud grin from ear-to-ear. "He was interviewed as having access to the school after hours, but clearly nothing about him screamed *doer* back then. And to top it off, Sal, this guy lives in the Lake Osceola neighborhood, you know, that big lake in east Tampa that's connected to the Hillsborough River."

"Oh my God." Benitez knew her partner was fully aware that the dumpsite of Laura Diaz and the two others were along the river bank of the Hillsborough River which earned the killer the obvious moniker. She waited for him to say more, but the other end went quiet. Sal was impressed, she thought and didn't need to see his face to know it. She realized that the senior partner had just experienced his own "ah ha" moment.

Finally, he spoke, "Let me get dressed and I'll head in."

Chapter 34

With the ropes that bound her wrists gone, Rachel rubbed them, hoping the pain would go away. Moye circled her slowly like a shark testing its prey. His eyes were full of lust but remained cautious. He still gripped the K-Bar knife tightly in his hand.

"My ankles?" she asked gently.

Moye contemplated the request and continued to size up Rachel. She remained still, ready to give herself in sacrifice to save Curt. She let her arms fall back to her side, letting Moye take in her womanly form with his eyes. Unable to help himself, Moye reached up with trembling hands to caress Rachel's breasts, her stomach, waist, neck, and lips. His glaring eyes ogled along with his groping hands. Rachel shot a glance over to Curt who watched helplessly from the corner of the room.

After he was done, she reminded him, "My ankles? Cut them loose."

Moye hesitated, but only for a second before dropping down and running the blade of the K-Bar between her legs and the rope, slicing them away in two quick movements. Rachel stepped away from the chair and stood as if she were a prize model on the runway trying to catch the eye of a Hollywood producer.

Drinking her in, Moye stood there. His face was flushed and he let out a lustful shudder. He stepped over to Rachel, stopping only inches away from her face. He inhaled, taking a slow deep breath of her essence as if she were fuel for his body to survive. Rachel stood still, allowing him to do as he pleased. Both hands, his right still gripping the knife, reached up to her shoulders and peeled away her bra strap, letting it fall down her arms. He pressed the knife to the top of her left shoulder and gently ran the flat part of the blade down and across her chest. He moved it back, lightly scraping against her skin. The sensation sent alarming shockwaves through her body, knowing that with a simple turn and thrust, the knife could end her life.

"You like the way that feels, Rachel? The sharp blade rubbing against your soft skin?"

"Yes," she said, giving in to the danger.

Moye moved behind Rachel, but kept the knife against her body, moving it to her back. Moye ran the knife down her back, over her underwear, and along the back of her legs. Moving down her left, and up her right, continuing the sickening foreplay.

Moye stood up and then pressed his body against the back of Rachel's. He swung his left arm around Rachel's neck in a hug but held the knife in front of her face. He twisted it around giving her the full display.

"You know what they say about knives right?"

"No."

"You're not playing coy again, are you?"

Rachel shook her head slowly. Moye kept the K-Bar directly in front of her face. "Well, they say that a man's knife is in direct proportion to his genitalia." Moye dangled the knife loosely in what she believed was an attempt to impress her.

"Oh yeah?" she said.

Rachel turned around to face Moye. She gave him a playful grin and a flirtatious glance downward.

Moye grew uneasy at the advance but smiled in acceptance, ready to travel this road he had created. Rachel reached out for his crotch, rubbing him from the outside of his pants. Moye exhaled and trembled. Most of his prey had been inexperienced and obligated out of fear as opposed to desire.

"I'm ready," Rachel said. She eyed the knife and Moye understood, instantly dropping it to the floor.

"We are a part of each other, Rachel and finally will finish what we started."

Moye reached around Rachel's body to embrace her half-naked physique.

"Yes, we will, but first...." Rachel released his crotch and stepped back stopping Moye's advance. Rachel's arms disappeared behind her back, reaching for her bra clasp. "You want to see the woman I've become?"

"Oh, yes."

As Rachel reached behind her, Moye's devilish eyes became fixated on her breasts. His mouth gaped open, and he ran his tongue along his lips in lustful anticipation. Taking a half step backward, Rachel dropped her arms by her side but her bra remained. She planted her left leg, took a quick step and let loose a mighty kick that landed directly between Moye's legs. His body leapt up from the blow and fell to the floor in agony.

With Moye writhing on the floor, Rachel turned and ran to Curt's side. He sported a smile underneath the gag as she fiddled with his bindings trying to work them loose, pleased at her deception.

"We have to find a way out of here." She said.

"Up da sayers," he managed.

"Huh?"

"Da sayers." He nodded behind Rachel. She twisted and saw what he was talking about.

"Oh, the stairs. Yes. Obviously."

Struggling to get his hands free, Rachel wasn't having much success.

"Watts out." Curt said.

"What?"

A shadow grew over Curt. The kick to Moye's groin didn't last as long as Rachel had hoped. She rolled forward, falling over Curt just missing a would-be fatal slash of the K-Bar knife.

Scrambling to her feet, Moye hissed, "You bitch! Now, I'm going to kill you. But it'll be slow and painful, just like your sister!"

221

The rage inside Rachel never subsided. It reached its pinnacle, but Moye held the advantage, being armed. Rachel scanned her surroundings for a weapon while Moye crept closer, knife held steady, poised for an attack. Backing up to keep space between them, her frantic search for a weapon came up empty. The wooden counter she had spied behind the stairs had abruptly stopped Rachel's retreat. Moye stalked closer. Trapped, she reached to her right and left while she kept her eyes fixed on Moye. Finally, she found something that felt weapon worthy. She grabbed it and as Moye lunged forward, leading with a thrust of the razor-sharp blade, she blindly swung it forward. The head of a rubber mallet crunched the backside of Moye's knife hand, sending the K-Bar skidding across the basement floor. Before Rachel could reload for another swing, Moye's right hand shot out with lightning quickness and grabbed her throat in a viselike squeeze.

Instinctively, Rachel dropped the mallet and used both hands to fight against Moye's clutch. A sinister glower burned in his eyes as Rachel struggled against his grip. The strength the demonic man possessed was astounding, and Rachel began to panic as she suddenly got light-headed. She tried to kick, but with Moye's anomalous power, he lifted her half-naked body up off the floor. Pinning her against the wood counter, Rachel tried to kick her legs, but with no room for leverage her efforts were futile. As she clawed at Moye's hand, she gasped for breath, feeling the edges of her peripheral vision start to fade.

"Stop fighting it, Rachel." Moye added a cocky smile to the malevolent hate. "Once you pass out, the real fun begins."

Her opposition resulted in a pathetic gurgling sound, not the battle cry she intended. The dark edges were closing in. Rachel got so close, only to fail.

Kicking, clawing, and pulling at Moye's hands, Rachel fought and decided to fight until everything went dark. Focusing on the porthole of vision that remained, Rachel didn't understand why suddenly she was at floor level; her breathing was unrestricted and her vision widened. She pushed up off the floor, looked back to find an answer and continue the fight.

"You're going to pay for that, friend," Moye sneered, while collecting himself up off the floor. He stood tall over Curt, looking down with hate burning in his eyes. Still bound at the wrists and ankles, lying on the floor next to Moye, Curt was helpless. Before Rachel could react, Moye grabbed the rubber mallet and struck down toward Curt's head. From her angle, Rachel couldn't see where the blow landed, but Curt's body went limp, and she feared the worst.

With her bearings back, Rachel stood up and spied a wooden, butcher-block cutting board with blood stains sitting on the counter where the mallet was found. She peeled it up, reared back, and while Moye was hovering over Curt, she let loose an unbridled swing smashing the corner of the cutting board against the back of Moye's head. A wet thud emanated as Rachel followed through and brought the board up over her head. Moye staggered forward, the impact not quite enough to knock him out, but he moved sluggishly. Rachel stayed in step with him, aiming the makeshift weapon to the back of Moye's head as he tried to get away. Keeping in striking distance, Rachel slammed down the heavy wood board against the back of his head, but it missed, hitting him flush along the neck and top of his back, mitigating the damage. Rachel re-gripped the wood for another try, but a swift kick landed in her stomach expelling all the air in her lungs.

Gasping for air, Rachel backed up quickly and weathered the strike. Moye clambered away, and Rachel stepped forward and let the board loose, sending it hurtling toward Moye like a Frisbee. It crashed against his jaw in a perfect throw, knocking him to the floor. Rachel enjoyed a moment of elation before realizing that she needed to keep going. She needed to end Moye.

The contrast of the black K-Bar blade against the wooden plank floor caught her attention. She ran past Moye to retrieve it across the basement. A leg kicked out tripping Rachel, sending her crashing to the floor. Moye leapt up and pounced on her, grabbed her hair in a malicious rage, pulled her head back, and slammed it down to the floor with all his weight. Rachel held her hands to soften the hard landing, but the pain caused flashes to pop in the corners of her eyes.

Through clenched, gritted teeth, Moye spat, "You're not going to get away from me this time, you little bitch!"

A violent flip of Rachel's body sent a hard elbow smashing into the other side of Moye's jaw, knocking him back with surprise. Completely on her back, she kicked, with both legs landing in the center of Moye's chest. He flew back, tripping against the base of the stairs and falling from exhaustion. Rachel crawled over to the knife and grabbed it. She sat up gripping the knife outward. She eyed Moye as he winced in pain and exhaustion. He glared back, studying her as an adversary and not prey. Rachel sensed his fear sending the pendulum of control toward her.

She stood up and began approaching Moye. Glancing over at Curt, she saw he hadn't moved and was lying still. She wanted to go to him, but she had to deal with Moye first. Turning her attention back to her captor, she squeezed the knife in her hand ready to plunge it into his black heart. Moving around the chair in the center of the room, she saw a wicked smile crease Moye's face. An uneasy feeling seized Rachel, erasing the control she had felt a moment ago. She froze in place, preparing for another attack. Moye jumped, but not toward Rachel. He moved to his side, next to the staircase, grabbed the mysterious stick in the floor and yanked it backward. Rachel braced herself for the repercussion, but a sensation of weightlessness came over her. The floor gave way. Suddenly, Rachel was falling helplessly into a black abyss.

Chapter 35

The blow from the cutting board caused an incessant ringing in Moye's ears, muting all other sounds in the basement. His head ached and his heart hung low, having had to flush Rachel down into the depths of darkness. *It was her decision*, he thought, it was she who resisted their connection, and it was not his fault. Sitting on the bottom step of the stairs, he rubbed his jaw and tried to catch his breath.

Replaying the scene from moments before, he grew angry. She had tricked him. She was his most prized beauty, given their history, and she failed to see they were a part of each other. She said she did, but that was part of her treachery. Twenty years of longing to complete the connection was all for naught, he realized. It was time wasted, fulfilling his desire through unworthy substitutes. An emptiness that began to consume him.

A slight movement caught his attention. Turning toward the intruder, Moye saw he was fighting his way out of the dredges of unconsciousness. Still alive. A soft moan let him know his hearing had returned, and he realized too, he needed to dispose of this filth before he caused any more problems. Remembering his coveted knife fell into oblivion with Rachel, he needed to get something else to do the job. Moye stood and ascended the steps, returning to the main part of the house and turning his back completely on where Rachel had been. Stopping in the kitchen, he pulled the butcher knife from its block to assess its potential savagery. He thumbed the edge and knew with a powerful slice, he would drain the life of the intruder instantly.

Another thought occurred to Moye as he set the knife down and went to the living room. As he rounded the corner, the image of Rachel, the fake reporter sitting on the couch, excited him, but a sharp sense of disappointment followed, realizing the final outcome and her demise. Shaking off the reverie, he knelt by where she had sat and reached underneath the sofa. Finding what he was looking for, he disconnected a plug, unhooked a hose, and pulled it out. It was one of many machines he'd built over the years, this one the most updated version. Its beauty was in its simplicity and commonplace usage.

Moye opened up the housing and removed the liquid tray inside. Taking stock of the clear watery liquid, he calculated there was enough left to effectively deal with the intruder. Snapping the housing shut, he gathered up his tiny machine and stood to return to the basement.

The sound of a car door slamming shut came from just outside of the house. Worry gripped Moye. He set the machine down and peeked out the window. A maroon Chevy Impala with tinted windows sat across the street. Detective Benitez was back, accompanied by a fat, dark-haired man walking toward the house. Had she found something on her last visit that warranted a closer look? Damming evidence, perhaps? He was convinced she planted that ridiculous pink barrette. Keying in on the man, Moye recognized him, but from a distant past. Searching, scanning his memories, he remembered, never forgetting a face. The name came to him just as quick, Detective Salvatore Monroe, homicide unit for the Tampa police. Monroe had come around the school and questioned him about a missing girl who had in fact been one of his beloved beauties sent off to the far reaches of the netherworld. He had pacified him with faux sincerity and a plausible alibi, it had been quite easy, actually.

"What the hell are you doing here?" Moye asked no one.

The detectives discussed something at the back of the car while staring at the house. Whatever they had planned, Moye felt he had to cut ties and run. So much had gone wrong in the last few hours, a bitter anger left him reeling in frustration. It all started when Rachel knocked on his door. He took it as a serendipitous moment to take advantage of, but it resulted in the complete opposite. An utter disaster.

After the first visit by the female detective, he had been able to fully disguise the truth, but with their return, he questioned its effectiveness. What had he missed? What had they found? Moye scanned the living room looking for damning evidence but saw nothing. He kept watching, trying to figure out their plans. Daybreak was approaching and cops don't show up to your house at that time without the intention of taking action.

The two cops looked to the side of the house and began their approach. Moye had to act fast or face the police and subsequent consequences. Taking stock of the situation, he realized he hadn't sanitized the basement, erasing any evidence that Rachel was held captive. The presence of the intruder added to the exposure and the likelihood of the truth being unveiled grew exponentially. It was time to cut and run, but unlike last time, the cops would be close behind.

"Shit!" Moye dropped the machine on the couch and tip-toed to the master bedroom on the opposite side of the house from the detectives. He grabbed up a few essentials, knowing he would never see the rest again. He listened out for the detectives, and when he couldn't hear what progress they were making, he slipped open his window and climbed out into the darkness of the pre-dawn morning.

***

"What do you mean you've already searched it?" Detective Monroe asked with a sharp edge in his tone. Detective Benitez told him about Melinda Dalton and the mysterious three who told her that Harold Stephens was actually Harold Moye and claimed a colleague had been ensnared by Moye.

"It was late. I didn't want to bother you. Plus, you haven't exactly been Supercop on the missing girl case. So, I made a judgment call," Benitez answered.

"Okay, fine. What's done is done. Tell me how that went?"

Benitez relayed her detailed search of the house and the cat and mouse game she and Moye had played. She hoped her account would elevate her respect level in the senior detective rather than lower it because of her actions, but he held a flat look on his face while listening and thinking. It was impossible for her to tell which way he was leaning.

"Okay, we'll… It's going to be hard to get a judge to sign a search warrant if you've already searched it and found nothing."

"What would we need? Something new?"

"Yeah, or something exigent."

The silence of the pre-dawn morning was peaceful and reminded Benitez of the long nights she spent on the midnight shift. The early morning hour was her favorite part of the shift. Even the cretins had turned in and the rest of the world was just waking up. Standing at the back of her Impala with Monroe, she looked up toward the sky to see the smoke-colored clouds racing by, bringing a cool gust of air with them.

As the wind whisked by, Benitez heard a faint yell coming from the side of the house. Unsure if it was the wind, her imagination, or real, she paused for confirmation. The breeze trailed off and the silence returned.

She heard it again. She looked at Monroe for his reaction, but he kept the flat face.

"You hear that?" she asked. Worried that her older partner would further chastise her for "making up" an emergency as an excuse to enter a home, she waited.

"Actually, yeah. I did," he replied, giving her relief.

The two detectives crossed the street and made their way down the driveway that ran along the side of the house. The sound was still distant. Making their way to the back of the house, there was a privacy fence with a wooden gate latched shut. Closer to the noise, it came again, it's origin beyond the fence. Benitez looked back to her partner for validation that they could continue without a warrant. The case was too big to lose on a technicality.

"Sounds like exigency to me, Sandy." Benitez smiled and pulled her weapon from the holster. She pulled the gate open and stood at the threshold. She fished out a small handheld flashlight and led the way in the darkened back yard. The yard immediately sloped down, making its way to the water's edge. She scanned the back of the house, shining her light in the windows before crossing in front of them. With blinds or curtains on the inside, the light couldn't penetrate further into the house. The back of the house jutted outward over the water, but there was an enclosure held up by concrete stilts below the main house that struck Benitez as odd. There was a small deck off the back door; it too was covered with vertical blinds.

The noise, clear but still faint, returned. It came from the area of the water. Scanning the rest of the yard, she noticed that the near side of the yard was built up, to hold the foundation of the house, a detached garage set in the back, and the driveway led to the road. The far side of the yard fell at a sharp decline to an inlet from the lake. She could tell that water ran beneath this part of the house.

Standing on the edge of the abutment, she looked down to the water. Shrubbery, reeds, and overgrowth at the rim of the lake made it difficult for her to see, but she stood there waiting for the sound one more time. All she heard was the sloshing of water, too heavy and quick to be the slow tiny waves of the still lake lapping at the edge, but like something moving in the water itself.

"You think it's coming from down there?" Monroe whispered.

"Yeah." Benitez nodded and then met her partner's eyes. He was on edge just as she was. "That's not part of the house that I searched. That's another part, because I never saw any stairs or anything going down." She replayed the earlier search in her mind, verifying she didn't miss any stairs or access to a basement or any type room under the house. She turned to Monroe and whispered back, "Matter of fact, I have no idea how to get down there."

Chapter 36

If this was hell, Rachel thought, it wasn't anything like she expected. It was dark, cold, and she had arrived as she was, dressed in just her underwear. The weightlessness remained, which seemed odd, but a dull ache began to build in her shoulders that she couldn't explain. Something didn't register. There wasn't a final exit, and there was no curtain fall other than the trap door opening up and her passing through. Was it a gateway directly to hell? Was this the entrance to the abyss?

Then she blinked. The earthly realm she thought she vacated came back, assaulting her senses all at once. The light from the basement flooded downward giving shape to some sort of macabre grotto. As she remembered the creatures that stirred below the floorboards, she looked down to see her feet dangling several feet above water. Wrenching her neck upward, she found she had managed to grip a support beam under the trap door opening and was holding on for her life. The creatures below materialized. She saw a long, scaly back with a spiked tail slowly sloshing on the surface. The unmistakable sight of an alligator sent a wave of panic shooting through her body. Twisting around, she looked for a landing suitable to avoid the carnivorous animals but found nothing other than the water. Her only option was to go back up, into the dungeon, to face Moye.

She reassessed her grip and knew she had only a few more moments until her grip weakened and she would plummet down to face the gators. Pulling herself up was the only viable option, but just as she prepared to hoist herself back through the trap door, peering at her through the darkness was a simple, set of eyes. Beyond belief, Rachel didn't trust her own eyes, and she reconsidered the possibility of her falling into hell. But, as her pupils dilated on the dark face, a form took shape around the eyes. It was a girl.

"Layla? Layla, is that you?"

The eyes came to life. She was wedged tightly in a tiny nook just under the floorboards on top of the muddy embankment that helped support the house above. Rachel could see scratch and claw marks just below where she hid, knowing the alligators had tried to reach her but failed due to the steep incline.

"Layla! Oh thank God. It is you."

Rachel began to breathe heavy as her hold on the cross beam began to loosen and fire burned in her forearm muscles.

"Um…, well…. We got to get you out of here." There wasn't enough room in Layla's hiding place for the two of them, and if Rachel swung down, she doubted the muddy embankment would allow her to stay out of the reptiles' reach.

The girl didn't budge. "Layla, can you move, honey? Are you hurt?"

Reacting slowly, she shook her head. Her teeth were clattering uncontrollably. Rachel recognized the sound from earlier.

"Okay, listen. I can't hold on here for much longer, and I don't know when he's coming back, so we have to hurry."

Layla didn't move. *Shit*, she thought.

"Curt!" Rachel cried. "Curt, can you hear me? Please, we need help."

There was no reaction. Rachel yelled out again and waited, but nothing. She feared he was dead. Surely, Moye would have moved onto Curt after sending her hurtling through the trap door.

"Goddamnit, Layla. Listen to me!" Rachel snapped. "We are getting out of here, and I'm getting you back to your mother." Rachel ignored the muscle fatigue as she clung to the crossbeam. She had to think quick, she needed to get Layla up through the hatch. With her grip sure to fail, she had to act fast.

"Now, you have to jump out to me. I'll catch you and help you up, then we can get out of here."

Rachel readjusted her grip, giving each arm a reprieve by dangling by the other. Her strength was leaving her fast. She feared if Layla didn't hurry, she would jump too late and pull them both into the mouths of the hungry gators. Looking down, she counted at least two circling the surface.

"Layla, c'mon honey. Please!"

"You'll take me to my mom?" She asked, her voice weak.

"Yes, honey. Of course. But please, hurry."

Pushing out of her little pocket, she moved as far to the edge as she could. She was sizing up all of the space and judging whether she could make it.

"Just jump as far as you can and reach for my hand. I'll catch you." Rachel sounded assured but was scared she would fail.

Layla retracted back into her nook and locked eyes with Rachel. Rachel read a determination in the girl's eyes.

"You can do this."

Layla shot out from the dark crevice and leapt forward, arms pushed out far toward Rachel. She focused on the girl's hand and hanging from her left, held out her right arm. With the skill and precision of a trapezist, Rachel grabbed Layla's wrist as she clamped tightly to hers. Her momentum swung both of them wildly under the opening of the trap door like a pendulum full of speed. Too excited that it worked, Rachel failed to realize Layla's feet dangled only a few feet from the surface.

Looking down at the girl, Rachel spied movement stirring in the water. An open elongated pink and white mouth rose out of the water aimed for Layla's left leg. Rachel pulled the girl up as much as she could at the awkward angle and the gator fell back after snapping inches away from Layla's leg, and catching nothing but empty air.

The move sapped just about all of Rachel's strength, and she feared she'd doomed them both in her haste. She let Layla back down, still holding on to the crossbeam with one arm.

"Okay, listen. You need to help me. Please, climb up me as best as you can. I can't lift you anymore. I need my other hand to help hold us up. Do you understand?"

"Uh huh." Layla's eyes were wide with fear, but ready to follow directions. She reached around Rachel's waist and hugged tight. As soon as Rachel could, she reached up, gripping the crossbeam with both hands. She felt a little stronger, but knew the girl had to do the rest of the work.

Rachel spread out her legs to give Layla more of a base to climb on.

Layla started moving, scrambling to get her feet somewhere near Rachel's hips but settled on the crease of her knee. Readjusting her grip on Rachel's shoulder, the sweat made her hand slide off. Layla lost her balance and felt back down.

"No!" Rachel, held her legs out wide to help hold Layla as she squeezed her midsection tight.

"I can't do it," she whined.

"Yes, you can. You don't have another choice, honey."

Layla whimpered, "I'm scared."

Rachel let out a quick chuckle. "So am I, Layla. But, if we don't, we're going to be those damn things' dinner."

The earlier determination that fueled her jump returned. Rachel's grip was sliding, and there was an inferno burning in her forearm muscles. Layla clambered again, stepping on the inside of Rachel's knee, then pulling up on her shoulder. Before she slipped again, she planted a foot on Rachel's hip and pushed up. The girl's navel was moving past Rachel's face and she could feel the relief of the lightened load as Layla had a hold on the crossbeam herself.

Underneath, Rachel saw the same pink and white mouth shoot out of the water and go straight for her leg this time.

"Oh, shit!" she cried as she twisted out of the way. The gator missed again and fell back into the water on its side. "Okay, seriously, hurry and get out of the damn way."

Layla stepped on Rachel's shoulders with her bare feet and then pulled herself up into the opening. Rachel prayed Moye hadn't returned, and they had time. She had survived so much when it came to her captor, for it to end now would be unfair, she thought.

A cramp seized her right arm and she lost her grip of the crossbeam. Letting go, her left arm barely hung on with the strength of three fingers, and they too began to slip.

There was a calm acceptance that embraced Rachel, like that of a gentle touch of a loved one telling you, "It'll be okay," in times of need. Death no longer frightened her. She had set out to save Layla Bragden and so far, she had. If the girl managed to survive the trap door and a pit full of alligators, she could make it out of the house. Then she thought of Curt. If he was dead, she would soon join him, and maybe they could help save children from heaven, and if not, then he would see to it that Layla got back to her mother safely. It would all be worth it, she thought. Then she thought of Rhonda. Rachel had gotten her answer, albeit a vague one, but she knew her sister was dead, and Moye only said those things to further incite her. Images of Melinda, Beth, Louis, and Alexis floated in her mind, and she was happy to be a part of their team. Even though it was a short life, she was ready.

Two fingers were left holding her entire weight and she contemplated letting go. She looked to the opening for anyone to help her, but there was only the bare light bulb that shone brightly. She looked down, spying one bony-plated back snaking through the water. She didn't see its friend, but then a dark green nose pushed up through the surface straight under her, its mouth opened wide. She could see the pink of the mouth and tongue, the razor-sharp teeth, and the tiny dark of the animal's throat.

Two deafening pops boomed from above Rachel, causing her to jump, even while suspended in air. Blood sprayed from the gators mouth, and its ascent toward Rachel's dangling leg was cut off as it snapped its mouth shut and fell back in the water.

Rachel's two-fingered grip gave way, and she began her descent downward but was abruptly halted with a violent jerk as something placed a vise-grip around her wrist. She looked up and saw the silhouette of a person bent down in a squat holding onto her with both hands.

"Curt?" Her eyes failed to adjust in the light. "Is that you?"

There was a second person standing on the opposite side of the opening, aiming a gun down at the water.

"I got you." It was a woman's voice, with a hint of Latin, not Curt. There was a sincerity and compassion behind the voice that Rachel instantly trusted. Incredulous, Rachel was speechless, but worried about the absence of Curt. Her strength renewed, she gripped the strong hands that held her and allowed herself to be pulled out of the grotto and back into the basement.

Climbing out of the alligator pit, the two silhouettes materialized into two people with badges clipped to their belts. Her mind raced trying to connect everything together. This must be the detective that was working Layla's case, Rachel thought. As the rest of her senses refocused, she saw one cop knelt next to her while the other was helping Curt up. She was relieved he was alive. Rachel spun around in a panic until she saw Layla standing at the foot of the stairs, pitiful and emaciated, but also still alive, and with a vibrant smile across her face, silently thanking Rachel for her heroinism. Rachel smiled back.

Catching her breath, the female cop asked, "You must be Rachel?"

Ignoring the question, the reason that brought them all together suddenly dawned on Rachel. "Where's Moye? Did you catch him? Is he under arrest?"

The detective's face frowned and answered, "No. We looked but I think he escaped out of a window in his bedroom. We heard you and came down here first."

"He got away?" she asked with heavy disappointment.

"He couldn't have gone far. We have a shit ton of cops on the way to look for him. Even a helicopter and a K-9. This bastard's not getting away this time."

Rachel found solace in the detective's enthusiasm.

"Here miss." The male half, a heavy Italian looking fellow with a brilliant mustache offered a blanket to cover herself with. Rachel had forgotten she was still in her underwear.

The two detectives began barking orders through their radios, ascending the stairs and back out to the front of the house. They coordinated a manhunt for Moye, summoned EMS to the scene for Layla, Curt, and Rachel, and called in a slew of personnel to work the crime scene. Benitez escorted Layla Bragden back through the house so she could later be delivered back to her mother. On her way out, Rachel heard the Latina detective curse at the top of the stairs, "The Goddamn door was hidden by the deep freeze. Can you believe that shit?"

Curt was still woozy from the violent blow to the head and Rachel was drained from the acrobatics and reptile dodging. Battered and bruised, together they managed to help each other up the stairs and outside. There, Louis, Melinda, and Beth awaited them with open arms and tear-soaked eyes.

Chapter 37

The mechanical roar of a delivery truck downshifting and its large tires splashing into a day-old puddle woke Lucas Millwood from his drunken stupor. Only half-way aroused, he leaned forward in the seat of his Mustang and looked around, trying to get his bearings as the truck pulled up to the front of the store. It was still dark as the blue-gray sky of the morning hadn't yet transitioned into day.

"Where am..." As soon as the fog cleared his eyes, he remembered he was in the usual hangout parking lot of the shopping center. His head was still swimming from the beer. He wiped his face, trying to lessen the inebriation of the emotional night. His stomach churned, feeling volatile like a rumbling volcano. In his mind, he imagined the bile, beer, and last night's dinner mixing in a tumbling action. The imagery was too real, and he fumbled for the door handle. Grabbing at the handle, he fought back the urge to vomit, but only managed to delay it until the door was opened. Luke retched outside onto the ground several times. Afterwards, his head felt like someone had smashed it with a hammer. However, the swimming feeling from a moment ago had gone.

He grabbed the stale, watery Coke from the center console and sipped the warm soda to combat the vomit taste in his mouth. It was that or more beer, and the mere thought made him gag.

Luke cranked up the car and the dash clock read six forty-nine a.m.

"Holy shit. I'm in so much deep shit." He laughed to himself. He'd missed his curfew by over six hours, and he knew there was going to be hell to pay.

A cool breeze, wet with the morning dew blew through the interior of the car. He sucked in a deep breath, trying to clear his head completely. He looked around the parking lot and up toward the store front. Several of the employees had already reported for work and more vendor trucks were parked out front, bringing in their wares for the day. The thought of food made his stomach churn in a bad way.

He reached over and pulled his door shut. He fished out his phone, but the battery was dead.

"Dammit."

Searching the center console, he removed a car charger and plugged in his phone. The battery symbol lit up his screen but wouldn't power up. It needed more of a base charge to turn on. Luke imagined there'd be a million text messages and missed phone calls from his mom or dad wondering where he was. A month, or two months of being grounded, he weighed. Whatever, he thought.

Wiping his face one last time before driving, knowing the effects of the alcohol were still present, he hoped he was well enough to drive. Remembering what a buddy told him to do to sober up faster, he slapped the side of his face hard, then again hoping to invigorate him to the point of sobriety. Surprisingly, it worked and hurt at the same time.

Before putting the car in gear, Luke figured if he took the bridge back west, it would save time instead of the toll road home, knowing morning commuters would soon clog up the highway. He pulled out onto the street and headed home.

He looked over at the empty passenger seat, wishing Layla had been there with him. Her disappearance was his fault, and he had no idea how to rectify that situation. Then a thought occurred. He would try to contact those women who came up to him at the Circle K and help them look for her.

A determined smile came across his face. "Yeah. That's what I'll do," he said aloud.

The early morning traffic was light, and Luke took no chances, driving under the speed limit and gripping the steering wheel tight with both hands. Despite his best efforts, the car was hard to keep steady.

Making the left turn toward the Hillsborough Bridge, he checked his phone. The battery outline was still on the face indicating it wasn't ready. It was only delaying the inevitable ass-chewing he was due when he got home. Strategizing, he hoped to explain how distraught he was over losing Layla to a kidnapper and be granted some leniency.

As he reached the foot of the bridge, his cell phone chirped. Then buzzed, chirped, chimed, and buzzed some more as its connection to the network was flooded with all of the missed texts, alerts, and calls.

That's not good, he thought. He grabbed the phone and turned it over. There were over fifty texts messages and sixteen missed phone calls. He scrolled down on the screen seeing the notifications stacked on each other. Most of them, as expected, were from his mom. Trying to read a few to gauge how bad the impending punishment was going to be, his left hand failed to keep the car steady. He veered into the oncoming lane and a motorist blared his horn back at Luke. He pulled the Mustang back into his lane and focused on driving. He was near the crest of the bridge and began his descent when the allure of the phone messages pulled him back. Especially the one from the 813 area code that wasn't a known contact. It read: Luke, this is Investigator Garzinetti with the Tampa Police. Please call me back or your mother, ASAP.

"Investigator?" All hope for merciful sanctions just ended if his mother had contacted the police, he figured. "I'm in deep shi—"

The Mustang veered back into the outer opposing lane and two vehicles were coming head on. Luke yanked the wheel back to the right causing the back end to fishtail. A deafening screech came from the tires sliding sideways on the roadway. A vision of an old man standing on the side of the bridge flashed through the windshield. Luke wasn't sure if he was real or a beer-induced illusion, both options worsened his panic. Luke tried to overcorrect, but in his frightened state, hit the accelerator instead of the brakes and slammed into the steel braces of the bridge. The Mustang leapt up off its tires from the collision and fell back to rest.

Pushing away the suffocating airbag, Luke tried to look out of the windshield for the old man. He was certain he was real. He pulled the door handle, but the door wouldn't budge. A terrible pain radiated from the side of his head and he touched his hand up above his ear. There was a wet, sticky liquid, and Luke realized it was blood as he held his hand down to study it further. But the old man, he remembered. Luke shouldered the door open, rubbing metal on metal, crunching something extra in the hinges so he could extricate himself from the vehicle. Other motorists were stopping to help check on him and he waved them off as he moved to the front of the car. He spun around looking in all directions for the old man but didn't see him. *Was he real?*

Luke stepped over the debris and glass as the pungent odor of radiator fluid assaulted his nostrils and checked over the side of the bridge. It was still too dark and the water looked black from the roadway. He looked at the front of the Mustang in case the man was squashed within the grill, but there was nothing but a broken car.

"Hey kid, are you okay?" asked a Samaritan.

"Um, yeah." Luke touched the side of his head again, the blood still seeping from a wound. "I think so."

"C'mon, sit down for a minute. I already called 911, so just sit there, okay?"

Luke did what the man said, confused about if there really was an old man or if it was just his imagination. He looked over at his prized possession, and it was a pitiful sight. Mangled, broken and hideous. The front bumper laid hanging down as if it were a dislocated jaw broken and hanging from the skull. His vanity tag, though, still held on to its housing and proudly read: *Lucile*.

***

There was a sense of urgency about this situation that bothered Moye. Harold Moye was calculated and methodical, rarely took chances and learned from past mistakes. He had violated just about every rule when Rachel Goodwin came back into his fold. After all those years, he knew nothing of her existence, her routine, her fears, her pleasures, but yet when she showed up at his door wearing that phony media lanyard, claiming to be a reporter, he couldn't help trying to ensnare the one that got away. It was truly a miracle. Having pined over the mirage that was Rachel Goodwin since she got away that day back in Texas, Moye let her in and planned her entrapment on the go.

After he returned to his house back in 1993, he quickly disassembled all of his tools, gathered all necessary items, and stored them in his car for a hasty escape. He doubted, and was later proved right, that the delirious girl would be able to retrace her steps back to him. However, he wouldn't take that chance, so he left to regroup elsewhere in the country. He even thought about setting fire to the house to cover his tracks, but that could have raised too many flags. He didn't want anyone looking to close and not passing it off as coincidence.

Heading east on I-10, he had passed through the southeast and settled on Florida, but he wanted, he needed, a more populous area than what north Florida offered. He took I-75 South until he came upon the Tampa Bay area. It was perfect.

Changing his name had been the easy part, simply convincing the clerk at the DMV his forged out-of-state birth certificate was legit. He counted on the fact not many in the Florida office had ever seen documents from Montana, so with a little effort, and a new age color printer, he had become Harold Stephens. Transposing two digits within his social security was the easiest way to remember a new number, and he knew just so long as he kept his head down, no one would notice. He had already established a practice of going unnoticed and loved the fact he appeared unsuspecting. Being invisible gave him more confidence.

Moye had taken his time adjusting to the feel of the area, the speed of life in the south Florida town, but soon the pangs of his paraphilic desire ached to be fulfilled. He tried his hand in Tampa's seedier neighborhoods, finding a prostitute that flaunted her youthful looks, adding to the persona with a plaid mini skirt, white blouse, and black stilettos, she was perfect for his needs. Being intoxicated and high on whatever narcotic she fancied, she was overly suggestable. She made herself an easy target and was not much of a challenge. Although she was mostly willing, his desire went unsatisfied. Dumping her body became the chore and having found a house on the water offered the

241

perfect disposal site. Gaining confidence again, he began looking for his next real beauty on the campuses of the high schools. Staying over at work one day, he overheard a troubled girl express her hatred for home, acceptance in the streets, and willingness to experiment with narcotics. The girl made her routine easy to follow and never grew aware of her surroundings, making the abduction go easy and unnoticed. She put up a fight, but still, Moye went unsatisfied. It wasn't until he found the next girl, Laura, that his inner desire was reborn. While conducting an upgrade of equipment at her school, she forced Moye to do a double take as he was certain she was Rachel Goodwin. She had the same hair, same height, weight, and seriousness about her as Rachel. Before getting confirmation that she wasn't Rachel, the idea of having Rachel was planted, and it excited him to the point of release. She was the ultimate beauty, but why, he wondered? He didn't care, because it elicited a fire within and gave his desire direction and purpose. Like Rachel, Laura also had a little sister and with that came the leverage necessary to get what he truly wanted, his prey to desire him back.

Dumping her like the other two was his first real mistake. The cops, unintelligent and lazy, surprised him when they began sniffing around in his neighborhood looking for ties to the three murders. He managed to stay off the radar when the fat Italian detective questioned him about his job and residence both being associated with the victim. Giving him plausible answers and feigning ignorance made the encounter a one-time deal. They would come around again a few more times over the next two decades, but nothing ever materialized from those contacts.

In his self-proclaimed genius, Moye made some alterations to his basement, hiding the door that led down to it, and digging out underneath the house between the concrete pillars. This new inlet expanded the lake's reach and brought in its reptilian inhabitants to help him get rid of the evidence of his disregarded beauties. No bodies, no trail.

All that was in the past now. The sense of urgency irritating him to the point of madness was before in Texas he had had time to make that escape. This time, the cops were actually in his house where they would undoubtedly find enough evidence to label him the killer he was.

Making his way down the dock that ran off of his neighbor's back yard, he untethered their electric motor pontoon boat and steered toward the entrance of the neighborhood. Figuring the cops would set up a tight perimeter around the house initially, if he could use the water to get outside their dragnet, he could easily slip out undetected. He ran the pontoon up on to the gravel and dirt boat ramp at the public access ramp and headed up to the main street. He checked for any cops on post and continued along the main roadway toward the bridge. Returning to the old man façade, he slowed his gait to the innocent looking hunched shoulder shuffle. He was just an old man out for an early morning walk. It was the cornerstone of how he remained invisible. Cops are looking for an agile killer, able to physically subdue his victims, not an elderly man unsteady on his feet.

Sirens wailed in the near distance but came in from the other side of the neighborhood. Approaching the bridge that crossed over the Hillsborough River, he looked back across toward his house. Through the tree-lined lake, into his alcove, he could see the strobes of blue and red flickering in the early dawn sky. But, he was safe. He would escape and live to regroup. Again. He had no idea how, but that was a secondary problem at the time.

The early morning traffic was still in its beginning stages, but there were cars on the road. Moye figured if he could get across the bridge into the next town over, he could hail a taxi or pretend he was lost to an unsuspecting motorist to put more distance from the area.

As he neared the top of the bridge, he actually recalled dumping Laura's body off this very spot. He paused to relish the moment, reliving all the excitement and feelings the memory brought back.

Looking into the black water below, he let the reverie run its course. He needed to keep moving.

Headlights washed over him, but Moye kept his head down, not wanting anyone to recognize him or advise the cops once the news media had hold of his story and blasted his face all over the world. The thought of being identified as a notorious killer had a satisfying feeling of accomplishment. It was the highest compliment in his mind, and even with the utter disaster that led to his discovery, he felt confident he could continue finding more beauties to satisfy his lustful desire. It wasn't the first time he'd been exiled.

A tire squeal broke his ego boosting moment. Moye turned to the road just as a pair of headlights came barreling toward him, the engine revved up high. Unable to escape the path of the car, Moye braced for impact. There was no pain as his body went numb, but Moye couldn't breathe. Falling backward, the blue-gray sky of the new day was the last thing in this world he saw before plummeting into the dark watery grave below.

***

The car settled, crunched, broken, and steaming from the head-on collision with the steel guard rail of the bridge. Fluid dripped from the car; parts and pieces were scattered over the roadway. Lying just at the edge of the bridge was a right leg appendage, severed cleanly just below the knee. The shoe was still tied tightly to the foot, and the bulk of the calf muscle was suspended out over the edge. The shoe acted as an anchor to the bridge, but the weight of the lower leg was too much for the lifeless foot inside the shoe to hold. Slowly, before anyone noticed, the leg, as if it had a magnetic draw to its master, slid off the side of the bridge and plunged into the dark waters that had swallowed the rest of the body.

Chapter 38

The EMTs were done checking out her vital signs, telling Rachel she should rest from her ordeal while taking in plenty of fluids. Curt was holding an ice pack on the side of his head. He refused, even after the paramedics urged him, to go to the hospital for a possible concussion. Rachel didn't know what to think. She was glad he was up and talking after seeing Moye slug him with that mallet. Layla Bragden had been whisked off by another ambulance headed straight for the hospital. Rolling past her on a gurney, Layla gave Rachel a hopeful smile that said thank you for saving me. Being on the team for over half a year, Rachel had come to recognize the look and learned to covet the moment. It was fuel for the crusade.

The sun was just barely setting over the tree tops, bringing the reach of daylight to the scene. Rachel sat in the Sprinter Van and watched the circus unfold with Detective Benitez and Monroe directing. They set up a large perimeter aimed to catch Moye, coordinating additional resources to help them on scene and other peripheral locations. There were mostly uniforms buzzing around and as far as Rachel could tell, none were high ranking. Up the block, a patrol car sat blocking the road with yellow crime scene tape stretched across the street. The media were setting up cameras and live remote posts for the breaking news.

"We need to get out of here." Louis whined from his seat in the back of the van. "The news is already flying around. See?" Louis turned his screen to show an aerial shot of Moye's neighborhood on the news website, his house in the center and the black Sprinter Van an obvious black dot in the suburban landscape.

"Let's have a little faith in our friend, Louis," Melinda spoke. Everyone knew she meant Detective Benitez.

"Putting our faith in the police isn't what we normally do," Louis rebutted.

"True, but if we just leave, it'll probably make things worse. This is a pretty big hornet's nest we just kicked over." Melinda looked to Rachel to settle the decision. Rachel noticed that she didn't even glance in Curt's direction.

"We sit tight for now, but depending on how they want to play this out, we may need to make a quick exit," Rachel said.

Rachel had been following Detective Benitez's movements since stepping out of the ambulance. She moved from the unmarked Impala, to the front yard, to the front door, and back out to the street orchestrating the chaos. She was impressively calm in the swirling maelstrom. She stood sequestered from the activity next to her partner and discussed something intently. Benitez kept pointing back to the van and the house while Detective Monroe nodded, spoke, and then twisted around to look at the van. Rachel's instincts said they were discussing what to do with her and the team. Monroe threw up his arms and nodded to his younger partner, then walked off to handle something else.

"Looks like we may have an answer," Rachel announced. She slid open the side door and stepped out, meeting the detective in front of the house. Melinda followed.

"How are you feeling?" Benitez asked Rachel.

"Actually, a little sore. But overall, fine. How's Layla?"

"She's good. I just heard back from the hospital. She was very dehydrated, but all else is good. Physically, that is. I'm sure she'll need some therapy for everything that went on. Apparently, when Moye dumped her through that trapdoor, she was somehow able to swing far enough under the house and climb up into some hole before the gators could reach her. Damn lucky little girl."

"I'm just glad she's alright."

"Yeah. I am too."

"So, um. . . detective?" Melinda asked.

"What?"

"Well…, like I mentioned last night, we prefer to work off the radar, and we kind of want to know where you stand on that?"

"We just stumbled on a serial killer who's been operating undetected for the last two decades and rescued his last victim, who was still alive because of *your* intervention, and you want me to somehow just let that slide?"

Melinda and Rachel stood there, silent, unsure of what to say. Rachel began to worry that all of their anonymity would vanish because she went against Moye on her own. After everything was finalized, Alexis might have no more use for them. The disappointment in herself began to weigh her down.

"Actually, I was thinking of letting it slide," the detective said, softly.

"What?" Rachel sounded surprised. "You are?"

"Let's just say that I'm feeling very generous after you've handed me a career case," Benitez smiled. "When Melinda told me what you guys do last night, as a team, going around the country looking for missing children, I didn't believe it at first, but now that I've seen the work you've put in, the research and information you were able to dig up, I believe you. Your willingness to go up against someone like Harold Moye takes some serious courage. And although I question your tactics which undermine what I do, I can still appreciate what you guys do."

"So, what does that mean?" Melinda asked.

"What that means is, and as long as she's up for it, Layla can cover everything I need on my end, and we just pretend you were never here. The only person to contradict that would be Moye himself and something tells me that's unlikely."

Rachel was puzzled and glanced over at Melinda, it was obvious she was confused too.

"The way I see it is that we received a tip that a young girl, possibly the missing girl Layla Bragden, was spotted at this house. My partner and I arrived to investigate, as it is our case. So, when we arrived, we heard yelling for help which gave us cause to enter the house without a warrant. We find Layla under the trap door, Sal shoots the gator, and we rescue the girl and discover Moye is the Hillsbo River Killer. It's all the truth." Benitez smiled and added, "Only with some *slight* omissions."

"Wow," Rachel said. "Thank you, detective."

"I told you, I was on your side. Plus, Layla was under those floorboards for over a day. She overheard how you stood up and fought back against Moye."

"She did?" Rachel hadn't thought about that.

"She did." Benitez added, "And that included hearing Moye confess to everything."

"You think that'll hold?" Melinda asked with skepticism. "I mean, who's going to believe you guys came on an unsolicited tip in the middle of the night?"

"I think it'll hold, but if that gets challenged, I'll use your phone call to me at the station. Technically, *you* did provide me a tip when you called, and that is what prompted the follow up. Plus, if some dick defense attorney wants to call us on it, I trust you'll come back and help out the cause."

"Oh, of course we would." Rachel said.

"Good."

Rachel nodded toward Monroe. "What does he think about everything?"

"He's fine with it. When I explained how we didn't need you and that we should have more than enough evidence inside to put this guy away for three lifetimes, he actually suggested it."

"Really?"

"Yep."

Rachel felt like a guardian angel was looking down on her. Maybe it was Rhonda placing a guiding hand on things, she thought. The idea of her sister, robbed of life on earth and looking down on her from heaven made her smile.

"So, you guys haven't found him yet?" Rachel asked.

"Well, no." Benitez had an obvious degree of annoyance in her answer. "We've got a perimeter over a mile wide, the chopper up for the last thirty minutes and several K-9's on the ground trying to pick up his scent. But, no. Nothing yet."

The notion that Moye had not been located was disheartening. The thought that he could be out there hunting for his next victim to supplement his fantasy was unbearable. Or worse, him out there planning revenge on Rachel and the team. But the more she thought about Moye being free in the world, the less frightened of him she was. She had returned to the darkness that plagued her for so long and yet she was able to survive. Again. She was able to fight back, despite his best efforts, and although it was extremely difficult to walk away, she did so rather unscathed. It gave her a confidence that she had never known before. She was no longer afraid of the faceless monster who had ruined her childhood. The power he once held over her had vanished, and in this she sought comfort.

"It's okay, Detective. You'll find him."

Two male detectives exited the house and headed toward Benitez. Rachel and Melinda shied back, knowing their presence inside a major crime scene warranted explanation. They asked how she wanted to handle the crime scene and the canvassing amongst the other detectives. Rachel noticed the position of decision making was somewhat new for the detective but saw she was enjoying it. She gave the two men their orders and they walked off.

"Sounds like you've got a handle on things. We're not leaving town just yet, so if you need us—"

"Oh, the pictures." Benitez remembered. "The pictures. I wanted you to take a look at them before you left. You know, a victim's perspective?"

"Uh, yeah. Sure, but what pictures?"

"Yes, the pictures." A groggy voice spoke from behind Rachel. She turned to see Curt, still holding the ice pack to his head. "That's where I was standing when that asshole knocked me out the first time."

"You saw them?" Benitez asked Curt.

249

"Yeah." He answered, then looked down at Rachel. "I definitely think *you* should look at them."

"Yes, but before the brass show up, alright?" Benitez offered.

As Detective Benitez, Rachel, and Curt walked up to the house, one of the uniformed officers on scene yelled out to another detective standing with Monroe.

"Hey Garzinetti!"

"Yeah?" The detective shouted back.

"Garz, they just rolled up on a crash over at the Hillsbo Bridge. You working a missing kid by the name of Luke Millwood?"

Rachel stopped in her tracks, recognizing the name. She immediately tuned into the conversation.

"Yeah, why?"

"Well, he just fucked up his Mustang, running it into the guardrail on the bridge. Couple of my guys are over there working the crash. What do you want done with him?"

"He hurt?"

"A little banged up."

"Tell them to get him cleared by a doctor, and I'll call his mom to meet him at the hospital. Have them do the recovery report since we got this going on."

"Sure thing."

Rachel remembered when Beth told the team how aloof Luke was when they went to talk with him. They had gauged whether he actually cared about Layla and was worth talking to. She tried to find meaning in the two occurrences, the rescue of Layla and the crash of Luke's Mustang, but nothing took shape, so she passed it as mere coincidence.

As Rachel reentered the front door, she put the nightmare from the night prior out of her mind. A mantra of, "He can't hurt me anymore" repeated in her head. It helped maintain the survivor's confidence.

Walking past the living room toward the bedrooms, Rachel saw what she believed was a nebulizer lying on the couch as if dropped. A crime scene tech knelt beside it taking samples from its tubes. It was right where she'd been sitting to *interview* Moye.

"What's that?" Rachel asked.

Benitez glanced over to see what she was asking about. "Oh, we think that's one of the ways he incapacitated his victims. You said in your earlier statement that you were just sitting there when you felt dizzy and eventually fell to the floor like you were paralyzed?"

"Yeah, it was so weird."

"We think he had that nebulizer set up just underneath you on the couch. There was a tube clipped to the underside, there." Benitez pointed. The crime scene tech overheard the explanation by Benitez and pointed for Rachel's sake. "We think it was remote controlled," the detective added.

"That's pretty clever," Curt said flatly.

Rewinding the reporter ruse, Rachel recalled Moye using the remote but the television not responding. That must've been it, she realized. She shook her head at how she had been so easily trapped. That'll be the last time, she resolved.

"I'm betting a month's pay it'll be Rohipnol or some type of highly concentrated date rape drug," Benitez said with confidence.

Entering the room, the collage of pictures was a little overwhelming for Rachel.

"Whoa." Rachel scanned the wall, taking in the randomness of the images.

"Look at the one in the center," Curt said.

Wondering why but listening to the direction, Rachel moved her eyes to the center of the wall. Once she found it, her breath left her for a moment. "Holy shit!"

"What?" asked Benitez. "What is it?"

Rachel stepped closer studying the center picture, then moved on slowly to each photo surrounding it.

"That was where she hid from Moye back in '93 when she escaped the first time," Curt answered for Rachel.

"Really." The detective crossed her arms, deep in thought. After a moment, Benitez, spoke. "That's right. Oh my God. The red bench. Laura Diaz."

251

Rachel looked back. "Red bench?"

"Yes!" Benitez stormed out of the first bedroom and into the other one. Breezing past a second crime scene tech photographing the house, she stood in front of a second picture mural on the wall. She scanned the lot and then pointed to a picture of an empty red metal bench. "That. That is a bench outside of the tennis courts at Northlake High. Laura Diaz was last seen at tennis practice after school. Matter of fact, her coach saw her sitting at that bench as he was packing up the equipment. He was the last to see her until her body was found several days later."

"How do you know that's the bench by the tennis courts?" Curt asked.

Benitez flashed embarrassment, but replied, "Let's just say, I learned I wasn't going to be the next Martina Navratilova at Northlake High. So, this can't be a coincidence, can it?"

There was an excitement within the detective that burned bright, on the edge of enlightenment. Rachel grew excited as well, hoping to help the detective better understand this monster. But then she saw another image, burned into her brain as significant as any milestone, especially when it led to such a horrendous nightmare.

"No, it can't." Rachel answered. Curt and the detective turned to her. "There." She pointed to the image of a sidewalk, a white fence and some green space.

"Is that…" Curt's questioned tailed off.

"Yeah. That's where Moye grabbed me and Rhonda as we walked home from the store."

"It's just a sidewalk. How can you tell?"

"Look past the fence. It's the steeple of the Baptist Church in the background, and plus, you never forget a place like that. It's where me and my sister's innocence was stolen."

A somber silence took over the room. Rachel stared at the picture while the detective looked at the others.

"So that's it, then," Benitez said with confidence. "These are where he took the girls, and the other room that's—"

"That's where he buried them," Curt said. "But with Rachel, it was the heart-shaped rock because that was the last place he knew she saw her."

"So each one represents a different girl?" Benitez said with reverence.

"I think so."

Benitez pulled out her phone, put it to her ear, and excused herself from the room.

"So, she's gotta be here somewhere, then?" Rachel said to Curt.

"Rhonda?"

"Yes."

Curt didn't reply but had a pained look on his face as if he were afraid to say something to Rachel. Finally, he said, "You know it'll be…"

Rachel bowed her head solemnly. "It'll be just her body. Moye confessed as much to me, that she was dead. I still have to find her. Ya know?"

"I understand." Scanning the wall with Rachel, Curt added, "Let's find which picture is hers."

Chapter 39

Absent the sick feeling in the pit of her stomach, Rachel thought the area was quite peaceful. Looking past a worn, barbed-wire fence, there was a sweeping hill that rose in the distance with velvet green grass blanketing the ground. A lone oak stood proudly in the middle of the field, accenting the pictorial countryside. What was once fertile farmland was now undeveloped land in the middle of nowhere, but Rachel knew its beauty hid the horrors of her past.

"It's actually very pretty," she said. Curt stood next to her and gave a head nod, silent.

Rachel held up a picture from Moye's collage that depicted the open landscape and compared the two. The picture was of the same hill, but the oak, the emphasis of the image, was in a more youthful state. Its placement on top of the hill was the same as the scenery. The tree line in the distance was shorter, she noticed. An indicator of the picture's age. There was no doubt it was the same place.

"This is it," Rachel said.

"You sure?" Curt asked. Rachel handed him the picture so he could see for himself. A quick comparison and he handed the photograph back, offering no argument.

A stillness fell on Rachel. "I don't want to go any further."

Curt looked down at her with a puzzled look on his face. "Why not?"

"I don't know," she said. "If I don't go over there, she's not dead, ya know? There's still that last ounce of hope that she survived and is just waiting somewhere for me to find her."

"But, if you go over there—" Curt added.

"Right, if I go over there and we find her, then that's it. That hope vanishes and then…, she really is dead."

Curt inhaled deeply. Rachel sensed that he was uncomfortable too. "Wouldn't it be better to know?"

"Yes. But, it'll hurt more."

There wasn't a chance, not even a slight chance in Rachel's mind, that Rhonda's remains wouldn't be found. In the last two weeks, along with the Tampa Police Homicide Unit running point and the FBI coordinating with the Texas Department of Public Safety, they'd identified and searched almost all of the burial sights gleaned from the picture mural on Moye's wall. Each one that had been identified resulted in the bodies of Moye's victims being found. Benitez and her team came to the horrendous realization that after Laura Diaz, Moye used the hunger of wild alligators to help cover up his crimes. The presence of the trap door and grotto under his house made that painfully obvious. The burial sites within the murals were from his earlier hunting ground in Texas. Rhonda Goodwin's was the last.

This place, however, was different and took longer to find. The others when carefully studied, were easily identifiable by the Texas cops riding around Moye's old house and area of operation. Each site being within a ten-minute drive from his house. Rhonda's proved to be an anomaly.

Figuring it was because of Rachel's unplanned escape, Moye was forced into ridding himself of her body on the run or facing potential exposure. Knowing the dump site could virtually be anywhere, they narrowed the search to the southeastern United States. Coupled with the fact that Moye moved to the Tampa Bay area, emphasis was put around Interstate 10 which ran through Texas all the way to the east coast. But it was the genius of Louis Melton that found this particular burial site. Using the same code and software utilized in facial recognition programs, he used the picture found in Moye's mural as "the face" and integrated it with Google street views and came up with this area as a possible match. Seeing it in person, Rachel knew Louis had been right.

A few miles inside the Louisiana state border from Texas, the roadside grave had been hidden in plain sight. Alexis Vanderhill had made arrangements for men, cadaver dogs, and excavating equipment to join the team. A lone FBI agent and a trooper from the Louisiana State Patrol stood by, waiting for them to make the discovery, rule Rhonda's death a homicide, and add it to the final count.

Alexis had also joined the team in person. She stayed back in the van talking on the phone, trying to put out another fire. Melinda, Beth, and Louis all hung back as well.

"How can one person be responsible for so much death and hurt?" Rachel asked. "When I knocked on his door, I was caught off guard, because he was so…"

Curt finished her thought, "Normal?"

"Yeah!" She shook her head. "I don't get it. And he'd been doing it for so long. There were so many girls after me. How does that happen? And how do we stop it from happening again?"

"I don't know," Curt answered. "What we do here on this team, is more than just find missing kids. We bring light to the darkness. People like Harold Moye, they survive in the shadows, in a place where light cannot reach."

Rachel inhaled in the cool damp air, trying to accept the existence of men like Moye in this world, but she resolved to be that light Curt spoke of, no matter how dark the path grew or how dangerous the monsters became.

"So that's where we have to go and fight…? In the shadows?"

"Yes," he answered. Curt looked back toward the field and nodded, "You ready?"

After a long moment of thought, she replied, "No."

The morning gave way to early afternoon when finally, one of the cadaver dogs gave a positive alert. Much to Rachel's annoyance, the dog handlers insisted on working on a grid system of searching, starting with the outer perimeter instead of going to the obvious area surrounding the tree. Rachel grew impatient on top of her apprehension when they ignored her pleas to start near the tree. She gave the handler a wry look when his dog gave the signal only a few feet from the base of the oak.

The men, along with the excavating equipment took over, setting up markers, taking test samples of the soil, and prepping for the dig. All which prolonged Rachel's agony. Curt calmed her by telling her these workers usually didn't perform this with actual victim's families present, but explained it was not a short process.

Two hours later, a bony hand, small and thin, that of a small person was found. Workers cleared the area around this, anticipating where the rest of the body lay. When enough of the dirt was cleared away, the full skeleton of an adolescent female was found. Her flesh had long since been absorbed by the earth, leaving only the skeletal frame behind. Torn and faded fabric was intertwined with the remains, the tattered leftovers of her clothing. It was all that was left of being lost for twenty-two years.

Rachel stood at the edge of the shallow grave. The workers backed away for a moment to allow her time to grieve. Curt stood behind her.

She wiped away tears but didn't say anything. The afternoon wind rolled along the sweeping hill, brushing over Rachel. There had been so many memories that never happened, good times never shared, and dreams that never came true. Rhonda's life had been violently cut short, and along with her memory, Rachel still carried the guilt of surviving. Nothing highlighted that more than standing there looking down at her final resting place.

Looking past the bones, and the ghastly sight, Rachel envisioned her sister's infectious smile, radiant eyes, and her innocence from long ago. That was how she was going to remember Rhonda, not what remained.

Rachel wiped more tears away and sniffed deeply to curtail the emotions from overriding the moment. She looked around, once again absorbing the beautiful landscape. She looked back at Curt. He had an endearing look on his face and smiled.

"She's no longer lost," Rachel said. "Now she's found."

***

After the body of Rhonda Goodwin had been properly removed from her unmarked grave and delivered to the nearest morgue, night had fallen and the hour was late. Curt answered a phone call, and with a sense of urgency, left the recovery site headed for Tallahassee. She assumed the reasoning surrounded the health of his son. He left Rachel with a quick hug and a promise to meet up soon.

A low rent Cajun restaurant and bar just off the interstate drew the team's appetite. The air was smoky and swampy rock and roll emanated out of an antiquated juke box sitting in the corner. It was the kind of place that served deep fried food, full of flavor and character, on paper plates with checkboard parchment paper.

Rachel wasn't hungry, but she ordered fried shrimp with the house's remoulade sauce on the side. It would be easy enough to nibble on, she figured. The raucous laughter, loud conversations, and the hillbilly music were enough to drown out any casual talk amongst the team so Rachel used the noise as an excuse to stay quiet, to reflect on the day's events. She had finally found her sister. It wasn't the joyful reunion that is afforded to most of the people they helped, but a reunion all the same. It didn't end in a loving embrace, and she wondered what she would trade in her life to make that happen. It ended the way it ended, and she would have to finally accept that. Given the circumstances, she wouldn't allow anger to take charge. Instead, she thought of her mother. The vision of her, passed out drunk on her own couch, made her feel alone.

The old idea of Rhonda being out in the world, lost and wandering, had given Rachel an odd sense of comfort and belonging. The hope she was out there had fueled the connection between sisters, but now, with the confirmation of her death, that connection had been severed. The only other person to share that tragedy with was her mother. But instead of comforting each other, Rachel knew her mother would rather drown in a bottle of alcohol and continue living inside a lie. Rachel felt alone.

"You alright?" Louis leaned over after finishing an ear of corn, then yelled through the noise.

Rachel gave a quick smile and nodded. She picked up a shrimp and popped it in her mouth so she wouldn't have to actually answer. Louis leaned back letting it go.

As the team finished up their late dinner, the restaurant crowd thinned. Most of the remaining patrons filed out to the patio bar. The jukebox had been turned down to give way to a guy strumming a guitar.

After taking care of the bill, Alexis walked back to the table to say goodbye. She had disappeared through most of the dinner, walking outside to talk on her phone.

"Alright guys, I'm going to catch a cab back to the hotel and hit the road. I'm heading out for Baton Rouge tonight. Stay as long as you want. I need to handle something," Alexis stated. She glared at Rachel before turning and walking outside.

The look irked Rachel, like Alexis' irritation was because of something she had done. Finding her dead sister better not be it, she thought, or else she would make her sorry.

"You guys want to hang out longer or head back too?" Louis asked.

Rachel looked at Beth, not ready to let that glare go and asked, "What was that look about?"

Beth's eyes looked uneasy for a moment as if answering would break some type of trust. It told Rachel that she knew what it was about.

"What is it?" Rachel asked. She could sense Beth's hesitation.

"Well, she didn't tell me, but while you were at the scene today, she kept getting phone calls from Barbara Green. You know, the ones that took in our little street girl, Holly?"

A foreboding feeling dropped in the pit of Rachel's stomach. She didn't want any bad news, not on the same day she found her sister. She remembered the genuine smile Holly had on her face when she first met the Greens. The hope that putting them together would give the girl a real chance at life was promising. Holly was rough around the edges, and she feared that the generous couple had abandoned their commitment after realizing the girl was too much to handle.

"What about her?"

"She ran away from their home?"

259

"What?" Rachel snapped. "Why? What happened?"

Thoughts of hidden abuse or neglect on the part of the Green's came to Rachel, which made her angry.

"From what I could tell, the girl just up and left," Beth answered. "No rhyme or reason, according to the Greens. Alexis was floored. That's why she's going to Baton Rouge tonight, to figure out what went wrong."

"There has to be a reason."

"They had just enrolled her in a nice private school, and the last Alexis heard was that everything was fine." Beth shrugged her shoulders in disbelief. "They are good people."

Rachel knew Beth was right. She'd seen the open acceptance and love in the couple's eyes when Holly stepped out of the Sprinter Van. That was what gave her the hope that was now gone.

"Should we head that way?" Rachel asked. "I mean, I found... we... found her and brought her in."

"No, Alexis wanted to take care of it herself. Plus, she's been handling all the facetime with the Green's."

Rachel scowled. Holly had not held up her end of the bargain. She shook her head.

"Dammit." Rachel said. "How could...?"

Her anger overrode any rational answer she could come up with. Holly was a damaged girl who turned to drugs and prostitution to escape a life of sexual abuse at home. The reality was that it would take more than the open arms of complete strangers to help her.

"Ugh!" Rachel stood up. "She didn't even give it a chance."

Rachel walked away from the table and headed to the bathroom. She stopped at a sink situated under a dirty mirror, turned on the water, and splashed her face. After patting her face dry with napkins, she stood in front of the mirror, staring at herself. It was there. She could see it, even in herself. She looked away but came back. There was a darkness within the depths of her eyes. She thought about her life, going over the highlights. The kidnapping, subsequent recklessness, maturation, joining the team, and lastly finding and surviving an evil that had haunted her most of her life. Locked in her own stare, she realized the darkness had been there for a long time. Most of her life.

When Rachel returned to the table, Beth was standing up by herself.

"Hey," Beth said. "We're headed back to the hotel. You coming?"

On this day, Rachel felt more alone than any other day she could remember.

"No," she answered. "I'll meet up with you guys later."

"Um, okay." Beth looked puzzled. Rachel didn't care. "Call if you need anything, okay?"

"Sure. Thanks."

Beth left going out the door, and Rachel stepped out to the patio. The guitar player was on a smoke break, chatting up some floozy in a short black dress. Rachel ducked into a small corner and pulled out her phone. A compulsion she had been ignoring since that afternoon gnawed at her. She decided to give in, finally.

She dialed the number and put the phone to her ear. It rang and rang on the other end. As the voice message kicked over, Rachel decided to leave a message rather than call back. She took a deep breath before the final beep.

"Hi, it's me Rachel. Um, so…, I found Rhonda today, Mom. She's dead, Mom. She died a long time ago. She was buried about twenty-five miles west of Baton Rouge in a shallow grave. It… it was actually really pretty there. She probably would've liked it."

Rachel turned her body to shield herself from the small bar crowd. She wiped a tear that leaked out.

"And, um…, I found the guy too, Mom. I found him and tried to take him down, but it didn't quite go the way I wanted. He's on the run from the cops, but they know everything about him and everything he's done. We've found about ten other girls he'd taken before… us. But, I'm not afraid of him, Mom. I fought back this time."

Another tear ran down her cheek, but this time she let it fall.

"Anyway, I just wanted to tell you. I thought you'd want to know." Rachel ended the phone call and shoved the phone in her pocket. She turned back to the crowd who were completely unaware of her heroic exploits and wiped her face. She scanned the crowd and saw an empty chair at the bar. She knew the consequences of staying as opposed to leaving, but without thought, Rachel made her way across the patio and sat down at the bar. She didn't want to be alone.

The bartender gave her a head nod.

"Vodka tonic," she ordered.

He nodded again and made the drink. He held up a lime wedge offering it to Rachel. "Lime?"

"Sure," she said. "Not like it matters."

The bartender smiled and placed the drink in front of Rachel. She stared at the clear drink as the tonic bubbled, intermixing with the vodka. She reached out for it and spun it around on the bar. Standing at a familiar set of crossroads, she knew where each path led. She thought about Moye getting away, Holly running away, and her place on the team. There was success, to a degree, but in either outcome, she realized nothing changed. Moye was free to prey on more victims, and Holly was back out on the street. She wondered if she ever made a difference.

Rachel put the drink to her lips and let it pour down her throat. The cold liquid came with a fiery bite. She reloaded for another pull and then a third until the drink was gone. Being out of practice, she coughed quietly into her shoulder in reaction to the alcohol.

"Another one, please." She waved to the bartender.

The guitar player began another set, starting with his rendition of Tom Petty's *American Girl*. He had a nasally voice that came close to the original. Rachel soon tuned him out as the thoughts of her failures forced their way into her mind. The second vodka drink didn't disappear as fast as the first, but after emptying the glass again, she ordered a third.

As *Free Fallin* started, Rachel wondered if it was Tom Petty tribute night. She turned in her seat to scan the small crowd. There weren't many people left.

"Hey," a smooth voice said from Rachel's left. "Mind if I sit here?" She turned to see a guy, short brown hair, clean shaven face, and kind brown eyes, smiling with anticipation. She gave a polite smile. He sat down and ordered a bourbon on the rocks.

"Sure." He was attractive and smelled nice, she thought. "Thanks."

Rachel turned around and watched the back wall of the bar. A thin sliver of mirrored glass ran the length of the bar, allowing her to watch the guy without him knowing. He kept glancing over at her, as if he were thinking of something to say.

He leaned over. "My names Drew."

Rachel turned back to face him. "Rachel."

Drew stuck out his hand and Rachel offered hers. His grip was firm but gentle. He is trying hard to impress me, she thought. She turned away to hide a grin. A glance back at the mirror behind the bar showed Drew had also found it and was watching her.

Rachel giggled.

"So?" Drew asked. "Are you really a Tom Petty fan or did you get lost coming off the interstate?"

"A little of both, I guess."

"Me? I come for the gumbo." Drew smiled. "Seriously, it's world famous."

"Oh yeah?" Rachel played along.

"Yeah, the menu says so." Drew flashed the inside of the restaurant's menu. "I mean, they can't put that on the menu if it's not true, can they? I mean, there are laws against that stuff, right?"

Rachel giggled again. His timing was comforting. She let Drew go on about himself but committed no details to memory. He was a young financial advisor for a large corporation with dreams of breaking out on his own. He came across as charming and harmless, but his confidence told Rachel that he was no stranger to picking up women. Somewhere between her fourth and fifth vodka tonic, she peered into his eyes. Mistaking it for a moment, he leaned in for a kiss, but Rachel was looking for something else. The absence of darkness eased her concern, and she allowed Drew a simple kiss, before drawing back and finishing her drink.

"Sorry," he said.

"For what."

"I think I misread that look. I just thought—"

"It's okay." Rachel looked away and studied her drink. "I was looking for something."

"Oh?" Drew asked. "Something good or bad?"

Rachel shook her head. "Just looking is all."

"Did you find it? Whatever it is you're looking for?" Drew turned away on his barstool, taking a drink.

"No," she said plainly. "But, that's a good thing."

Drew nodded. "Okay, so you were looking for something bad… and didn't find it." He emptied his drink and waved to the bartender for another. "Good to know. Is that something you do with everyone you meet?"

Rachel laughed. She just smiled back at him for her answer.

Rachel got the attention of the bartender and made a writing motion. He nodded back and stepped over with the tab.

"You're leaving?" Drew asked. There was a pathetic tone in his voice that sounded hurt. It almost changed her mind.

"Yeah," she answered. "I'm ready to go."

"Okay, well…" Drew looked as if he were thinking of a reason for her to stay.

"So, how about your place?" she said.

His eyes widened, but otherwise, Drew remained cool. He threw down a twenty-dollar bill for his tab and stood up.

"Yeah, I got a best of Tom Petty album just waiting to be played."

Rachel smiled and followed him out.

Once at Drew's, Rachel walked in and took stock of the townhome. It was a clean, typical bachelor pad with sports memorabilia and superhero movie posters. It coincided with the personality he portrayed. The vodka tonics caught up to her. Her head was swallowed in a thick fog and she moved slowly, but her mind was crisp and held onto control. A current of sexual energy flowed through her body, top to bottom.

As if he was reading her body, Drew came up behind her, running his hand down her sides and pulling her body back against his. He matched her in height, thin but athletic. Rachel turned around. The next few minutes were a torrent of clothes ripping, deep kissing, and physicality. There was no apprehension, only submission to the moment.

Held up against the wall straddling Drew, Rachel held on tight to his strong back as he moved with enthusiasm. She found her image watching her in the foyer mirror. Moving past the shame, she noticed that the darkness still loomed within her own eyes. It would always be there, she realized. It wasn't going away.

Allowing herself to get lost in the throes of a stranger, she reciprocated Drew's enthusiasm until they collapsed to the floor, following a climatic finish.

They moved to the bedroom for another round of equally intense sex. Laying in the afterglow, Rachel didn't feel the level of guilt she did during her reckless period, but it was there nonetheless. Drew was a wonderful distraction, but her thoughts quickly returned to Holly running away and Moye in the wind. Again, she replayed all the events as they unfolded, second guessing her decisions, and she wondered if she left, would she be doing the team a favor? Lastly, she thought of Curt. Thinking of him while lying next to another man added to her frustration, but she didn't stop. She admitted only to herself that she would never stop thinking about Curt Walker.

Chapter 40

The orange glow from the interstate lights weren't welcoming in the late hour. As Curt pulled off onto his exit, there was a sudden urgency to get home. Tracy had called detailing an argument that she and Josh had gotten into, and she wanted Curt home. Rushing his good-byes with the team, he immediately left and was nearly there.

Tracy explained Josh had gotten upset about whether his father should come home or not. Josh had overheard Tracy venting about Curt's absence to someone on the phone and confronted her.

Curt was ready to be home for a while and spend more time with Josh. Plus, he had a hell of a story to tell him.

Curt's phone buzzed as he made the light onto N. Monroe St, heading toward his home. Tracy's name appeared on the caller ID.

"Hey," he answered. "I'm almost h—"

"He's gone. Again." Tracy was panicking.

"Dammit, Tracy. What happened?"

"We had the fight earlier, and he went to his room. I thought he was in there doing whatever so I checked on him and now he's gone."

A sinking feeling fell to the bottom of his stomach.

"Are there any knives missing?"

"Oh shit—"

Curt could hear Tracy's quick footsteps moving through the house. He braced himself for the answer.

"No." There was relief in her tone. "No, they're all here."

"Okay, well, maybe he's out walking around, letting off steam."

"I don't know, Curt. That argument was about five hours ago. I don't think he got that mad."

Curt's frustration grew. Not knowing his son's motives proved maddening. The boy was damaged, not through his own faults, but by the hands of another. He thought of the men responsible and seethed with anger. It was in these moments, Curt thought, had they been in front of him, he wouldn't hesitate to end their lives. As he turned into his neighborhood, he had to refocus on finding his son.

Curt slowed down and scanned each house as he passed, hoping for a glance of Josh. He wasn't ready to accept that his son wasn't as strong and resilient as he believed. He cursed the whole situation over again and blamed himself for being the reason the boy was kidnapped in the first place. A tear welled up and fell down his cheek. His resolve, no matter the difficulty, was to help the boy get back to his normal self.

Five minutes later and no signs of Josh, Curt called Tracy back.

"Did you find him?" she asked.

"Not yet."

"Dammit."

"Where was he before? Last time he wandered off like this?"

"The interstate overpass."

Curt whipped around the car and sped down the road. The overpass was around the corner. As he neared the bridge, he saw Josh, but the scene froze him with fright. The sun had long since set over the western horizon so it left Curt with one real possibility of why his son was at this place, and it scared him beyond words.

"Curt? Curt? What is it?" Tracy's voice called out, but he let the phone fall to the floorboard and jumped out of the car.

Josh was standing on the concrete ledge of the overpass, staring down at the passing cars of the interstate, seventy-five feet below. Curt was overcome with fear.

"Josh!" Curt cried out. "What are you doing, buddy?"

With unsteady footing, Josh slowly turned toward the voice of his father. His face was hollow, drained of hope.

"Dad—"

"Josh, get down, buddy. Please?"

Curt took a quick step toward Josh, but Josh flinched, becoming even more unbalanced.

"No, Dad." Josh held up his hands, palms out. "Don't come closer. Please."

Curt stopped. His elongated shadow from the headlights stretched out to the edge of the bridge. The roar of speeding cars rushed by underneath them.

"No, Josh. I can't do that. You're my son, I won't let you do this. I will fight for you. You have to know that."

A light flickered somewhere in the recesses of his soul. "I do know that, Dad. I do."

"Then come down from there, and let's go home." Curt extended out his hand to Josh, willing the boy to take it.

"Did you save her, Dad? Did you save Rachel?"

His concern for another in this moment confused Curt. Feeling it was somehow important for the boy to know, he searched for a response. "Um, yeah, buddy. Of course. She's going to be okay. Come down and I'll tell you all about it."

A smile creased his face, almost like a balance had been restored. "That's awesome. I knew you'd save the day, Dad. I knew it."

Subtly, Curt inched closer to his son. If he made an overt attempt to grab the boy, it could startle him and would cause him to fall. He had to get closer to ensure that didn't happen. He just needed to keep him talking.

"Dad," Josh said, "I'm sorry."

Curt could feel his pain. "Sorry for what, son? You never did anything wrong."

"I'm sorry I can't stop thinking about them…. Those men. I can't stop thinking of all the bad things they did. I want it to stop. Why won't it stop?"

If he held the ability to pause time and space, he would break into those men's jail cells and execute them without remorse. He'd do anything, if it meant it would erase his son's pain.

A set of headlights broke the ridge of the hill, casting a light down on the dramatic scene. Josh studied the lights as they crested the hill and drove toward them. With an audience, Curt feared that would aggravate the situation, and he prayed the car would turn around and disappear.

Looking back at Josh, he saw him stand up taller. A calm resolve washed over his face. There was determination in his eyes and that scared Curt to the brink of collapse.

"Thank you for finding me, Dad," Josh said as tears clouded his eyes. "I waited every day for you to find me. I went to sleep each night knowing that you'd never give up until you found me. And you did."

"That's right, Josh. I never gave up. I never will. And I'm here now, too. Please?" Curt kept his hand held out.

"Go help the next kid. He or she's out there waiting for you, just like I was."

"Not until you come home, Joshua. Please!"

"Thank you, Daddy. I love you."

Curt held his son's stare, reading his intentions. He leapt forward as Josh slowly leaned backward, submitting to the abyss below. Curt dove to the edge and reached out for Josh, but he was too late. He was forced to watch helplessly from above as Josh fell into the depths of darkness, never to return.

The End